I0677812

THE ASSIGNMENT TWO:

KEEP YOUR ENEMIES CLOSER

DJG

Enterprises

2

Dear Diary,

New job new me! I'm finally living the life I have wanted to live. I have a job that blends my writing ability and passion for international social justice! I am making a more than liveable wage! Only thing missing is a man. So, I went online to find a man because that's what everyone said I was supposed to do. But I don't think that is for me and I really did try. I ignored the spelling and grammar mistakes. I excused the opening lines like "shy brotha looking 4 his queen". But the screen names like Darkthunda and Alottabrotha tested my patience. Mommy said look for someone at church but (and I feel bad saying this) a lot of the guys my age who go to my church are weird—at least the single ones and there aren't even that many of them. There's like a 2 to 7 ratio of men to women so even the guys with visible facial tics and speech impediments get snapped up quick. No! I decided to try the old-fashioned heathen way—I went to a club, and it worked!

I have a puddle (can't call two a pool) of men sniffing around me.

The first guy, we'll call Prince because he said his father was the king of his tribe in Nigeria and he kept telling me about his friend's

Mercedes Benz. That was code for "I ain't got no car." I'm not that interested in him but figured maybe his friend . . . Just playing.

The second guy is a med student from Cameroon. We have good conversations on the phone, so I decided to invite him to a dinner I had to go to for work last night.

Can I tell you that my organization has MON-NAY. The dinner is a the Corcoran Art Gallery. Very Swanky. Very formal. Very Bougie!

Siti, good big sister that she is, said I should tell my friend how to dress because, not for nothing, African men have no problem mixing prints and colors which I'm generally cool with but . . . not at the Corcoran Gallery in front of my bougie colleagues. I told him to wear a dark suit.

I looked great in a black, long sleeved, boat neck, moderately bodycon dress (showing lots of curves but conscious of the fact that some curves are actually bulges and need to be hidden) and pearls. Siti had freshly permed and styled my hair. I was going to look great on his arm and together we were going to look like the next cover of Fly Blackness. So, tell me why that Negro rolled up to my door wearing a pair of black pants and a navy jacket? Yes, they were both dark colors, but this was not a suit! I was mortified but Siti said it was too late to cancel.

"At least he's trying. Plus, he's a med student and you said he is nice. Just go and have a good time," Mommy said as Siti freshened my makeup. Then Mommy gave me a kiss on the forehead and Siti pushed me out the door.

I knew they were right and on the ride to the dinner, I remembered why I had invited him. He was confident without being cocky. He was highly conversational and a good listener. When we got to the Corcoran he just kept raking in the cool points as we walked around the gallery and had intelligent, interesting and entertaining conversation about the art.

As I write this, I'm struck by the fact that guys have it so easy. Good conversation and I forget about his mismatched suit. I wonder if he'd have been as into me if I had been wearing a multicolored moomoo just because I had good conversational skills? I think not.

I was feeling really good about my date by the time we were seated at the dinner table with all of my colleagues and their spouses. I had envisioned him regaling us with funny/interesting stories and me walking away at the end of the evening being the envy of all of the women there—"he's such an interesting and NICE young man!" I imagined them saying. But, when the conversation began, this man who had been such an attentive and appropriate date suddenly clammed up. Like hermetically sealed. You couldn't get a word out of him. I even set him up in conversations and he'd just smile and nod and look down at his plate.

That is, until dessert came.

There was a piece of chocolate cake with a thick dollop of cream on the side and a sprig of mint, all on an elaborate plate. We were all commenting on how good the food was (all except my date of course who by this time I was pretending wasn't there) when out of the blue, from behind my left ear I heard a squeal of delight. It startled everyone at the table, and we turned to look in the direction of the sound. There he was, my date, Mr. Blue and Black, looking down at his dessert plate with a delighted smile on his face, clapping his big hands like a little girl. He looked up and said incredibly animated, "It's chocolate!"

Huh?

"See, it looks like part of the plate but it's not. It's chocolate!" he said pointing to the designs on the plate.

And just when I thought it couldn't get any worse, he said "mine is different from hers and hers is different from his and his is different from hers . . . " all the way around the 12-person table until he made it back to "and yours is different from *mine*! It's Chocolate!" I'd never seen anyone so happy and satisfied. I swear I even felt him swinging his long legs in glee under the table.

The entire table looked at me with the indulgent smile I gave the mother in the supermarket whose child lifted her dress above her head and yelled "Me and mommy gots ba-DINE-as! Daddy and Billy gots peeee-nitis!"

After the chocolate demonstration, Doctor Chocolate was more animated. He ate his dessert and even reached over and took a forkful of mine—all smiles. After that he even talked to people about things other than chocolate.

3

Dear Diary,

It's been a while I know but things have been GRRRREATTT!

I can't believe my time in Guatemala is over. So grateful for the opportunity to take down the stories of folks really in the struggle. I love my job!

It's been hard but what an education. Talking to people in the Ixcan and the Communities in Popular Resistance (CPRs). The stories were harrowing and incredibly sad. They have made me really proud to be an American (I know! GASP!). But I can't imagine the things I saw there happening in the US and I am so grateful to those slave owning forefathers who developed America. (GASP!)

The story that haunted me for a while was of this guy who rode through this town in the Ixcan daily at noon, like clockwork. People would stop when he came through on this beautiful huge healthy horse. The horse looked like it ate better than most of the people we met. The guy would just gallop jauntily through the town like he owned it. Turns out he did own it, or at least he'd stolen it, and his daily ride through was a reminder that if anyone tried to rise up, he would take everything they had and kill them.

The horse used to belong to the mayor. A good man. An indigenous man. It had been his pride and joy. The horse-guy was a collaborator with the army and when they rolled through, they killed the mayor, the town leaders and their families. Burned them alive, in a pit, in-back of the church. Their properties were given to collaborators, like the guy on the horse. The poor folks of the town lived alongside those who had been installed as their masters and the horse-guy rode through on the mayor's horse to remind them, daily.

Nobody told me that my family and friends couldn't handle stories like that. After I told Mommy about the horse guy, crying the whole way through it, she shook her head and left the room but not before she said, "I can't hear anymore! I don't want to know anymore." Mommy is one of the most compassionate people I know. If she wanted to NOT know, in such granularity, about the suffering of others, I knew I couldn't share those stories with anyone. So, I stopped talking about Guatemala and the Ixcan, at least until I stopped feeling guilty about the funny stories. Now, this is the story I tell when civilians ask me about my experiences in Guatemala.

The best thing about Guatemala, was that Lin was there. Lin is a staff attorney with the Cairing Coalition, my organization. She was dating Calixto, much to his wife's chagrin.

One day, Lin announced that Calixto's wife's brother's cousin or somebody was getting married and after much cajoling, aka sexual with-holding, Calixto had "invited" Lin and her ameba-riddled sidekick—me—to the reception! We knew we shouldn't go. This was a family affair of the man she was having an affair with but there was NO WAY we were NOT going.

"We'll just slip in and sort of watch. No one will even notice we're there," we told each other.

Now, it bears saying that we had been in Guatemala a long time and our fashion sense—at least mine—had suffered.

I broke out my reddish maroon-ish knit empire waist low cut (stretched out from so much hand washing and line drying) dress. Because it was a special occasion and nobody knew how to do Black hair, I had a yellow and brown piece of fabric wrapped around my head and tied with a flourish on the side. To make the outfit extra-special I wore pantyhose—L'eggs—that had been sent from home because apparently there is no need for queen size pantyhose anywhere in Guatemala. It didn't matter that they made me look like I had prosthetic legs. Tonight was special and called for pantyhose. When I was finished dressing, Lin, who is petite with big boobs and long hair, (aka always cute), gave me a once over and said, "lovely!" (Really good friends lie to each other sometimes.)

We got a cab to the party and giddily, holding hands, opened the door to the hall. I don't know what Lin expected but I thought people would kind of be milling around drinking and talking and well . . . happy and welcoming. That way, I thought, we could slip in unnoticed. We opened the door which was in the back of the hall to find that everyone was seated already, and they looked like they were playing the game, "I bet you smile before I smile." There were some people standing at the dais addressing the crowd, but at the sound of the door creaking opened, all heads turned to look at us: the little white woman and the big black woman with fake legs and a towel on her head. Calixto, who was at the head table, closed his eyes and slid down in his chair.

Lin and I took a couple of steps forward desperately looking for friendly faces who would welcome us to their tables but there were none. Thankfully, we both zoomed in on a pair of empty seats. The problem was that I was on Lin's left and had noticed chairs to her right and she had found seats to her left—on my side of the room. The result:

17

we looked like we were in some crazy pinball machine as we kept bumping into each other trying to get to the safety of the chairs.

Thank God someone at one of the tables, sort of in front of both of us, took pity on us and offered two seats so we were able to pin ball bump ourselves to the table. Our saviors must have been Calixto's leprous cousins, but they were nice to us. By that I mean they talked to us a bit. I want to say that we danced but it was marimba music all night long so we just kind of jostled around on the outskirts of the gathering for a bit then went home.

Guatemala: Good times. Good times.

4

Dear Diary,

I went to a Tea with Mommy to get introduced to International Bible Fellowship (IBF). I went to keep Mommy company. Siti went to protect me and Mommy from being scammed or forced into a cult (cuz ain't nobody gonna mess with us as long as she has breath in her body and the strength to beat the hell out of them). None of us (not even my Christ-loving, saved at the age of nine, Mommy) had any intention of joining but it actually sounded good. An international Bible Study. Classes around the globe studying the same thing. I could go to class even if I had to travel. We all signed up for the next class. Then I got a call from the leader asking me to be a Bible study leader!

Yeah, I know. Me? I mean I love the Lord but mine is kind of a personal/quite/internal faith not an out loud one. I believe, but I know that being a "practice what you preach" Christian is hard, and I am usually in the remedial class.

I asked the lady, Betty, if she was sure that she wanted me to lead it. She said, and I quote, "Yes. When I saw you at the tea party, I heard the Lord clearly say, 'Ask her.'"

What do you say to that?

Ummm . . . Ok?

5

Dear Diary,

Haven't slept in like two weeks. I've been like a mad woman!

I went to a conference and this woman at my table was talking about dinosaur brains. How evolutionarily fear has been used to keep us safe but sometimes it cripples us. She drew this great word picture of a cave man experimenting with making fire. Just as he's about to succeed a dinosaur eats him. Everyone thinks that the fire caused the dinosaur to eat him, so nobody wants anything to do with fire. Their fear kept them from doing anything. She said we do it today. We keep ourselves and others from dreaming and striving because we are afraid it will end up in pain or misery or death so our "dinosaur brain" stifles us.

I thought it was genius. I told her she should write a children's book about it because I could see the scenes. Do you know what she said to me?

"YOU should write that book!" she said.

It was like she spoke a prophecy or something over me and I have been working on the story since then.

Finished it last night!

Now to figure out what to do with it. Would love to publish it. Imagine that?! Me with a book.

Dinosaur Brains, by Trina Pardo. That would be crazy!

6

Dear Diary,

We're studying Isaiah in IBF this year—loads of references to the End Times. Makes me wonder, how close are we to the Rapture of the church? Where are we on the prophetic timeline?

"The granddaddy of all the signs—Jews back in Israel."

Check!

"Earthquakes, famines, disease and signs in the sky."

I mean, not really. I'mma say nah

"Perilous times."

Define perilous. I mean slavery, Jim Crow, the Holocaust—*all perilililious en fleek*. Now? I got a great job. Economy is ok. Yes, this is a US-based evaluation, and my friend Liz would hate it but we kind of are the center of the world, the canary in the mine. If we are ok—the world is ok. Yes, I hear the flaw in that thinking but whatever.

"Wars and rumors of wars."

I mean . . . maybe but again, I'mma say nah.

"Violence and sexual immorality"

So . . . Check-ish.

"False Christs."

Nah.

"The whole world will turn against Israel."

No!

So, we are ok. We got time.

Happy and a little disappointed.

Happy because, until we get raptured, Christians get a front row seat to the shit show the world is gonna become in the end times. I'm not really feeling like I wanna go through that hell. My life is still pretty good. Like I said, I have a good job, I'm happy to have the world stick around as is for a bit longer. Give me time to get married, have kids . . . yadda yadda yadda. None of that happens for Christians after the Rapture I don't think. It's all God all the time which I'm sure will be great (I guess, maybe?) but I'm not ready for all of THAT . . . not yet.

So, yeah happy. AND . . . it would be kind of cool to see the stuff happen:

Sun and moon turn black (scary but kind of cool)

More signs and wonders—albeit on the evil side

The two witnesses who will turn water to blood and then be killed and then resurrect? Come on.

More supernatural occurrences—again more evil than good but God's angels will be no joke. Incredible miracles for the saints.

And the big daddy of all the occurrences of the end times: HARPAZO! The Rapture of the Church! What will that be like? Crazy!

I know it won't be like watching a movie. So, I am really happy that it still seems far off, but . . . Maranatha! Even so, come quickly Lord Jesus.

7

Dear Diary,

I fell in love with him when he cried.

"The sound of military coming to get you—official or rebel—is unmistakable. There's a heaviness to their march—even when the majority of them are barefoot. The knock was simultaneous with the door splintering. I still don't know how they did that or even why. I've thought about that a lot since it happened. They could have either knocked or just shot the hole in the door. Why do both? When it happened, there was no time to think about it. Now it's like a riddle that repeats non-stop in my head.

All of us except my parents were in the house when they came. My sister, her husband and their two children.

When they shot the door down, something—bullet, splintered wood? Who knows—struck my nephew and he fell to the floor in a pool of blood. My sister, who was 7 months pregnant scrambled awkwardly on the floor toward him screaming and then there were 8?

10? 15? Men with guns piling into the small front room where we all stood.

All had proper uniforms although not all of them were new or clean. The commanders—2 of them—had sunshades on even though it was dusk. The left lens of the taller commander's shades was chipped, covering only half of his eye. All of them were tall and thin—Mende men.

This was the army—not the rebels.

It could have been either group, because my brother-in-law wrote about both sides. He was a journalist. He was the reason they were here.

"Which is Adamu Koroma?" Chipped Shades said.

Adamu and I both looked up at the same time. I don't know why, probably because we had both been looking at the floor where my sister was wailing, cradling the body of my 3-year-old nephew.

Two groups of soldiers moved forward and grabbed us roughly.

"I am Adamu!" my brother-in-law said and as soon as the words were out of his mouth Full Lens sunshade shot him in the head. A fight started between the sunshades as Adamu crumpled to the floor at my side. Apparently, the task was to bring Adamu back alive. The government had begun to make a spectacle of torturing and killing reporters. They wanted to make an example of those who opposed President Momoh. But at least the army let families live.

The sunshades were low level commanders but Chipped Shades was crafty.

'Nobody care who we bring back. Take he and kill the rest. Make it look like rebels.' he said indicating that I was to stand in for my brother-in-law's torture and public execution.

Rebels kill in a haze of juju and drugs. Like the mythical Kamajors fighters, they want to take the power and soul of the ones they kill. So, they destroy them. Drugs just make the process more chaotic.

It took over 3 hours for it to be done. They tied me down and left me guarded in a corner. The soldiers peeled off two at a time when it was their turn to rape my sister and her 7-year-old daughter. One of the younger soldiers cried when his turn came. The little girl screamed for her mother and me—Uncle Jo-Jo—to help, until her voice gave out. I tried not to, but I involuntarily looked up into my sister's eyes just as they slit her belly and took out the baby—a classic sign that the rebels had been there. I saw the light of life leave her eyes. Then they grabbed me up and we all moved out of the house. The carnage around me was unbearable."

I took down his story as he gave his testimony. I'd learned that the best way to get through these horrific tales was to disengage. Just write it down. Plenty of time to interact with the story when I had to write the article for the annual report. The air had gone out of the room as he fell silent, letting us imagine the moist heat of a room filled with the salty tang of blood and the stench of filth that must accompany the scene he'd just described. The gasps and sighs from those who had gathered to understand the horrors of war quieted and the room was suddenly shrouded in silence.

When I looked up, I was startled to see these almond shaped eyes looking directly at me. His eyes weren't beautiful. They were small, and the whites were slightly yellowish-brown, set in a face that was deep chocolate, angular and round at the same time. I noticed that his mouth was lovely. Medium full brown lips hiding just a hint of brilliantly white teeth. Random thoughts ran through my mind.

"Why's he smiling?"

"He's fine."

"Are the eyes a sign of jaundice?"

"Was he really on the right side of this conflict?" This thought is a result of hearing too many horrific tales and frankly a few shady tale tellers.

Then he said, "All I could think of was how my mother would come home to the stench of her child and grandchildren rotting in her living room" and tears poured down his cheeks.

My breath caught in my throat and my heart opened wide to him.

8

Dear Diary,

His name is Fallubah (Fallu, for short) and he calls me "HONEY!" There's always an exclamation point after he calls me. "Honey!" No one has ever referred to me by ANY name that conveys such love and raw desire. I'm done! Stick a fork in me.

He's beautiful. Tall, slim and chocolate with slightly bucked teeth which is endearing and makes him approachable. He smells salty, like the ocean. I imagine the sun on my skin when he smiles.

He's smart too about things I have no idea about. He knows African history like a champ. He knows the intricacies of American history and politics way better than me. He's more interested in it than I am, but I don't mind listening to his theories and ideas of governance AT ALL! This stuff means something to him because of his history and his history is AWFUL. There's a lot of pain and dysfunction because of it but I love the fact that he has SURVIVED! His story makes him more interesting and real—like Guatemala was—and when I'm with him that's how I feel too. Kind of sick huh? Whatever, it's true. Again, thank you Dr. Progoff for championing journaling so I can admit all of this without anyone judging me.

My International Bible Fellowship (IBF) ladies have been praying for me to find someone. I didn't say anything about him because it's embarrassing to fall and then not have it work out in front of long-time married women. But, today in fellowship someone straight up asked me if I was seeing someone. They said I'm glowing! He loves me and treats me like I'm precious. I feel special and I'm so happy it's like fire shut up in my bones, so I guess it makes sense that they noticed.

I must admit . . . I LOVES ME SOME FALLU!

9

Dear Diary,

Next month is the family reunion in Alabama. Not excited about going, especially since it's too soon to invite Fallu, and that means a week away from him. I'm driving down and by I, I mean my beloved big sister, Siti, my brother-in-law, Mark, Mommy, the five kids and I will drive down together in the van. It also means that I will entertain the kids. Note to self: remember to pack the kiddie Benadryl to entertain the kids with. I'm joking. As long as we have books, hot wheels, pacifiers and dry diapers we'll be ok. Just may have to dose Mo, the oldest, cuz she likes to talk and talk and talk.

10

Dear Diary,

Crap! I am SO not looking forward to this trip to Alabama.

Mark has already pissed Siti off by telling my father's stepson, Calvin, that we will be driving through Memphis and suggesting that we visit him and Daddy. I don't know why he would do that. He knows we don't speak to them. And by we, I mean his wife, Siti. Her hurt, which looks like white hot anger with Daddy for throwing us away, gets me off the hook for speaking to our father who, since I can remember, has always found a way to turn every phone conversation into a condemnation because I'm not slim and pretty—like Siti.

"Daddy! I made Honor Roll!"

"Good. You still fat?"

"Yes, Daddy."

"Daddy I won first place in the poetry contest!"

"I never really liked poetry . . . how's your diet coming?"

Silence

"Not so good huh?"

"No Daddy"

"Daddy I'm going to the dance! Mommy said I could get a new dress."

"You should wear one of your sister's outfits. She's very fashionable."

"I . . . her clothes don't fit me."

"You wouldn't need a new dress if you lost weight. Then you could fit your sister's clothes. Your mother doesn't have money to keep buying bigger and bigger dresses for you"

"I'm sorry Daddy."

"I'm valedictorian of my class of 700! I have to give a speech at graduation!"

"You are gonna lose weight before you have to stand up in front of all those people I hope."

"I'll try Daddy."

"I got a job writing for a human rights magazine!"

"I guess writing is a good job for someone who doesn't like to move around a lot. It'll be harder for you to lose weight sitting behind a desk though."

Thank You Lord that you made him divorce Mommy, even though it still crushes her spirit 30 plus years later. She wouldn't have left him until he physically hurt me or Siti. Thank you for doing the hard thing that was for our good.

Thank you again Lord for moving us to Boston away from him so his access to me was limited!

God please don't let us stop in Memphis! Please don't make me see Daddy! Please, please, please, Lord. In Jesus' name I pray. Amen.

Maybe I can drive my car then I'm in charge of when and where I go.

Who am I kidding? My car wouldn't make it to Alabama. Neither would I.

I could fly.

No. The family is driving, and everyone's feelings would be hurt if I didn't go with them. Like I'd be saying something—judging them/separating myself—if I didn't go with them. Plus, Siti could use help with the kids . . .

God please don't let us stop in Memphis! Amen.

11

Dear Diary,

I told Fallu about Memphis and Daddy. He pulled me close, rubbed my booty then rumbled, "I like you heavy" in my ear.

Thank you, Lord. Amen.

12

Diary,

Ok, so guess what! I loves me some Fallu! I know I don't say it much right? But we took the kids out to lunch today—his idea! Yes. This man suggested and orchestrated that we take five kids ages 3 -10 to lunch. Deciding where to go was, in and of itself, a herculean effort. In the end we decided on Chuck-E-Cheese which meant it was going to be at least a three-hour outing, not including travel time. But my baby wanted to do it and had even saved his money from his job as a parking attendant to do it. Tell me that is not sweet!

I picked him up and we headed to Siti's house. The man was giddy! He said he was always around little kids in Sierra Leone. "Family was everywhere, Honey!"

When we got there the twins were still taking a nap, but the other kids were ready, especially Manny who loves hanging around other men, surrounded as he is by me, mom, Siti and his four sisters. He and his dad regularly sneak away to quiet corners to steep in their masculinity. For Manny, the steeping usually culminates in him getting naked and running through the house shaking his little penis at everyone, especially guests. Especially his paternal grandparents who

36

are much more proper than Mommy is. Mommy told Siti to "let the boy go naked. There'll be plenty of time for him to conform later."

I was grateful to find him clothed and playing with Legos when we arrived. Not sure how Fallu would have responded to a naked five-year-old.

Beans and Mo were ready. I beamed when I saw them. I always do. I love their little personalities. Mo, perfectly coiffed in a nice pair of jeans and a sweater. The bows in her hair perfectly matched her sweater and her hair was in two ponytails, not a hair out of place. At 10 she is discovering make-up so her lips were super shiny with Bonnie Bell lip gloss.

Beans was laying on the couch, legs akimbo, reading. She wore white on black polka dotted tights under a purple tulle tutu with an oversized green sweatshirt that had a giant purple sequined dinosaur doing a jig and saying "super-dee-doo-per-dee!" printed on the front and back. To top off the ensemble she had her sparkly purple and silver cowboy boots. Beans never went anywhere without them. Her hair, which is curly and shorter than Mo's, was in two pony-puffs. She had released a tuft of hair at the front of her head which she twirled around her finger.

When they saw us, the girls ran to give me and Fallu hugs. Fallu stood awkwardly with Siti (she wants to like Fallu but she's wary of him. Wary from Siti looks frosty). The girls as I chased Manny around the room to get my hug and kiss. After a few pleasantries, Siti and I went to get the twins and Manny led Fallu to the living room to play Legos with him. Fallu told me later that he had never played with Legos before. He'd seen pictures of them once in a magazine but, "In Africa we *use* plastic, Honey! We don't play with it." Turns out he loved them. I am already planning to buy him some for his birthday.

The twins, Milga and Carma, were lovely as they woke from their nap. Siti does such a nice job with them. They were so excited about Chuck-E-Cheese that they had slept with their shoes on. "So ve vill be veady ven Poohpie comes!" Siti mimicked their pacifier induced speech impediment. They sat up at the same time and each raised a dry cloth diaper to their noses and sniffed—their security blankets along with their pacifiers. Just like Beans went nowhere without her boots, the twins always—ALWAYS—have their pacy and their "dry diapee." After a hug and a kiss for each, Siti and I let them dress each other for the date. They each made sure the other's shoes were tied tight and smoothed down the other's hair. Then they walked to the potty and at the door informed that we were to wait for them in the living room.

"Ve need some piricy. Ve vill be vight zeah"

Translation: We need some privacy. We will be right there.

True to their word, they came to the living room a few minutes later with their coats on, ready to go. The older kids took a little bit more time to get ready but finally Manny had chosen the appropriate hot wheel to carry in his pocket and the girls had packed their pocket books. Morgan's full of tissue paper and lip glosses. Bean's with a tiny notebook, crayons and an orange, just in case there was a storm and we had to hide somewhere and she needed a snack and got bored.

Fallu watched the whole thing in amused silence.

After one more bathroom check we were finally ready to go but at the door Milga saw Carma sniff her dry diaper and instinctively went to sniff hers, but it wasn't in her hand. She checked her pockets. No dry diaper. She looked down at her feet, but it hadn't fallen there. The first utterance was calm, "Dry Dipee?" I saw my little sweetheart turning in a circle calling softly to her love "Dry Dipee?" Then she patted her chest the way her dad does when he's looking for his glasses. "Dry Dipee?" Undaunted she hit her knees and called out authoritatively as though to a dog, "Dry Dipee?? Dry Dipee!? Dry Dipee!" When Dry Dipee didn't come wagging his tail the panic rose in her voice and she began running through the house yelling for her friend, her baby, her love.

Dry Dipee! DRY DIPEE!

All of us, except Fallu, had been through this before and we manned our battle stations. Carma followed Milga to the bathroom, the last place they'd seen Dry Dipee. I could tell by the wails that he wasn't there.

Beans and Mo ran to the kitchen checking cabinets and the refrigerator. Siti and I looked between couch cushions and under toys. Manny walked around calling for Dry Dipee and laughing because he knew it wasn't like a dog and wouldn't respond. Fallu, assuming Dry Dipee was a dog, followed Manny calling out hoping Dry Dipee would respond. This sent Manny into fits of laughter.

Meanwhile Milga was in full meltdown mode on her knees looking for Dry Dipee. Her sisters offered her other dry diapers, but Milga wanted HER Dry Dipee. Carma helped Milga get her pacifier in her mouth, and this helped but after a couple of sucks Milga bit down on the pacifier and through clenched teeth screamed DRY DIPEEEEEE!

After five minutes of looking, and afraid Milga was going to send herself into convulsions from the panic, Siti took command of the situation, picking up Milga who was now rigid, arching her back, screaming around her pacy. Siti sat and cuddled her. Carma held her hand while Mo, Beans and I stroked her hair and legs. She was calming down when from the back of the house we heard Fallu's deep voice demand, "Dry Dipee! Come heya!" followed by peals of laughter from Manny. Reminded of the trauma, Milga pitched her head back and moaned "DRRRRYYY DIIIIPEEEE!"

One look at Siti's bucked eyes and pursed lips, sent the girls from the room. A minute later they returned to the living room, Mo holding Fallu's hand, Bean's pushing Manny forward.

Then the most amazing thing happened.

Carma cupped Milga's cheek and Milga stopped crying. They were looking into each other's eyes. No words transpired but they were apparently communicating. Carma cocked her head to the left and Milga nodded yes; to the right and Milga hunched her shoulders as if to say, "I don't know." A few more seconds of looking intently at each other, then Carma reached forward, unzipped Milga's jacket and pulled Dry Dipee out!

We all sat there stunned for a second until Milga laughed. Crisis averted.

Chuck-E-Cheese was fun.

Fallu was amazing.

The kids had a great time. Fallu had a great time! He even tried to go in the ball pit—he'd never seen one of those either—but I pointed out the sign that said it was only for kids.

Later after we'd dropped the kids off, he asked me where Dry Dipee had been hiding. When I told him he'd been in her coat all the time he asked how a dog could hide in her coat the whole time, and nobody know.

I can't wait to tell the kids tomorrow.

13

Dear Diary,

"When they discover a way to take a fertilized egg from my body and keep it alive OUTSIDE of my womb then birth it WITHOUT ME . . . Then and only then can you tell me that I can't have an abortion!" I railed at the tv as some white old man talked about the imperative to make abortion illegal.

I knew I was loud, but I was mad. I was tired of the debate about law that was settled before I was even born. I'd never had an abortion, but I was glad that I could have one if I needed one. I know I shouldn't get into a situation where I would need one, but that ship sailed years ago. I'm trying to be good with Fallu and so far, so good-ish, but . . .

Once I said my, I thought powerful, pro-choice statement, I realized that the vehemence may raise a question as to whether I'd had an abortion, so I backed away from the TV, sat back down at the dinner table and smiled at my family in apology as I took a bite of a roll.

Uncomfortable silence, and then . . .

Mom

Aka Lovey

Five foot three inches.

183 lbs.

Short salt and pepper afro with impending male pattern balding.

Spiritual head of household said.

"Trina, how does your stance on abortion jive with your Christianity?"

UHHHHHHH . . . well . . . it . . . Damn.

14

Dear Diary,

I guess now was about the best time to hear from Daddy as ever. I'm inoculated from him by Fallu's love.

Seems like Calvin, my stepbrother, told him we might be stopping by. I'm sure this set off all sorts of alarms for dear old Daddy. I'm sure his congregation doesn't know that Pastor Bob is a deadbeat dad with two children he effectively abandoned and an ex-wife he beat, at least once. Siti and I have always fantasized about standing up when they recognize visitors and announcing our relationship to dear old Daddy, aka SWoMM—the Sperm Who Made Me.

He called out of the blue. I think it's been at least 5 years since I spoke with him.

"Hey Baby, how are you?" (no exclamation point after the "term of endearment". Barely a comma just a throw away trying to get to the rest of the sentence.)

It took me a minute to register who he was then I heard the kind of hiccupping laugh that is uniquely Robert Lee.

"Daddy?" I say, then think that I really must find another way to address him. I think to call him SWoMM but the thought of sharing that moniker right now makes me sad.

"It's been a long time." He says somewhat accusatorily, and my sadness turns to guilt then anger that I should feel guilt. A beat passes before I can muster a word.

"It has been." I croak tightly. "How are you?"

"Things are hard here. People are going crazy. Are people going crazy there too?"

"Yeess..?" I say but can't keep the question out of my attempt at politeness because I have no freaking idea what he is talking about.

He talks for a while about the news in Memphis. Shootings, crime, vice—all the effects of the breakdown of the family and the absence of fathers in the household. He actually says this to me, the child he would have completely abandoned from the age of two. The only reason he didn't is because Mom insisted that we visit him for the summer and paid for us to do so until she couldn't afford to send us to him any longer. By that time, he had a wife and three sons (having adopted her two sons, and the one they had together) to take care of so he damn sure wasn't going to pay the two or three hundred bucks for the bus for me and Siti to come visit him.

I just responded with silence which to me is deafening but he didn't hear for about ten minutes.

"So enough about that. What is going on with you? Your brother tells me you are seeing someone pretty seriously?"

Dag, Mark has shared a lot with Calvin. Is this all he shared or is this the only thing that matters to Daddy?

"Yeah. He's pretty great. It's kind of new but we're serious." I can't help it. My voice brightens and I beam as I think of standing before my father with Fallu who is holding me tight. Proud of his Honey! With an exclamation point.

"Your brother says he is from somewhere else?"

"Yeah. He's African" I say.

"I guess that makes sense. They like big women. I'm guessing you're still fat? Where in Africa?"

"Uhhh. . . " I stammer, trying to get my bearings. I'm a grown ass woman and he still insults me and makes me feel like an ugly little girl. "Sierra Leone." I finally manage.

"Oh! Calvin didn't tell me that. They are animals in Sierra Leone baby. Don't you watch the news? He's probably just trying to get a green card and get away from that place. Be careful. I wouldn't stay in that relationship if I were you," he says.

I'm lost for words.

Hot tears run down my cheeks, and I feel like I'm going to vomit. Where do you start? What do you say? Apparently, nothing.

"Well baby. Good talk. Take care of yourself. Don't let him make a fool of you. I gotta go. Your stepmother is calling me. It's time to prep for Sabbath school. Don't be a stranger to your Daddy. Call me sometimes. Love you."

"Love you too Daddy." I say, providing the obligatory response to his call.

"Bye."

"Bye Daddy."

15

Dear Diary,

Back from Alabama!

So funny because I had straight up flashbacks to road trips when I was a kid. Back then I would be terrified when I saw the "Weigh Station" signs on the highway. I just envisioned everyone getting out of the car and lining up in front of giant scales and having their weight announced aloud. I didn't know what they would do if you were found to be too heavy. Was it dangerous to drive around with fat people in the car? Were the tires going to burst? Is that why there was rubber on the side of the road earlier in the trip? Had a car gone over a bump in the road with a fat person inside and when they came down the tire gave up the ghost and burst—like sitting on a balloon?

Would they pull me out of line if the scale said I was too heavy? Would my family be allowed to keep going and I'd just have to wait for them to return? How would they get me from the weigh station back home if I was too heavy to ride in a car? Mommy and Siti would never leave me—ever. I knew that for sure but how humiliating if we had to call and tell family and friends that we couldn't come visit them because Trina is too heavy to ride in the car!? Oh God My God! How heavy is too heavy? I didn't know but I knew for certain that I probably was.

I would be struck dumb with terror at the first sign and then pray and pray and pray that we would get to a sign that said, "Weigh Station Closed." In the event that we never saw the closed sign I would redouble my prayers and will/force Jesus to stop the driver from veering right, off the highway and onto the access road toward the Weigh Station. When we passed the station, I would promise God that I was going to lose weight and not put my family in danger again. But first I would eat a Twinkie or a Ho-Ho or both, to manage the aftermath of the anxiety and celebrate escaping the dreaded Weigh Station.

I never told anyone, not even Siti, about the terror of the Weigh Station. I don't know how I figured it out. I wonder if Siti would have told me it was to weigh trucks or if it would have been another thing she used to terrorize me and force obedience. Like telling me I was adopted and showing me rolled up papers that proved it. "If you tell Mommy that I was cursing I'll give the papers away. Then THEY'LL come and get you!"

I wasn't afraid of the Weigh Station this time, but I was terrified that Mark was going to take the exit for Memphis! Not only would Siti have been red hot pissed and the car dreadfully uncomfortable in her seething silence, but I would have to see Daddy and we all know what that would have been like. Even the idea of outing him to his congregation didn't make it worthwhile. He'd just say he hadn't wanted a fat daughter and I'm sure they would have understood his abandonment—at least of me. I saw the sign 140 miles before the exit. So did Mark and he mentioned it. There was a rumble of argument from the front seat then opaque silence coated the car for the next two hours. The closer we got to the exit, the more frequent his suggestions that we just pull off and have lunch with them. The silence turned jet black. The babies even pooped their pants, and the stench lay on top of the tension—choking us all. I was grateful when he pulled the car over to the side of the road so we could change them but we were only seven miles away from the exit so I couldn't breathe.

"There are three of us," I thought, "what if we just tied Mark up and put him in the trunk until we passed the exit?"

I looked at Siti, but her pupils had narrowed to pinpricks and I knew she was only seeing red as she changed the diaper. I cleared my throat to get her attention. When she looked at me, I widened my eyes meaningfully and cocked my head cryptically toward Mark who was smoking a little ways away from the car. She rolled her eyes and refocused on the task at hand, obviously not comprehending my ambush signal.

"All set?" Mark said, startling me.

"Does it look like we're all set?" Siti snapped, pointing at the little crap smeared tushy in front of her. I put my twin back in her car seat as Siti finished changing her twin's diaper then we all climbed in the car.

When we started off again, I prayed and prayed.

At mile marker 5 I could see that Mommy was praying too.

Mile marker 2 I reached out and held her hand. We prayed.

When I saw the exit, I closed my eyes and invoked scripture, "Lord where two or three are gathered you are there. Please please please"

I heard Mark chuckle and Mommy let out a deep breath. When I opened my eyes, we were cruising past the exit toward safety. It took days for Siti's wrath to pass but nobody called me fat and ugly the whole trip.

Thank you, Lord!

16

Dear Diary,

I was torn today. Black v Christian and proud of both. I left Sonia's house around 7 this morning to get back home to get dressed and go to work. We had a great time last night just hanging out. It's been a minute since I just hung out with friends. Most of my time has been taken with Fallu. I don't think that's bad, but they were salty and started talking about how they don't see me unless "He" is around, and I don't have any time because I'm always with "HIM".

"You don't even go to church on a regular basis anymore." That was Sonia, like she goes to church. She's right I don't go as often as I used to, but she only knows that because I said something about it. Fallu says he likes a more holiness church. I don't. He hasn't found one he likes, and he doesn't like my church. "It's too white. Honey!" So, I end up spending most Sundays with him. Shoot me.

I still listen to ministers on the radio and that's why I feel torn today.

Rev. John Perry said flat out that he could not support the Black Man's March because it was so closely aligned with the Nation of Islam. I understood that and it kind of resonated with what I felt in my gut, but I was torn. Said aloud, that reasoning felt narrow, bigoted and white-washed. What about black Pride and Unity?

Fallu was no help.

"You need to go to a real church Honey! Listen to a real preacher. Your church is too white for God to be there!"

"Shut up. You don't go to ANY church and you're not even going to the march."

"That's too many American blacks in one place Honey! They don't know how to act civilized."

Yeah, it turns out Fallu hates America and Americans (Black, White, Yellow, Red and Brown) but he would slit his wrists if somebody told him he had to leave.

I get his disdain of America in the liberal side of my heart but there's another side of me that feels a patriotic anger that I'm not accustomed to, so I ignore it. Just like I ignore the fact that he says I'm different from other Americans. Sort of how white folks say intelligent, well-spoken black folks are "different".

Then I heard this black male preacher on the radio say, "I am a Christian black Man, not a black Christian. Christ modifies everything about me. NOTHING modifies my relationship with Christ." So, the matter was settled for me. It felt great hearing a man of God who is black speak life and truth and stand up for Christ in the middle of a difficult situation. I was confident in my stance . . . until this morning.

I drove down 14th street and it was awash with so many black men and they were kind and happy and gentlemanly and beautiful. They were crossing the street in a HUGE gaggle until a beautiful brown skinned, short, buff man in an Omega Psi Phi t-shirt parted the crowd and let me drive through. As I did, he caught my eye and bowed! Then ALL of these black men just bowed slightly in respect for what . . . an African Queen? Me. I cried and giggled all the way home. This is MY people. This is black manhood. This is how I am supposed to be treated.

Thirsty for Christian black manhood.

50

17

Dear Diary,

I don't know why the Black Man's March affected me so.

Maybe it's the being seen. Or maybe it's pride. The sense of possibility. Of history. Of purpose. Just seeing so many black men and being seen by them and valued. Protected by them. God! That was so lovely. It's been a month and I still have the vapors. I've made some decisions:

1. I'm going to self-publish Dinosaur Brains, my children's book.

Ok . . . that's the only concrete decision I've made. The others are just to walk in my truth. Ok, not sure what that is completely yet but it has something to do with not being afraid to call myself a writer and not shying away from the fabulousness that is Trina but that I tend to hide away under a proverbial rock.

Guess I need to figure out what the rock is so I can get out from under it.

18

Dear Diary,

I broke up with Fallu tonight. He just gets mean and nasty, and I don't like it. Nothing violent but just crazy mean out of nowhere. I know it has something to do with his past but . . . . It's tiresome.

I told him I didn't want to see him anymore and he started crying. I usually fold when he cries but I felt manipulated this time, so I said I didn't want to hurt him, but it was over. Then he pulled out the big guns.

"If you leave me, I'll kill myself."

Looking back on it I'm proud of myself. I was so scared. I mean I know he has thought of death before. If you went through what he's gone through wouldn't you have to? I was afraid for him, but I also saw the red flags flailing wildly like hurricane Andrew was at the door.

"If you did that, I would be incredibly sad. I probably would never get over it, but I'd be alive, and you'd be dead, and it wouldn't be my fault."

Then I hung up the phone and prayed that I hadn't just horribly misjudged suicidality to be manipulation.

Freaking out!

19

Dear Diary,

I think I figured out what the rock that obscures my fabulousness is.

Daddy—duh.

Fuck!

Tired of "discovering" how he messed me up.

So, what Fallu is doing is a Daddy trigger. If I just go with the trigger, I'll call Fallu and apologize or at the very least act like he didn't threaten suicide to manipulate me.

Fuck that.

20

Dear Diary,

Day two and no Fallu.

What if he's lying dead in his room? It'll be my fault. Will this mean that I killed him?

Shut up! You did not kill him. He killed himself. And he probably didn't even kill himself. He's waiting for you to call him and apologize.

Should I?

For what? You don't even know what he was mad about. What was it???? I truly don't even know. I remember that he was getting agitated then he pulled out the tried and true insults about my weight. Veiled threats of cheating with the Ethiopian girls he works with at the parking garage. How pretty they are, how thin. And then the coup de grace was that his manager is thin, pretty and smart. "In her country Honey! She was a journalist. A writer like you but recognized. Important. A *good* writer. She wants me. I could have her, but I stick with you."

Daddy? That you?

Then, suddenly he was threatening to kill himself.

21

Dear Diary,

If he killed himself one of his roommates would have contacted me. They're not friends but they look out for each other. All of them are in immigration proceedings so nobody wants a dead body in the house. And none of them would call the cops first. I'd have heard. NO. This is manipulation.

22

Dear Diary,

I was right. That Man didn't kill himself. He brought flowers to my office today and everyone pressured me into having lunch with him and blah blah blah . . . we's loving again.

23

Dear Diary,

I know I'm in love cuz this makes me laugh.

Homeless Man asked me to buy him some chicken wings for lunch. I was a bit taken aback by the specificity of the ask but thought I would rather get him what he wants than something he doesn't like. Plus, just cuz you're homeless doesn't mean you eat everything, I reasoned. How would I feel if I really had a craving for bacon and couldn't buy it? And there's also that thing about being kind to strangers cuz they could be angels unawares.

So, I got my lunch and 3 wings for him. I passed him and happily gave him the Styrofoam package. He barely said thank you before tearing into the package. I kept walking feeling happy and holy about being able to do a good deed. Then I heard "only 3?!" I turned to look at him and he said, not apologetically- matter of factly—"that's alright tho. I ain't mad at you sis"!

What the f . . . ?!

My mind wasn't quick enough but even now I want to shove those wings down his THROAT!

Next time I see Mr. Chicken Wing I wish he would ask for something, so I can say NO and keep walking.

24

Dear Diary,

Last week, Fallu and I were at Sunday dinner at Siti's and I was telling a story about the first time I slugged to work.

"I was scared so I announced my name loudly and made a scene before getting into a car. 'I'm Trina Pardo (P-A-R-D-O) and I'm slugging for the first time! I hope this red Honda Civic, license plate number ZPW-7F43 has the heat on because I'm cold even though I'm wearing a green bomber jacket and brown slacks. But that's the system, right? I get in and they take me to work for free? Ok, I'm getting in the car. I'm Trina Pardo! Oh Look! The driver is a white guy with long brown hair almost as long as my B1-colored box braids!'"

Everyone, except Fallu, was laughing. It hadn't been his finest evening. He was nervous and when he's nervous he's a bit of a jerk. But to be fair, he thinks my family judges him—which they do. I'm the baby. It was just me, mom and Siti until Mark came along. Then the babies came so now it is me, mom, Siti, Mark, Mo, Beans, Manny, and the twins, Carma and Milga. Fallu has to prove himself worthy of acceptance. It just makes sense. But today he was making a particular ass of himself.

"Honey! Why do you do that slugging? It's suburban hitchhiking. It's not safe." Fallu's sternness cut into the laughter.

"I used to feel the same way" I chuckled, "but it's a free ride to work and gets me there in a fraction of the time and"

"I don't like it! I disallow it!" he kind of bellowed.

Siti's side eye and Mommy's pursed lips were not lost on anyone. This was Siti's second side eye of the evening. The first came in response to the comment, "Honey! You need to wait for someone to say that about you!" when I stated that the potatoes I'd made were delicious—which, for the record, they were. When I heard Siti take a deep breath I jumped in quick because nothing good was going to come from anything she said at this point.

"It's really ok Baby. I've never had a prob"

"You gonna help her pay for the bus since you *disallow* slugging?" Siti broke in, eyes bucked, head cocked to the side, tongue slightly poking through tight lips and nails clicking against each other.

Crap!

Mommy and the kids looked up from their plates, on high alert waiting for Siti to explode. Thank God for Mark. I saw him place a hand on her hand, silencing the nails.

"The roast is good, Ter" he said then he looked at Fallu and gave a "don't push it Man," nod of his head, which, thank you Jesus, Fallu understood.

"It is good. Did you cook it before you cooked it?" Fallu asked and gave a fake smile.

I heard the kids giggle and I saw Mommy shoot a look that shut them down. If the moment hadn't been so fraught I'd have giggled too, it sounded funny: cook it before you cook it.

"Yes." Mark said even though he had no freaking idea that "cook it before you cook it" meant tenderizing the meat by boiling it before baking it. Apparently, the meat in Sierra Leone is tough so you have to cook it before you cook it. But who the hell knows that in America?

61

Mark gave a pursed smile that yelled, "Poo, you so hard up that you would date an idiot child?" Siti, mouth wide open, rolled her eyes. Mommy's face softened and she offered him a dinner roll. I could hear her reciting, and modifying, Hebrews 13:2 in her head. "Do not forget to show hospitality to strangers (and Dorothy, in this case, dimwits) for by so doing some people have shown hospitality to angels unawares. The kids giggled uncorrected by their parents who were also at this point on the verge of hysterics. Fallu took an embarrassingly huge bite of the roll Mommy had proffered.

Later after dinner I heard Manny say, "cook it before you cook it!" in a spot-on imitation of Fallu. Worse, I heard Mommy laugh—not the indulgent grandmotherly laugh—a real belly laugh. Everyone—even Mark—was laughing. When I walked into the kitchen they tried to stop but couldn't.

So . . . yeah. Everyone thinks Fallu's an idiot.

25

Dear Diary,

In the end it was just easier to give in. I pay $13/day and easily add 90 minutes to my daily commute.

Siti hasn't said a word to me for a week.

I'm beat, broke and sad.

26

Dear Diary,

Fallu had to leave for a while. Immigration sucks! He had to go BACK to his first port of safety—Ireland—and wait to be called for an asylum interview in the States. It's messed up and . . . just messed up. But, this entry is not about the tears because I've cried enough. This is about the strength of our relationship and our determination to make this thing work.

I sent him Polaroid pix of my boobies!

My sister, ever cautious, said that I could get arrested on international porn charges, but I was committed to it because I didn't want to give Satan a foothold in my marriage and Proverbs 5:19 said he should be intoxicated by my breasts—how can that happen if he doesn't see them?

Yes, I know we are not married but we love each other. We haven't done the DEED but close and I don't want some Irish chick turning his head.

Emboldened by the utter righteousness of the whole thing, I sent the pix and . . . he really liked them! I know because a week later I got the call. He was talking in code—because he was afraid of the possible porn charges too.

"Honey!" (Said with such love and desire. I just . . . wow)

"You know those things you sent me?"

"Oh, you mean the"

"Yeah! Send me some more huh? But lower next time."

OOOOH MY GOSH! Was he seriously asking for pix of my vijajay? I mean we got away with the tatas but vag pics were sure to get me arrested! And what happened if they got lost in the mail, pictures of my vagina could be floating around—they could end up on the internet!

No way!

If I did, I'd have to make sure my face wasn't in the picture.

No freaking way!

How would I even get pictures like that?

NO way!

But then, another verse popped into my head, 1 Corinthians 7:3-4. "Don't deny your spouse sexually; yield your body to your husband."

(Yes, Diary I know. Not married . . . Damn!)

I called Lin, my sexiest friend. She always had sexcapades to talk about. Once, she emailed sexy pictures of herself to a boyfriend and he opened them in the middle of a meeting. She has a good camera.

"Sooo, Fallu wants pix of my twat! Can you believe that?"

"That's really sexy."

"I know!"

"You're going to do it right?"

"Yeah. That's why I called you. You took those nice pictures at the wedding last year . . . I was wondering if . . . "

"NO!"

"Come on, you're such a good photographer, remember that picture of the Grand Canyon you took? It wouldn't be that weird."

"Hell no!"

Ok so I didn't think that through that well, but she did loan me her camera and show me how to use the timer.

All I had to do was focus the camera on something—I used a Hello Kitty stuffed animal the twins had left at my house—set the timer then exchanged my cootie for Hello Kitty. At first, I was all timid but with a couple of glasses of Shiraz and my imagination ablaze I got bolder. After 10 minutes I had resurrected a pair of old stilettos and figured out how to take the pix without the timer—action shots.

I can barely walk in those stilettos, so I know I looked like a baby giraffe wobbling around the room trying to balance on one foot with the camera pointed you know where—but I did it!

The next day I dropped the film at Walmart. I was so nervous and excited that I didn't really think it through to the end. I returned 2 hours later to pick up the photos. You drop the film off at the front of the store and pick the pictures up in the center of Walmart at the developing station.

The developing station is a giant machine with this conveyor belt. The pictures, once developed, fall to the belt (face up) and slowly ride around the machine until they plop in a pile on the table. All of this is enclosed by a transparent case that seems to magnify the pictures, so shoppers can easily share in the fun of the pictures of the cookout tug of war, the cutting of the wedding cake and, oh yeah, Trina's cookie! Then the 16 or 83-year-old Walmart worker manually puts the pix in the folder right there so you and everybody and their daddy can see. The kids love it! In fact, there was a HUGE crowd of kids around the station—it looked like a freaking field trip! All I could think was "I am going to be recognized and then arrested for the corruption of minors."

I prayed, "Lord this is a good time for the Rapture please" and waited to be harpazo'd into the sky to meet the Lord and escape sex crime charges.

When I opened my eyes and saw that the Lord had not chosen this moment to have his Church meet him in the air, I turned to leave; but I wanted those pictures! That's when it hit me! I could lie!

I did my most perfect impression of a high powered "I don't give a damn about you because I'm a doctor" arrogant stance. I strode to the counter ignoring the children around me who were probably traumatized and full of questions. I ignored the stares from all of the adults who certainly recognized my twat through my pants. And I ignored the voice screaming in my head that the pimple faced cashier KNEW, and said, "I am DOCTOR Trina Pardo, OB/GYN! And I'm here for my important medical conference photos—of someone other than me!" and I flung my ticket on the counter.

That's how it happened in my head. In reality, I shuffled to the counter and guiltily slid my ticket stub toward the little boy I had corrupted and I waited for the police to arrest me for lewd and lascivious behavior; for the reporter ready with the headline "COOTIE QUEEN BIBLE TEACHER ARRESTED!

To my surprise the Walmart guy said, "$5" and gave me an envelope full of pictures—just an envelope.

I ran out of the store giggling to myself barely able to resist showing my twat pix to the little old man greeting people at the door.

I was too embarrassed to look at them, but He liked them! (Fallu, not the old man.) He said it gave him hope and determination to keep fighting to get back here to me!

MY Cootie did that!

Take that Ms. Fitzgerald, Immigration heffa!

27

Dear Diary,

It feels weird not to do International Bible Fellowship (IBF) this year, but it takes up a lot of time and I want to be available to Fallu when he's able to come back to the US. I also need to be able to go see him in Ireland and that means my co-leader has to do the class on her own. Nobody said anything last year, but I know it was a problem from the prayers.

"We're just going to pray that the Lord removes all obstacles, so leaders can honor their commitment. Amen?"

I get it. Betty, my IBF leader, was sad when I told her I wasn't coming back, but something's got to give and it's not going to be my relationship so . . . .

28

Diary,

I was at Siti's house today and went to get the kids for lunch. Siti said they were in the basement but there was no sound coming from that direction. When I got to the bottom of the stairs, I saw Carma curled in Bean's lap and her twin, Camille, curled in Mo's lap. The older girls were petting each twin as if they were puppies. Midnight, the dog was sitting contentedly in the corner. It was the cutest sight.

When I tip-toed closer trying not to disrupt the scene, I realized Midnight was sitting on Manny's lap like he was a tiny shih tzu rather than a giant black lab. The scene went from sweet to funny and my cackles ignited chaos. Midnight started barking and ran to me looking for treats. Manny let out a wail—Midnight's tail had smacked him in the face. The girls, startled by the commotion, scattered. I saw Beans' behind, and chubby little leg go over the back of the couch as Mo reach out to drag Manny by the leg behind the curtains. The twins had bolted behind the chair, but they've grown taller, so I saw the edges of their afro puffs peaking above the pillows. (Siti's a little paranoid and they live in a very wooded, secluded neighborhood so the kids have been taught to scatter and hide when there is a commotion. "You never know

Poohpie." Mo had told me one day when she was three.) The whole scene went from funny to hilarious and I was bent over, legs squeezed together trying not to pee my pants laughing.

"What is going on down here?!" Siti demanded as she came bounding down the stairs—ready to annihilate who or whatever was threatening her seven cubs (the kids plus me and midnight). When they heard the savior's voice, the kids came running and hid behind Siti's legs.

Seeing her standing wide legged and holding a bat above her head, sent me to my knees screaming in hysterics. The kids fell on me, laughing.

After a stunned moment Siti yelled "What in the world?"

Siti wanted to laugh too, I could tell, but the adrenaline was still high so annoyance was all she could muster. She found her smile and laughed a little, but I saw tears escape her eyes—fear. Beans saw it too. She hugged her mom and we all followed suit, calming the mama bear.

After lunch Siti asked for clarification on what had caused the commotion. Anxious to ensure that I was not blamed for "riling up the kids" as I frequently am told I do, I recounted the scene that I'd come upon.

"What happened that made you all sit so quietly? There was no tv show going. Nobody was reading. You were just sitting quietly petting each other," I said.

Mo and Beans looked at each other a little sheepishly. Manny gave his twisted smile. In unison, speaking around their pacifiers, the twins giggled, "Ve vere playing Poohpie and Fallu"

Siti looked puzzled then smiled in understanding.

"You were playing Poohpie and Fallu? What is Poohpie and Fallu?" I asked completely lost.

"You know Poohpie!" Manny said and in a rare moment of cuddling, crawled into Bean's lap and she began to cuddle and pet him like she'd done to Carma. "I'm Fallu," he said.

"And I'm Poohpie!" Beans said.

"Vy is Fallu alvays ze puppy?" Carma asked.

"Yeah Poohpie? Do you get to play ze puppy?" Milga asked, concerned.

I was still completely clueless, so Siti explained that the kids had noticed that whenever Fallu and I were together I was touching him. Petting him like a puppy, and he always sat really close to me almost in my lap.

"It's one of their favorite games," she said, and one that she encouraged them to play, especially around nap time.

God, I love them! They notice everything about me.

God, I miss him.

29

Dear Diary,

Did budget.

Woefully overdrawn!

Effects of ticket to Ireland and cost of being there ten days. Found out that Fallu is living in an awful building. Very drafty.

Thankfully I haven't signed a contract to self-publish Dinosaur Brains. Spent some of that money to get Fallu some warm clothes and blankets and to try to insulate his flat. Didn't work. We were both sick. Colds. Left him with some money to take care of himself. There's just enough left to pay the bounced checks and overdraft fees.

I know I know . . . my dream. Fallu's my dream now. When things are better, I'll publish. Anyway, if I were a real writer—a good one—I wouldn't have to self-publish. I'd get a real publisher.

30

Dear Diary,

Heartbroken.

He called around 9 tonight. We were talking about the day, and I could tell he wasn't really listening. I told him about the Bosnian refugees I was working with. My job is to write their stories and humanize the issues for our funders and for the courts. He knows this. Duh that's how we met. Several of the Bosnians reacted negatively to having a black woman in the room so I was asked to leave, and the cases were given to another staff whiter, I mean writer. I was annoyed but understood that inserting race at this point is more problematic than helpful.

"Why didn't you know that, Honey! You are always trying to help but you don't help anyone!"

"What the hell does that mean?"

"It's nice of you and I guess you can't help it that's how Americans are. You get in the way, and you are nosey and don't help anybody," he said.

"Like we didn't help your ass? My organization provided free legal representation to your black behind, and I supported you when they deported your ass. But Americans and me specifically. We don't help anybody?"

I wanted to say all of that, but I held my tongue and just sat silent which felt like a betrayal of myself and everyone, but I did it, hoping he'd be quiet and we could just move forward and/or end the call.

"You are all so gullible. Those guys. Those Bosnian guys are lying to you. None of that stuff happened to them," he said and sucked his teeth really long the way he does when he's angry.

"What do you mean they are lying?" I said it before I thought. I knew his eyes had closed to slits and he was shifting in his seat. I'd seen and felt this mood often enough to know better. I should have just been quiet. I usually am. I don't know if it is a flashback or some other trauma process, but nothing good comes when he's like this. Best to let it pass but I couldn't this time.

"Honey! They are making all of that up! There is no war over there,"

"What about all the testimonies and pictures. I spent the last week looking at pictures of women and girls who had been raped and beaten! What do you mean it didn't happen?"

I tried to prove to him and myself that he was wrong. As if I doubted the war. I didn't. But in that moment, I wasn't absolutely sure.

"They make that stuff up and you Americans are too stupid to know it! You are all dumb. And idiots!" he was yelling now. The anti-American rant went on for a good 2 minutes.

I felt like I was losing my mind. He's been back three months and each day he seems more dissatisfied with me, America, everything than the day before. Did I really do all that I did to get him back here for this? All the time and heartache. All the humiliation from Ms. Fitzgerald, the immigration heffa who repeatedly said Fallu was only after citizenship and didn't love me? All the debt I've racked up? For this?

Unable to hold my tongue any longer I said, "All Americans are dumb?"

"Yes! All of you. You don't know anything!"

"I'm dumb? Mom's dumb? My family is dumb? Your attorney is dumb?"

"Yes. Honey, you know Mum doesn't know anything!"

Now you can do a lot of stuff to me but don't mess with my family—especially my mom.

"Ok," I said. "I'm gonna hang up now."

"You are just going to let me talk about Mum like that? What kind of woman are you? You should be ashamed of yourself! You are horrible! You will never be the mother of my children! NEVAH!"

My voice was so calm. I was distraught inside and in tears but all I could do was say goodbye and hang up the phone.

He called right back and for 20 minutes the phone rang. Finally, I answered, and he was out of his mind yelling. Cursing. Calling me and everyone I knew out of our names.

I did my fair share of yelling back and then I said, "Never call me again." Then he began to cry. I didn't care. I was tired, and something kicked in and said you are worth more than this. He's been calling all night, but I just can't with him anymore!

31

Dear Diary,

This was in my inbox today:

Hardkock57 wants to meet you!

Everyone is forcing me to go online and find a Fallu replacement. Donna wrote an ad for me and paid for 3 months.

Out of horror, and sheer curiosity, this is what I learned about Hardkock57. He is a black man. Aged about fifty (Hardkock? Fifty? That alone tells you he's a liar—sorry, smile). His profile picture is a selfie of him in a hoodie. I'll give it to him, he has a nice smile except for the gold upper front teeth. He took the picture of himself standing in a mirror. The room reflected in the mirror is a mess—clothes on the floor, a gold, 70s era carpet. In the full-length picture he is shirtless in tight red hammock shorts, with a picture of a hot dog in a bun accentuating the bulge between his legs.

Hardkock then informs that: he has a high school education, is "not looking for a relationship or commitment of ANY type;" and, in the "about me" section he says he wants "*to make you quiver and arch your back.*"

Oh yeah, he notes that he is a Baptist.

This is who looked at my profile and chose to write to me or (and this is even worse-er) may have been *chosen FOR* me by the wise folks at the dating site. My profile reads thusly:

"Conservative Christian, two master's degrees." The profile picture is professional and polished with my locks pulled into a bun. My full-length picture (which apparently is mandatory—ugh!) is from a family picnic last summer. I have my signature bodycon look. A fitted v-neck yellow shirt showing a bit of cleavage (body) and a flirty, above the knee multicolored skirt (cinched at the waist and showing leg; flouncy, covering tummy pouch and cellulite thighs—conscious).

In the "about me" section—interested in the arts, loves live theatre.

32

Dear Diary,

I almost signed up for IBF. Almost. I picked up the phone to tell Betty everything, but I just couldn't. I knew she'd be thinking, "Poor pathetic Trina. Why can't she keep a man?"

Well, I can keep a man, BETTY! And it sure as hell won't be Hardkock57, "Jesus lover on a dirty mattress," or any of the others who had bad grammar or wouldn't respond to a message unless I sent a picture of my body.

Fallu's difficult that's true but who wouldn't be if their family was killed in front of them? If you were in a Sierra Leonean jail and tortured for a year then escaped when they took you out to kill you Betty, you'd be difficult too! And God saved him and sent him here. If he can live through that I can love him through the hard times.

The dial tone-turned-into-an-insistent-beep broke into my thoughts.

I can't abandon Fallu. Especially not for judgmental women who already have their husbands and children. I'm sure they had to work through issues. Fallu and I will work through ours.

33

Dear Diary,

I don't tell anyone about our arguments anymore because I tend to get over them quicker than others do. Especially mom and Siti. Forget it. They are going online looking for men for me to date. (Surprise! They haven't found anything! I told them about Hardkock 57, but hey . . .) Still, they're done with Fallu. Mom said it would break our family apart if I stayed with him. For the first time ever, I had to read her and tell her that this is my life and I hope I don't have to choose between my future and my family. She was quiet after that. Detente.

I love him, and he says he loves me. I know he needs me and that feels as good as love. Even better. His love is about me. Nobody and nothing else. That feels great and even when it feels lousy it's better than not having it.

34

Dear Diary,

Fallu asked me to marry him yesterday, and I said yes.

Last night's dream.

I walk into the room. I'm in a white gauzy gown/robe deal. I'm me but not me. I'm a white woman a la Charlize Theron in Devil's Advocate but you can't see my face that well. I'm just in good skinny shape under the robe thingy. The room is hazy, and you suddenly realize it is a church.

I sit on the communion table in front of the altar waiting and willing something to happen.

The door opens at the back of the sanctuary and Fallu is standing there. He is broken and sad. He can barely stand. The sight of him so alone and hurting breaks my heart. I cry for him and hold out my hands to him. "Come!" I say but it seems like I am so far from him that my voice is but a whisper on the incense smoke laden breeze.

Then, somehow, I take his hand and lead him down the aisle to the altar.

HERE'S WHERE THE DISCLAIMER IS NEEDED. I'm NOT saying I am God!

I cry as he walks toward me and say, "Come let me heal you." And I lay on the table naked and wait for him.

When he gets there, he mounts me, and I keep saying "I will heal you."

35

Dear Diary,

Wedding planning has been tough. Who to invite? Fallu wants a big wedding, but he is sad—which means angry—that he doesn't have anyone to invite. He doesn't like Americans so doesn't make friends with them. "They are all white Honey! Even the black ones. And they hate immigrants. All of us!"

No sense arguing. But the problem is he doesn't like immigrants either!

"All of them are either tomato girls or teefman!" he is fond of saying with a suck of his teeth. (Took me months to figure that one out, 'teefman'. I thought he was calling them dentists. "Teeth Man". No. A teefman is a "Thief Man" My Krio is getting there.)

So, the guest list has been hard to make up.

I always wanted a big wedding but when it comes down to it I:

a. Don't have THAT many people I want to invite
b. Would prefer any money that we would spend on a wedding go into the bank; we want to buy a house. Fallu doesn't believe in renting. I guess I don't either.

36

Dear Diary,

I have to say that I have hated this wedding planning process and sometimes Fallu, until today!

We agreed to have a small ceremony in Siti's backyard. She doesn't agree with the marriage, but she loves me so she's doing as much as she can. Still, I feel the tension and I know the family is praying that I'll come to my senses and end it . . . or Fallu will. Everyday there is an argument about something but today we unanimously chose the ring bearer.

The kids, especially Mo, have befriended the little neighbor boy. His name is Ngoc. The cutest little thing. He follows Morgan around like her shadow. When his parents found out about the wedding, they let it slip that Ngoc has wanted to be a ring bearer since he went to his cousin's wedding 3 years ago. His cousin wouldn't let him be his ring bearer because Ngoc has Downs Syndrome—the wife's family didn't want to mess up their wedding pictures. Why did they say that? When the kids heard about it, they were livid and went on a campaign to have him be my ring bearer.

I have to admit, I was afraid to ask Fallu. I wasn't sure what he would say but God is good and so is Fallu. He agreed! One of his childhood friends had a little brother he said looked like Ngoc.

"Short with eyes like him and the same little waddle Honey! He was always sweet. I felt sorry for him because they kept him in the house. He always cried when we went out to play but he liked my mum's banana akras so I would always slip him one when she made them."

Can you say I fell in love with him? HARD! I forget how sweet he can be when he gets into his angry spells. I don't care what else happens with the wedding. Ngoc is going to be the ring bearer and that's all that matters.

NO IDEA what an akras is.

37

Dear Diary,

It's akara. Thank you, Google.

It's a banana fritter. Pretty easy to make. Just a little messy because you deep fry them. Yep, I made them for Fallu.

He came over for dinner. I was going to try my hand at cassava leaf soup again but I hate Cassava leaf soup. So I just ordered a pizza and then fried up the akara while he was watching a soccer match on tv.

They came out beautifully and really tasty. I walked out into the living room where he was sitting on the couch and stood in front of the tv proffering my gift of love.

"TADAH!" I said and put the plate of akara under his nose so he could get a good whiff.

He looked like I'd smacked him.

"I-I tried my hand at akara." I stammered, terrified I'd just made a giant mistake.

He didn't make a move he just sat there, face inscrutable.

"I'm sorry. It was stupid. I thought you liked them." I was trying to turn and scurry away before he said something awful, when I felt his hand on my arm, stopping me mid-pivot.

"I do. I love them, Honey!" He kind of whispered. Then he reached up and took one. It felt like slow motion as I watched his hand move to his mouth holding the golden-brown dense puff of fried dough. He ate it in two bites and when he pulled his hand away there was powdered sugar on his mouth and there was a smile. When my eyes scanned up from his mouth, I saw the tears in his eyes a millisecond before they rolled down his cheeks.

"They were my favorite. I was the only one in the family who liked them. My mum would make them special for me and no one else." He said and the tears just flowed and flowed.

God, I love that man!

Telling myself that I will not make banana akara every day.

38

Dear Diary,

It took some sleuthing, but I found a Sierra Leonian lady who will make akara for our wedding. It'll be a surprise. That way his mom will kind of be there with us.

Ngoc and akara.

I can't wait for the wedding.

39

Dear Diary,

I's Married now!

It was such a beautiful day. Bright and sunny but not too hot. It rained two days before, so the lawn was an emerald green. Ngoc was so excited that he started crying. Mo had to hold his hand and walk down the aisle with him. I could hear the "aaawwww" from inside the house as I waited my turn.

When the wedding march started to play, I stepped out of the patio door. Fallu was at the far end of the yard next to Pastor Farmer. Fallu looked so handsome in a white grand boubou with brilliant gold embroidery. I could tell he was nervous aka mad by the set of his jaw, the wideness of his eyes and the tenseness in his stance. He looked like a rabbit about to bolt. But then he looked at me.

I heard him gasp then saw the smile spread across his face. He was all teeth! I took a step toward him and to my surprise he took a step then another toward me. The next thing I knew he had sprinted up the aisle and was holding me and smiling down at me. I noticed a tear in his eye before he kissed me. It was a glorious kiss. For a second it was just the two of us and when the kiss ended he nuzzled my neck and whispered "you are so beautiful!" in my ear.

I could have stayed there forever but Pastor Farmer cleared his throat and effectively broke the spell Fallu and I were under. We looked up and the entire gathering was looking at us smiling, some had tears flowing. Embarrassed, I smiled at Fallu and then he broke into this perfect little giggle that made me love him in the core of my being. The giggle turned into a belly laugh full of happy tears and all the while he held on tightly to me. The whole gathering laughed and finally Pastor Farmer said, "Who gives this woman to be married to this man?"

My whole family said as one, "we do!"

To which Pastor Farmer said, "good cuz by the look of things he ain't letting go!" and the crowd burst into laughter again as Fallu and I walked hand in hand down the aisle to the altar to get married.

Yeah. No.

None of that happened.

That's an excerpt from a romance aka smut novel I'm writing.

Wedding was trying. He didn't like the akara. Said they were soggy. Wondered if the lady's house was clean. "Honey! You don't even know her. She could have poisoned us! Americans!"

Crazy Fallu showed up with a vengeance on the honeymoon.

Arguments.

He disappeared for three days then looked crazed when I saw him on the street. I begged him to come back. He did.

We barely touched.

What the hell have I done?

40

Dear Diary,

I know it's been a while, but I need to share this dream:

I am a little girl crying and saying all that has happened to me. I'm all alone it seems, then I realize that I am trying to talk to someone and tell them what is wrong. The scene pans out and you realize that there is a giant man in the room. I yell at him trying to be heard, "Daddy! Help!" But he can't hear or see me. He turns his back on me, so I start yelling at another person. Trying to get help/comfort.

"Fallu! Fallu!"

He's a giant too and even though he looks down at me he's indifferent and looks away as if I'm invisible. In response I scream louder and climb up on a chair and wave my arms.

Finally, I get off the chair and just plead to be seen/heard/helped . . . loved. Then mom walks up to me. She is the same size as me. We barely reach the top of the soles of Daddy and Fallu's shoes. She puts her arm around me and says, "They can't see you sweetheart. You don't exist for them." Then she leads me away from the giants.

I woke breathless.

Sick.

I *wish* I could pretend that my subconscious isn't telling me that Fallu like Daddy is going to break my heart.

47

Dear Diary,

He caught me.

I started going to church again. It's been a while and I have to say I missed it. Fallu doesn't go. Won't go. It's funny what we swallow when we are in love. In my gut I knew he was lying about his spiritual walk. He only pulls out God when he wants to chastise or control me. It has worked for a long time, but I know who God is. I've allowed myself to be stupid—questioning everything I know to be true. I'm trying to wake up now.

I don't tell him where I'm going. I go to the early service so he's usually asleep when I leave. I bring coffee home and act like I've been going to the gym.

I knew something was wrong this morning—he was out of bed and dressed when I got home.

"You went to the gym?"

It was a trap. I could hear it in his voice and his eyes were small and red.

"ummmmm." I said wagging my head in a slight circle. It wasn't a yes or a no, but regular folks usually feel as though there's been an answer.

"ANSWER ME!"

Shit! Fallu's not regular folks.

"I went to church!"

"LIES! If you went to church, why would you tell me you went to the gym?"

Good question! Why did I lie about going to church? Then there was my answer.

"Are you going to that white church?! I forbid it. It is a devil church. God is not there. I thought you were a Christian! If you go to church, why aren't you singing in the choir? That is not a church, and you are not a Christian! You don't sing!"

Wait, what?

How do you respond to this level of crazy?

You don't. You sit and take it until he gets so mad he leaves. So, I sat and eventually he left me alone—a penitent child sufficiently scolded . . . for now.

When he returned, he was still angry but able to accept my apology for not telling him I was going to church. He tried to tell me not to go—at least not to that church but he didn't push. I know it's not the end of this but I'm not giving up church again.

42

Dear Diary,

I can't stop drawing pregnant women. Distended, life-filled bellies cover every open surface I get my hands on. I'm getting quite good too. The last drawing was so beautiful with the hand resting lightly on top of the belly that I cried, wishing I could feel life moving inside of me. I keep it in my wallet.

Since the terrorists attacked New York and the world changed, my heart has been on getting pregnant, but my head and uterus scream NO! The baby's daddy would be Fallu and I don't know what he would do to the soul of a child. More and more his crazy is coming out. More and more I'm isolated from my family—my fault. I can't defend him anymore and I can't bear the humiliation. Also, deep down I'm afraid to have him around the girls. I don't think . . . ok I HOPE he wouldn't do anything inappropriate, but Bat Shit crazy Fallu could get my husband Fallu killed and me in jail . . . so best to isolate.

He pinched me yesterday.

I keep checking to see if there is a bruise. So far so good. I can still pretend it was playful, but I'm scared. Nobody knows that but you,

Diary, so keep your mouth shut about it. I don't mind spanking kids but if I'm afraid that a pinch is a harbinger of doom for me, what would he do to a kid?

The worst is the spirit killing. I feel like a husk of my old self. I can't think anymore. You know it's a problem when I look at work (8 hours of hearing/reading/writing about torture) as a relief.

I'm always tired. He wears me out. We argue all the time. I can't even tell you what he is mad about. He blows a gasket and walks out. At least he still walks out . . .

Last month he cleared out our bank account and packed up his shit and left while I was at work. He left $20 in the account. Thank God it was pay day, so the bills didn't bounce. Thank God Siti had convinced me to open a secret account in my name, so I had something. He contacted me 3 days later told me it was my fault he stole all of our money and I heard myself begging him to come back. I didn't want him back, but I didn't want to have a failed marriage. I know what that looks like. I don't want to be alone.

I guess it is already failed since I'm afraid when we have sex now –I don't know where he was, what he was doing, or who he was with then, now or ever really. He has already given me chlamydia. Fool me once . . . but I still have sex with him—when he will. God help me I still want to be married just maybe to the IDEA of him—not the reality of him.

So glad I can finally admit this, Diary.

No. Nobody knows this.

43

Dear Diary,

Two weeks after vacation to Sedona with Lin.

You know it's time for a divorce when you write, read and re-read this to fall asleep. To get out of bed. To get through the day. To fall asleep . . .

Tip Top Drive

When she stepped off of the plane she could feel the tension in her shoulders melt away. She was free, and her mind could be free too. She didn't have to think of anything that troubled her. Not her husband's lack of care. Not her sister's pain wracked body. Not her mother's need for money. Not the crazy people at work. Nothing. Was it her imagination or was the air thinner there? Not the thin that makes you nauseated but the thin that flows freely through the nostrils and up to the brain making synapses fire and bringing creativity. She'd been there for 8 days and 9 nights. Alone. What a wonderful vacation and now it was over. She was going back to her life, such as it was . . .

When she stepped off of the plane this time it was cold and immediately her shoulders hunched against the wind. She walked to the car which she had parked on the first level anticipating that her bags would be heavy, and she wouldn't want to walk too far. She'd had to get to the airport early to ensure that she found a spot where she wanted to be. That was ok though because it had given her an excuse to leave her life behind a couple of hours early.

Now she was back.

Funny, she'd climbed Camelback Mountain last week in the oppressive heat of August in Arizona and yet now she was winded just walking to the car.

"Hello!" She called voce sotto, not really wanting to arouse anyone. She had dreaded this moment for the entire plane ride. Part of her *wanted* him to come running like a dog, jumping on her with glee, panting his excitement at seeing her again. Most of her dreaded the anticlimactic "Hi Honey" she anticipated getting. No panting. No running. No exclamation point. Just a disinterested "Hi Honey" as if she'd only been gone to the store for a couple of minutes, not in Paradise for a week.

The house was silent. He wasn't even home. Was there a note? She checked the usual spots.

Nothing.

Just when she thought he couldn't surprise her anymore, he did. He was gone. No, not for good but definitely not there to greet her. Should she call the cell phone? Torn, she dialed the number she had dialed so many times before, seeking to open the lines of communication with her husband. He answered. His voice was light and happy, "Hell-lloo!"

"Hi" she said, voice somewhat dead yet expectant/hopeful.

"Oh, hi Honey" his voice dropped. That was it. . .

. . . When she stepped off of the plane, she could feel the tension in her shoulders melt away. She was free again and her mind could be free too. Thoughts ran through her head. Not of troubles but of possibilities. She could imagine herself a painter, sculptor, author . . . The ideas exploded in her mind in ways she hadn't experienced in . . .

how long had it been? The sun beat down on her skin and her body reverberated with the creativity which seemed to be bursting in her cells.

. . . Was it her imagination or was the air thinner there? Not the thin that nauseates but the thin that flows freely through the nostrils and up to the brain making synapses fire and bringing . . . freedom.

In the hills of Sedona on top of Tip Top Drive, she reinvented her future . . .

44

Dear Diary,

Driving home from Lin's I heard the most amazing man speak. (I rarely spend time at "home" anymore. Lin doesn't judge my poor decision to marry him. She was his lawyer and went through the crazy with me. Hopefully he'll leave soon, and the separation can legally start.) Anyway, I'm not even sure of the speaker's name but he's apparently from Chicago. Black and so eloquent. I almost pulled the car over to listen. I wonder if that is how it felt to hear Martin or Malcom speak— mesmerized, elated, riveted . . . PROUD. Wish he'd run for president, but America is not ready for a black President and even if he won, he'd be killed immediately, and we WOULD shut this place down. No, a white woman has to be there first, but talk about a winning team: Lawton/Otieno(?)!

45

Dear Diary,

I know I should be all up in arms about The Hurricane, but I just don't have the energy. Since Fallu finally moved out it's all I can do to get dressed and stay upright at work. I'm glad he is gone but wish he was here. Stupid.

I feel bad about not being able to care about those poor folks, but I just can't.

46

Dear Diary,

Divorced 6 months.
    Why do I still call/think of him as *husband*?
    Niggah gone!
    Why do I feel so tied to him?
    Not trapped.
    Tied. Still.
    There were Biblical grounds
    Abandonment.
    Probably infidelity.
    Thankfully, no violence—except the harbinger
    Niggah gone!
    Bullet successfully dodged.
    Why can't I be glad?
    Cuz . . .
    . . . .*Niggah gone!*

47

Dear Diary,

I did it! I called and asked to join IBF again!

I had to do something. The panic attacks aren't getting any better. I need to get myself back. The last time I felt like me I was firmly grounded in the Lord. Church. IBF. I want that back and I don't care if they feel sorry for me. They should. I feel sorry for me! I have to learn how to speak and look people in the eye and be ME again.

Before I called, I prepared for the panic attack. I was alone. I didn't have to be anywhere for the rest of the day, so I could just hide under the covers until it passed, and I could breathe again.

Betty's still the leader. She's still kind. She didn't ask any questions! She just said she'd missed me and couldn't wait to see me in the Fall. I started to cry, and she asked if she could pray for me! I said yes. She prayed. I don't know what she said. I was focused on not sobbing too loudly. When she finished, she said she loved me and that she was here if I ever wanted to talk. I thanked her.

I hung up and waited. When the panic didn't hit, I washed my face and went to the gym.

I can't wait for September 12. The first day of IBF.
Thank you, Lord!

48

Dear Diary,

OMG!

I'm not saying I'm psychic but . . . for a couple of weeks now, I have been seeing/imagining Otieno in front of a crowd like Hitler was in front of the Brandenburg gate. It's an iconic shot of thousands of people losing their shit in love with Hitler and for some reason I have just been imagining *him* there. And today it happened! They say 200,000 people came to see him. Listen to this line from a news article:

> Once the Glastonbury-style warm-up bands and DJs had quieted, the Democratic nominee almost floated into view, walking to the podium on a raised, blue-carpeted runway, as if he were somehow, magically, walking on water. Even from a distance, the brilliant white of his teeth dazzled, and his kind eyes made us all feel loved.[1]

That's Messianic speak.
I'm a little terrified.

There is no reason for him to be there and so freaking adored. He's not even president. What if he doesn't become president? What if He is too big for America alone? You should have seen how they were losing their shit over him. What if he IS the antichrist?

No Trina, the antichrist won't be the American president. America doesn't seem to be a big deal in the End Times of the world before Christ comes again. We're ok.

What if he's a false Christ?

Terrified.

Breathe.

49

Dear Diary,

I talked to Liz today. We only talk about once a month because she lives in Singapore, so timing is everything, but I wanted to talk to her about my concerns about Otieno. She's British by birth, a strong Christian, usually countercultural and thoughtful so I thought maybe I'd have another person I could talk to. Boy did I have another think coming.

"Otieno's beautiful and winsome but something doesn't feel right." I ventured cautiously.

"What could possibly NOT feel right about him?"

"Well, Ok, like his stance on abortion."

"I know it's wrong but that alone can't make you not vote for him."

"It actually could, but there's more than that."

"What?"

"Ok don't laugh but he's so popular. White people are losing their shit over him it just feels wrong."

"So, you don't like him because white people like him?"

"Yes. But when you put it like that it sounds so . . . it's just that the world is so weird now, terrorism and so much evil . . . I'm not usually hyper spiritual"

"Since when?"

"Shut up."

"Otieno is not the Antichrist, ok? Times have been worse than they are now. This is not the end times." I could almost hear her rolling her eyes in disgust.

"It's not the end times—yet, but we gotta go thru some stuff to get to the End Times and how do you know this isn't that?"

"Because I'm not an American Christian."

"That's not fair."

"You all are so focused on the End that you don't see today and who Christ is right now! Things get a little rough and you look for the Rapture. Things have been rough all over the world for a long time and the world hasn't ended. Two buildings come down and foreign terror (as opposed to the terror of slavery and capitalism and American imperialism and white supremacy all around the world) starts to hit US shores and, all of a sudden, it's time for the end? Give me a break. You know, maybe you're right. Maybe this is the time before the end. I hope so because during that time America gets humbled."

"What do you mean?"

"You know prophecy better than me. You know America doesn't figure in the Last Days in the Bible. Isn't mentioned not even once. What do you think happens to her?"

"Well. A lot of writers speculate that, as a Christian nation, America loses so many people in the Rapture that she can no longer function and loses her place as a leader."

Liz lost it and laughed in my ear. For a good minute she tried to get it together, but it was like she had never heard anything funnier. Finally, she gasped something about needing to get off the phone because she was gonna pee her pants.

Sometimes I hate talking to her.

Liz thinks America is the evil empire and Christianity here is dead. I know we're bad, but I have seen a lot worse around the world, so I think we are still a predominately Christian nation and not just in name. The Rapture will hit us hard.

50

Dear Diary,

Uncle Tom. Race Traitor. Coon. Oreo.

It's the mantra that keeps yelling at me in my head. My heart and head are at war.

How to vote Lord?

Heart says—you must vote for the black man.

Head says—you know you disagree with him on key issues.

Heart says—Who is your love? Your race or your Lord?

Head says—MacClan is a snake and will set you, black folks and the country back.

Heart says—Uncle Tom.

Head says—free thinker.

Heart says—Race Traitor.

Head says—Lord Traitor.

Heart says—white-washed.

Head says—baby-killer.

Heart says—Oreo.

Head says—Deluded.
I feel sick.

51

Dear Diary,

I haven't heard from Fallu in over a year until today. I can't believe it.

"Honey!" (as if we were still together. As if the last time he spoke to me wasn't when he came over, made love to me then he asked me for money. I haven't been able to bring myself to write about that particularly humiliating event but yes, that happened.)

"Hi"

"Honey! I thought of you the other day! There was this African guy and a white guy at the Social Security office. The white guy says 'Sir, are you this woman's husband?' And he points to the woman sitting next to him. The African guy says, 'No suh! She is my wife!'

'Right!' says the white guy. 'So you are her husband?'

'No suh! She is my wife!'

The white guy is really trying to help. You know, American style, so he says, 'yes. She. Is. YOUR. Wife.' the African guy smiles big and shakes his head yes like talking to an idiot child.

Then the white guy says, 'soooo you. Are. Her. Husband?'

'NO SUUH! She. IS. MY WIFE.

"Honey! They went on like this for 5 minutes! I wanted to help but I was laughing too hard. Finally, the white guy gives up and says, 'She is your wife?' African sits back satisfied and nods his head yes."

I was in hysterics. Fallu was in hysterics. He does this. He makes me laugh. It's one of the things I loved about him. He'd say things that were just hilarious. I missed this. I don't think I'd laughed like that in over 2 years.

"You are so stupid!" I said with way more love in my voice than I wanted to admit. "You called me at work to tell me this crazy story?" I was granted more laughter from the other end of the call and I was so happy to have made him laugh! I remember closing my eyes savoring the sound and imagining the beautiful smile I used to long for. Still long for if I'm honest. After a few seconds of his panting laughter he said,

"Honey, I don't have much time, but I wanted to ask you a favor?"

I waited silently for the second blow of this 1-2 punch to land.

"Honey! Vote for Otieno for me! Give me your vote! I know you probably don't like him because you a lot of times you're more white than black, but I want you to vote for him since I can't."

"NO! And what do you mean I'm more white than . . . No."

"But you are my wife! I demand"

"I'm not your wife anymore!"

"That was your choice. I didn't want that! In God's eyes we are still married and I'm telling you as your husband, you must do this!"

"NO"

"If you don't I will NEVAH talk to you again."

"Good" I said and hung up the phone.

I forgot how debilitating panic attacks feel.

52

Dear Diary,

I voted.
  I feel sick.

53

Dear Diary,

I saw Fallu at the mall last weekend.

He called me Trina. Period.

He introduced me to his girlfriend.

He called her "Sweetie!" Exclamation point. Then he smiled at her with the smile he'd reserved for me for so long.

She introduced herself as Sharon.

She's 7 months pregnant. White.

"This is going to be a wonderful year! My first child and Otieno is president! I never imagined I would ever be this happy!" he said as he rubbed her belly and smiled MY smile at her again.

I vomited in the restroom and stayed there until I could breathe again.

54

Dear Diary,

I just met (2nd time) with a guy who is me, if I'd stayed married to Fallubah. Wife is West African and has the same irrational—crazy—way of being that Fallu did. Difference—he's got a kid with her and he's completely conflict averse. It is scary to see myself in him. I recognize the heartache when you look at the history of the person and empathize with them and even understand WHY they are so incredibly crazy. You don't want to hurt them further. You want to heal them, but you can't see that *you are not medicine*. You want to take the high road even when you see that they are willing to completely steamroll you, ruin your reputation and ruin you in some crazy idea of protecting themselves and trapping you into being responsible for them (regardless of the fact that their actions quite possibly will stop you from being able to work and earn and take care of them). It is actually sickening. Then it also plays on your sense of self because you want so desperately to have a family of your own and want to think/hope/believe that this person will be that for you if you can just heal them and wait out the crazy. But the crazy is there to stay. It ain't going a damn where and it only gets worse and then WORSER! And here's a thought that sickens me.

I should have listened to that Immigration Wench Ms. Fitzgerald, who sent him back to Ireland and didn't want to let him come back to the US.

I shouldn't have FOUND the money (which was supposed to be student loan payments—plural- and my book) to fight her decision. It was probably God trying to help me dodge a bullet, but the heart wants what it wants.

Too bad the heart is Freaking Stupid.

55

So Diary . . .

I'm going to say it out loud, then I can get over it: I'm excited about the prospect of having a real live, tall, attractive, intelligent, STRAIGHT black man who likes to dance in my house tomorrow. Like Fallu, he has dark skin with reddish undertones and these bright white healthy teeth. He has an easy, beautiful, full faced, wide mouth smile that he shares generously. His swagger is like a cashmere pashmina, you wanna wrap yourself in it . . . in him. And, I have some chemistry with him. We met at a story-telling gig and while we didn't have lots of conversation, he did laugh out loud at the right time in my story, and I did the same when he told his story. What I'm saying is he's basically a zebra—not an UNHEARD of animal but certainly a rarity in these here parts.

The first since Fallu.

We have the first read through of my play tomorrow and Latif (aka "The Zebra") is supposed to be there. I am trying to keep in the FOREFRONT of my mind that as far as I know he is a Man-ho who may have a drinking issue. I've seen the panties in piles at his feet (It was impressive. Women just walked up to him and smiled as they tossed their figurative panties on the heap at his feet. I felt compelled to do the same but then remembered "I don't do that" AND just how jacked up my panties would look in comparison—I'm not knocking myself, but these women were PREPARED for the fight—I wasn't. Think cotton grannies vs. silk thongs) and the last time I saw him (over a year ago) he was talking about his plan to get "black out drunk" on New Year's Eve—a full 3 weeks in advance. SOOOO, unless things have REALLY changed I could likely, 1. never get that; and, 2. never NEED that. . .

But it do look good tho.

Trying not to write the script in which I find out that he:

- is a Christian who is black, socially conservative

- has given up his HO-ISH ways

- wonder of wonders, has been attending MacAllen Bible Church; and,

- really wants a *regalah* black woman to settle down with (his style *is* anything non-regalah, non-black with flowing hair; or, IF black: has an expensive weave, tight-body and is SUPER coifed. I'd have to work voodoo roots to be her.)

Again, not knocking myself I just know I'm UNIQUE, a special kind of zebra that you may not recognize as a zebra until you get up on me then you realize that I've got purple and peach and teal, etc. stripes. You just have to look closely.

In the script that I'm not writing, he also has a lot of disposable income and wants a woman who he can lavish with care (so sad, I don't want a big house just regular payments on my student loans and Verizon bill and I'd consider tossing my panties—psych/smile. I'm not a gold digger I'm just honest and real—financial security is a JINORMOUS turn on.)

He probably won't show up tomorrow. That'll be good. Cold water on a hot stove. Of course, if he does show, I'm ready. Hung some

119

mistletoe above my door. It's a little low-hanging and he's tall so his head will hit it therefore I won't have to point it out (it'll be ray-yal natchral like).

Ok, so I wrote the script a little bit and set up props a little bit, but I'll kiss the others who walk through the door too. It's just that with THE ZEBRA, he'll be standing under it (or maybe he will see ME standing under it—have to work out the staging bit) and he'll joke about it then look seriously deep in my eyes and cup my cheek with his over-sized hand, bend down and plant one on me—chaste but a promise of heat.

Hmmm. . .l'amour!

Wonder what I should wear.

Thinking of a jean skirt and sweater (showing a little skin but tasteful) with my Turkish embroidered boots to give him a reason to let his eyes take in the whole package and to let me *know* he took in the whole package without being creepy. I'm thinking hair up to show how kissable/nuzzle-able my neck is. Need some perfume that is musky and heady. Poeme? No, that was Fallu's favorite. Smiley! It has a chocolate undertone—makes people happy when they smell it. Sexy smell will come later.

Ok so that's wardrobe too but I'm REALLY not scripting this thing out.

Ok I am scripting a little but come on. . . he's a ZEBRA and he'll be in MY lair. (Smile.)

Note to self: Need to vacuum—nobody likes a dirty lair.

Pray this is my zebra or that a really good zebra will come along soon.

56

Dear Diary,

There were 3 women (and another Man who likely was also getting high off that zebra stank) at the rehearsal last night. One of us went off script and asked THE ZEBRA out. I lie to you not! No, it wasn't me or Siti. . . or the guy. The other lady has tickets to a formal dance and her date backed out. She doesn't want the ticket to go to waste so she asked him, AS A FRIEND (then asked me if I was ok with it. "Oh sure!" I said through gritted teeth, bucked eyes and pursed lips). He hasn't responded yet, but he has his own tux and DOGGONNIT he looks GOO-WOODT in it! (He was wearing it last year when I saw him standing in front of the panty pile.)

P.S. No the mistletoe did not work. It hit his head and did a wild swing which made it look like there was a bat in the house so we all kind of ducked and looked around cautiously then laughed and everybody walked in the house.

57

Dear Diary,

I think that heffa killed the Zebra. He just disappeared. He doesn't return calls/emails. They both quit the play. We're scrambling. He probably hit that and now they are both embarrassed and scared to be together. Drunken, "What the hell . . . let's do it" sex. Been there.

People suck!

Breathe.

Some Perspective Trina.

You are complaining about a little play when the death toll in the earthquake/tsunami in Japan is an estimated Twenty THOUSAND!

Ok. So, things could be worse.

How is all this possible? Lord!

58

Dear Diary,

I think I'm getting my voice back from the ghost of humiliations past AKA Fallubah but it may have cost me my Black Card.

First Ebenezer is the kind of church I grew up in. Upper middle-class black folks. Surprisingly even distribution of men to women. Lots of couples who have been together for decades. Sunday from 11-1:30 is full of smiles and hugs. From 2 p.m. onward you can hear a myriad of catty comments and judgements from and about the pastor, the deacons, the "urshers," the choir, and even Miss Nona in the cafeteria who "knows she can bake some biscuits but can't make grits to save her soul."

I don't attend because the sermons are usually more emotion than substance, but the music is good, and the people are nice. I know a lot of ladies who attend this church from IBF and sometimes I just crave the familiarity of a black church. It's also my safety net for when, as Siti warns, the race wars start. I don't believe that will happen but . . . it doesn't hurt to be affiliated—just in case.

I decided to go because my friend Dana was in town and frankly, I was embarrassed to take her to my church. She and I were pretty radical back in the day. We wore t-shirts that said, "Saddam never called you a nigger!" to the grocery store just to provoke conversations. She still wears hers. I am kind of ultra-black when she is around to avoid jokes about me being a "suburban black" which is somehow less than "full black".

We slept in and had Sunday brunch then I took her to a special evening service at First Ebenezer. The featured speaker was a guy whose bio listed him as a Social Activist Minister of the Gospel. The pulpit was full of black ministers from around the area. The packed church was hot after a rowdy praise and worship service.

"My Brothers and Sisters. During the Civil Rights movement our dear brother Martin encouraged us to imagine a Beloved Community in which racism and all forms of discrimination, bigotry and prejudice will be replaced by an all-inclusive spirit of sisterhood and brotherhood! Amen?!" the Pastor exhorted.

"Amen!" The crowd responded wholeheartedly.

"At this important time in our history as black Americans we must live our faith and not legislate our faith. For the Constitution is designed to protect the rights of all! Now, listen to me Church: there is no doubt people who are same-gender-loving occupy prominent places in the body of Christ! Amen!?"

The congregation murmured Amen as many frightened eyes looked down attempting to avoid the side eyes and knowing chuckles which floated in their direction. Nobody knew where this guy was going, and everyone was concerned. We gossiped about the "sugar in the tank" of the church but we didn't outwardly discuss it as this Joker was doing; as the black Church was being forced to do because of the President Otieno's *evolution* on the subject of gay marriage.

"I do not believe Biblical doctrine is equipped to shape civic legislation nor are civic representatives equipped to shape religious rituals and doctrine" he said cautiously

There was a gasp from the congregation. To me it sounded like an ancient door screeching open.

I nudged Dana, but she ignored me, so I whispered, "I'm supposed to leave my faith outside the polling booth?" Dana just patted my leg as if to soothe a fidgety child.

Enraged, I scanned the crowd and gratefully recognized the same incredulity and confusion that I felt mirrored back at me by many around me. The Pastor must have seen it too. He paused to take a drink of water and I saw his hand tremor.

"The institution of marriage is not under attack as a result of the President's words. Marriage was under attack years ago by men who viewed women as property and children as trophies of sexual prowess."

Yup! That's the button to push to get this crowd with him.

"Well!" one of the other pastors loudly intoned, and a smattering of congregants applauded. Encouraged, the pastor continued

"Marriage is under attack by low wages, high incarceration, unfair tax policy, unemployment, and lack of education! Marriage is under attack by clergy who proclaim monogamy yet think nothing of stepping outside the bonds of marriage to have multiple affairs with "preaching groupies."

BINGO!

The truth of that statement garnered shouts of "You better Preach!" and seemed to effectively shut down any potential mutiny from the men of God seated behind him.

"Same-gender couples did not cause the high divorce rate, but our adolescent views of relationships and our inability as a community to come to grips with the ethic of love and commitment did. We still confuse sex with love and romance with commitment!" he shouted then stepped away from the mic as if the word he had just delivered was too hot for even him.

Then, as if compelled to speak, he leaned toward the hot mic and, accompanied by the organist's punctuations, said quickly, lest he be burned by the truth, "The institution of marriage is not under attack as a result of the President's words!"

Wow! Just . . . Wow!

"Gay and lesbian citizens did not cause the economic crash! Foreclosures! The attack upon health care! Poor, underfunded schools were not created because people desire equal protection under the law!"

Economics trump morals. The crowd went wild, the organist played, the Pastor did a holy dance to celebrate the righteousness of the truths being extolled. The music fueled the crowd and men and women jumped to their feet waving handkerchiefs and holy hands in agreement. When the crowd calmed, the Pastor took another drink of water then grasped the sides of the lectern.

"We have much work to do as a community, and to claim the President of the United States must hold your theological position is absurd."

"Yes!" someone said for the congregation. The Pastor took a deep breath trying to stave off tears as he pondered the poignancy of the message he had to deliver.

"That's alright!"

"Take your time!"

"Jesus!" the congregation encouraged along with the haunting notes of the organ. Buoyed, the Pastor continued.

"My father, who is a veteran of the civil rights movement and retired pastor, eloquently stated the critical nature of this election when speaking to ministers this past week: Ministers who claim they will pull support from the President as a result of his position. My daddy said, 'Our ancestors prayed for 389 years to place a person of color in the White House. They led over 200 slave revolts, fought in 11 wars, one

126

being a civil war where over 600,000 people died. Our great grandmothers fought and were killed for women's suffrage. Our grandparents were lynched for the Civil rights Bill of 1964 and the Voting Rights Act of 1965. My grandfather never had the opportunity to vote and I believe it is my sacred duty to pull the lever for every member of my family who was denied the right to vote. I will not allow narrow-minded ministers or regressive politicians the satisfaction of keeping me from my sacred right to vote to shape the future for my grandchildren!"

"Preach Boy!"

Check and Mate. Civil Rights Movement for the win, Alex!

"We have much to do Beloved. November is fast approaching, and the spirits of Ella Baker, Septima Clarke, Fannie Lou Hammer, Rosa Parks, A. Phillip Randolph, James Orange, Medgar Evers and Martin Luther King Jr., stand in the balcony of heaven raising the question, "Will you do justice, love mercy and walk humbly with our God?" Emmitt Till and the four little girls who were assassinated in Alabama during worship did not die for a Sunday sermonic sound bite to show disdain for one group of God's people. They were killed by an evil act enacted by men who believed in doctrine over love. We must stand against the same."

The ministers behind him were on their feet and they shook his hand as he walked to his seat accompanied by the collective voices of the church singing the Negro National Anthem. Lift Every Voice and Sing.

There wasn't a dry eye in the place, including Dana's.

After the service there was a crowd around the pastors, glad handing and "God Bless you" all around. I was ready to go. In fact, I felt like I needed to run out of there because if someone asked me anything I was ready to take my big print Bible and beat them over the head with it. But Dana pulled me to the front of the crowd all the while saying, "This Man is a visionary. We gotta shake his hand."

127

Before I knew it, we were face to face with this false prophet in clerical robes. Dana was all geechy shaking his hand and heaping praise on him. Then he grabbed my hand and said, "Thank you for your support sister!"

Support? WTF! No. Hell no. There was no support here and that's when I heard myself say in a voice that was louder than I would have ever intended; a voice that drew the attention of the entire crowd of about 30.

"Must the Beloved Community exclude Biblical principles if they run afoul to public opinion?"

There was an acrimonious rumble behind me, but the pounding of my heart drowned it out and I knew it would come out of my chest if I didn't speak.

"Are you honestly suggesting that we sell out Christ for the pleasure and pride of seeing a black man in the White House?"

From behind me a voice said, "Come on sister. That's not what he was saying!"

Undeterred I said, "Pastor, you spoke eloquently but where is Christ in all that you just said?"

I saw the Pastor to my left slightly cock his head just as the speaker said, "Sister we are going to pray that the Lord makes himself clear to you as you think on what was said tonight." Then suddenly I found myself jostled to the outskirts of the group. No one had manhandled me; the crowd just found its way in front of me and the glad-handing resumed.

As I walked to my car alone, surrounded by the happy talk of people affiliated with each other and a group, I felt completely cast out and vulnerable. A few minutes later Dana got into the front seat, and we drove back to my house in silence. I'm sure she was just as relieved as I was that she was leaving early in the morning, so we had an excuse to get to bed as soon as we got home.

59

Damnit Diary,

Maybe Liz was right all those years ago. Maybe Christianity in America is a farce, and we won't be greatly affected by the Rapture of the Saints cuz all saints ain't Saints.

60

Dear Diary,

Good time to do this again:

<u>Rapture Nearness Assessment:</u>

How close are we to the Rapture of the church? Where are we on the prophetic timeline?

"The granddaddy of all the signs—Jews back in Israel."

Check!

"Earthquakes, famines, disease and signs in the sky."

Check-ish? I mean are they any more frequent than they always have been? It feels like it but didn't we just start measuring stuff like that? Plus the internet. Soooo . . . I'm gonna say no-ish, maybe

"Perilous times."

Again Check-ish. I mean haven't cops always killed black people? If anything, maybe we are more aware and because of that awareness AND our intolerance of the level of it—which, let's face it, was always high- actually feels really high now.

Note: I realize that peril is not just measured in black bodies but . . . in America, it's kind of measured in black bodies.

"Wars and rumors of wars."

I read a study once that said that we are a much more peaceful world than in mediaeval or olden times. So Imma say nah.

"Violence and sexual immorality"

Alright check AND wasn't ancient Rome at least as licentious if not more than us? Again: I realize that we are using America as a standard but . . . it's kind of THE standard, isn't it?

"False Christs."

Otieno? nahhh

"The whole world will turn against Israel."

Nahh.

Maranatha! Even so, come quickly Lord Jesus.

67

OMG Diary,

Today on CNN they showed a video of the Presidential candidate, Haedon S. Banner, grabbing a reporter's breast as he walked past her!

WTF!

He denies it but it's on tape! When pressed on the issue, he said he was waving at his fans when the reporter "jiggled her boobs in front of me. I didn't grab her. She's at best a 5. I don't even see less than 7's. She was probably mad because I don't call on her so the only way to get noticed was to shake her boobs. It happens all the time."

WTF?!

The awful thing is she's not very attractive. Worse than that is even though I watch the video and he clearly reaches out and grabs her boobs, when he keeps saying he didn't do it and his people say he didn't do it, over and over again, I get confused and think, "Wait. Did she jiggle herself in front of him? Was he just waving?"

I haven't felt that kind of confusion since Fallu. He'd say stuff that I knew was not true, but I would wonder if I had everything all wrong.

Presidential elections are more than a year away and it is (to quote Fallu) URGLY!

62

Dear Diary,

I gave a speech about Christian Persecution at a black church in Baltimore today. A conservative, Bible-preaching church. At fellowship one of the older sisters said, "I don't have a problem with Banner. I'd vote for him"

WT holy F?

Haedon S. Banner? The foul-mouthed, boob-grabbing, racist, reality show host freak who is running for president? The Banner who called all of Africa a "shithole"! That Banner?

I knew white evangelicals were behind him (the moral freaking majority sides with the would-be pervert in chief) but black folks? For real?

He might just win this thing. God help us.

63

Dear Diary,

Today is Sunday and I didn't go to church—again. I didn't even stream it. To be fair I was in a fair amount of pain. My period came last night so, crampy and I went dancing so feet and head hurt. I looked really cute though. My outfit was crazy expensive. I hadn't meant to spend that much money on it. African print high-low skirt, black shirt, gold plated cowrie shell jewelry and my Irinia Banner blue suede boots. I know. Banner. But I bought the boots 2 years ago, before it was wrong—and they are the most comfortable, highest heels I have so I was a sell out last night—but a cute one. I tried to craft a witty explanation as to why I wore the devil's child's boots but then realized that there was no stamp on them identifying them as such so . . . I let it go. I guess my penance is feet that can't be walked on today. The Devil always makes you pay.

No obviously single men at the event—SURPRISE! Lots of single women on the dance floor and the DJ was good because he played line dances and oldies that you just move and sing along to with the whole group, so you didn't look weird or "questionable" or pathetic dancing alone or with other women. Nice evening. Just had to watch how wild I got, and make sure that my booty wasn't gyrating in some woman's man's vicinity. So much to think about when you go out in your 40s.

Yeah, I still didn't go to church. Scared of what I'll hear or NOT hear; of what I'll see or THINK I see. Does white trump Christian? I am just not sure.

I'll go Next week . . . maybe. Certainly, after Thanksgiving. I know it's months away but hopefully the election will make things better. I don't think so, but keep hope alive. The Devil is playing this election and America like a fiddle. The choice is socially reprehensible or morally questionable.

Banner will win.

I hear the question. Why is my head hurting? Ok, they served champagne, and I had a dirty martini. Is it bad that I looked forward to/relied on the social lubrication of alcohol? I will think about that later and I appreciate your non-judgmental silence.

64

Dear Diary,

So glad I can write this to you. (Thanks again Dr. Progoff) I'm happy and I feel pathetic about being happy. I've been stalking this guy for a while. I call him *Low key Idris Elba, LoKIE for short.* He's fine! He's not as shiny and sparkly as the real deal, African-British actor, Idris Elba. Low Key Idris Elba is more accessible in his beauty, which is a good thing (don't need to work roots for it). I have smiled his way but no haps for about a year. Today we talked (well he talked mainly) for about 30 minutes. We rode in together (in silence—rules of slugging) and then he asked for my number. He flirted. I did too, but it was nothing uncomfortable. He whispers when he talks so I tried to read his lips but found myself just looking and smiling and trying not to lick my own lips. smile.

He's married (I asked, "is your wife from Cameroon too?" Yes, he was sort of non-committal about wife in his manner but—yes, married).

Cameroonian—which means African—which means Hell to the NAW! NO!—even if he was single, which he's not so No!

137

Didn't ask me much about myself. He did a lot of talking not so much about himself but his conceptualization of geopolitics and how the world is out to screw Africa (Boko Haram is a Chinese or American—I couldn't decipher the whisper—group aimed at getting oil out of Africa.)

3 kids.

Pretty. Tall. Chocolate. Slim. Nice bald head. Nice lips. Nice smile. He had an easy laugh. Well-traveled. French accent. Named Olivier which is kind of sexy.

So . . . No Haps. Nu-uh. Nagannahappen. AND I feel so happy. It has been a long time since a man I was attracted to obviously found me attractive. Welcome to black middle-aged womanhood. It's so nice to be SEEN.

He has my number. I didn't know how to say no and I didn't want to say no. It's not like he asked to have sex or even drinks. Just my number. To sanitize it a bit I gave him a marketing card for Dinosaur Brains. I may not get sex but maybe I'll get $14.95 and one less book to sell. I'll take it!

65

Dear Diary,

I haven't seen him in a while (4 years?) but the homeless man I call Chicken Wing is back! BIG AND BOLD as ever. Ok, so he's still scrawny but he looks healthy—nicely moisturized beard and shaved head, clean, pressed clothes. He's got a little bounce reminiscent of a crack head, but it could just be personality. ANYWAY, He's back.

I was walking to Au Bon Pain for some soup when I saw him. He's out of place for me cuz I used to see him at 20th and L but he's down here now at 12th and Penn. I saw him and smiled thinking, "Chicken Wing! That you Man?! Where you been? Rehab?" but he doesn't know me like that, so I just smiled. And. . . It's been a minute so I wasn't sure it was him until I heard his voice. A little raspy but confident.

"Eh, gimme a nickel? A dime? Quarter? Somethingtoeat?"

YEAHHH that's Wing! I was happy. Then I got up to him and he returned my smile like he knew me and said (cuz he's standing like the doorman of Au Bon Pain)

"Eh, eh sis. You got some change? Maybe when you come out?"

I thought, GOTCHA! I CAN'T GIVE YOU NOTHING. . . even if I wanted to—which I don't.

"Nah, I'm paying with a card." (I even waved the card so he'd see I wasn't lying.)

Then just as I walked past him into the door he said with a smile I heard rather than saw. "Cheedanish?"

It took me a minute to figure it out.

Undaunted, Chicken Wing was saying, "No cash? That's alright. Just buy me a Cheese Danish and we'll be good."

And just like that I was pissed (and laughing at the same time).

Is it wrong to be mad at a homeless man for begging?

66

Dear Diary,

I'm doing stuff to stay healthy during this awful election process. I'm kind of pumped because I led the first of 4 meditation kickstart groups and it went really well. You know I'm a fraud so I was scared I'd be outed as a zenfraud (I don't meditate. I need Adderall. My being is antithetical to meditation). I was so nervous I planned drinks for tonight thinking I'd be a nervous wreck. . . after leading meditation. I was nervous and so added 2 extra exercises (in vivo) that I had not planned to add to the 40 minutes (I was afraid they were getting bored). It went something like:

"Breathe and nO-tiss the space . . . between your breathes. It. . . is . . . a gap. Stay there . . . in the gap."

(In my mind: "shit. It's only been 3 minutes?! Crap! I planned the gap thing for 15. Shit shit shit shit shit. Crap! Ok)

"Now in the gap. . . place the word peace. So you are effectively breathing in peace and exhaling. . . peace. Peace. . . in the gap. Peace. . . in the gap. Peace in the gap."

(CRAP! How long am I doing peace in the stupid gap? I should have planned this better. Shit.)

"Now. . . notice your toes. And as you breathe in. . . let the air fill your body all the way to your toes. Relaxing and energizing them all at once *(is that peaceful? Shit)* In. . . .and out. Inn. . . and ooooout-ah . . ."

Writing out my script I realize that my meditation voice sounds an awful lot like Tina Turner's intro to Proud Mary. "You know. Everynowandthen. . . .we. . . think. . . you-might-like-to-hear-something-from-us. . . nice. . . and EAASY. But-there's-just one thing. See. . . We. . . Never. . . ever . . . do. . . nothing. . . NEYESSSSSSSS and EAAAASY. We-always-do-it..NEYESSSSSSS. . . and Rough."

Fifteen people and they all seemed happy. I know that shouldn't be my measure of "good", but it is. I want people to like me. What a wusss. I am doing research-ish for next week, but it all is sooooo soft and wishy washy. "The path is long and windy." blah blah blah. I need concrete. Even the Christian meditation sites are esoteric. Blah blah blah.

#Zen FRAUD

67

Dear Diary,

Left work to see a movie so had to catch the bus on 14th street. NEVER AGAIN!

I saw something that, paired with all that is going on with the election, tells me that we are in the last days. There was a squirrel that thought it was human! I swear he was going to crawl into this lady's purse looking for food. Everyone in line thought it was the cutest thing and folks were pulling out treats to give it. He'd stand still on his disgusting little hind legs and fold his little hands as if begging. It was like he was putting on a show!

When the bus came, he walked alongside the line as we got on the bus trying to get one last morsel of food. By the time he got to the lady ahead of me he ran in front of her as if demanding food! She laughed and clapped and gave him something and—HE LET HER PASS—but he jumped in front of me and demanded the same. I ran to the back of the line scared. Luckily the bus driver got tired of the delay, and someone shooed him to the side but he was still begging!

The lady in front of me at the back of the line was smart and just as afraid as I was, so she asked the guy in front of her to help us onto the bus. He had to stand in front of and then behind us as we got on the bus so that the thing didn't intimidate us!

City Squirrel,

AKA rat with a bushy tail,

AKA vermin carrier of plague that will survive the apocalypse eating the flesh of the fallen,

A-freaking-K-freaking-A just downright NASTY critter that (in this case) doesn't know it's a CRITTER!

Take me NOW Lord. I won't survive the meltdown of society if this is a foretaste of it! I blame the TOURISTS who feed them as if ALL of DC is a petting Zoo! Yes, I'm freaking out—a little bit! BAN TOURISTS!

68

Dear Diary,

Riding home with the negative chick today. She must have taken meds because she was all kinds of friendly. I told her about meeting Low-key Idris Elba (LoKIE) and she was all geechie. Then the lady in the back seat said she knows him! WORKS with him!

Young white girl—cannon fodder for fine African men—so I get a little jealous imagining that she's with or has been with him. Worse she's like a blackish white girl (Beanie calls them Dark Whites). Slightly nasal voice. Loads of swagger and attitude, tight body, tight clothes, rolls her eyes with the best of us. Think Rachael Dolezal, the white chick who got caught passing for black.

Racheal: "Hiss name iss O-liv-ee-yay. he-a-ho. But he nice tho."

Negative chick: "I thought you said he was married."

Racheal: He ii-iis. Three little boys but . . . he-a-ho."

Me and Negative Chick: "Really? How you know?"

Racheal: "He tried to step to me. We went out a couple of times, but he married, and we work together soo . . . "

Me and Negative Chick: low, judgement-laden rumble, "umph"

Rachael: He tries to talk to all the women in our office. I just laugh at him. We friends now. But . . .

Me, Negative Chick and Rachael: He-a-ho.

I looked back and Rachael was examining her multicolored nails nodding her head, yes, like a bobble-head puppy on a furry dashboard.

Damn.

69

Dear Diary,

Passed City Squirrel's hang out today and as usual watched to make sure he didn't get on the bus (I am vigilant when we pass his stop because I would FREAK ALL THE WAY OUT if he got on the bus but I wouldn't be surprised).

Today there are Loads of tourists. What is it about being in a new city that makes people think that a common squirrel is no longer Vermin but suddenly a Disney character?! These folks, aka fools, were gathered around City Squirrel taking pictures and offering food. Delighting when he scampered up and took it. Surprised and "geechy" when he didn't scamper away but stood there and ate as if he was at a restaurant and they were waiting for a drink. . . together. . . as equals!

It won't be so cute when he starts chasing them DEMANDING more treats. Or when he gets aggressive and bites. In short, when he acts like an animal.

I understand the temptation to act as if nature is suspended when on vacation. I did it in Cambodia this summer. I jumped off of a bus trying to give a wild monkey (may have been a baboon. He had teeth but I ignored that because he and his buddies were acting all cute and Disney-ish trying to get food from the stupid tourists like me.) I had some fruit and smiled when he smiled. I held out my hand and he took it all. Then he started stalking and intimidating me to give him more. He wasn't playing. He was an ANIMAL. My guide just chuckled when my big ass crawled on top/over/behind him trying to get to safety.

Tourists: Why CITY Squirrel doesn't know it's a Squirrel!

70

Dear Diary,

LoKIE-NOT-a-ho!

We met on the way to the slugline last night and we were just talking. It was nice. We were almost there—in front of Del Friscos—and he turns and says, "Do you wanna get a drink with me?"

Thank God it was Thursday so nothing to do after work!

"Really?

"Yeah. It's such a nice night and I rarely get to go out. It'll be quick. We can probably still get a slug. If not, I'll pay your bus fare." Suave!

We went to Del Friscos. I love their Dirty martini. He liked the way I ordered it "Dirty martini but make it *filthy* extra olive juice and extra olives please. With Gin." He just laughed. He has a great laugh! We talked. He asked me about myself! I watched his lips to decipher what he was saying. He's in IT (boring) but he's really interested in development and politics.

"I would never want to hold an office or anything. Plus, I'm an American Citizen so couldn't do it in Cameroon and I'd never want to be in American politics."

I wasn't interested in his politics because what I'd heard of them was kind of crazy and/or more sophisticated than I could comprehend so they bored me.

"Why'd you become a citizen? Did you not want to be Cameroonian anymore?"

"It was really expedience."

Ok, ok I know this is usually when I get mad, but he looked good and the liquor was working on me. I had a choice. I could be winsome and curious; or I could bring down the judgement hammer. You should be proud of me. I listened.

"My family pinned their hopes on me. I am not the eldest boy, but I was the smartest. My parents were teachers, they saved everything they had to send me to school. I got scholarships to study all around the world and ended up here. I always wanted to go back home and do something, but my family needed me here more than they needed my dreams of fighting the system in Cameroon. My father made me promise to make a life here and to bring family over to study and live and send money back to the others who couldn't leave. It was the same old trap, but I couldn't convince him to let me come back, so I got my citizenship to please my father."

"You can still go back and do great things as an American though right?"

"I like how you think." *(GO-JUS smile. Damn his teeth are big and healthy!)* "That was my plan, but my distant cousin's husband died, and she had 2 little boys. She was just a tomato girl. Do you know what that is? She sold produce at the market—subsistence really. My family convinced me to marry her and adopt her boys and bring them here. They reasoned that I needed a wife and she needed everything. Twelve years later here I am in a job that I don't hate with a wife and kids."

"Wow. Are you happy?"

"Happy is an American concept."

"Bullshit. Are you happy?"

He smiled the most beautiful, unhappy smile.

"I'm content. She is a good wife. She came here and tried to study but it just isn't her. You know? She keeps our house clean and feeds us well. She has some friends, but she never makes me worry about my reputation."

"Are you husband and wife—in any real sense?"

"We tried to be. We had a child together, but we have very little in common. That's why I asked you out. I . . . it's just nice to CONVERSE."

YES LORD! He said Converse not Conversate! You know panties were at my ankles. But seriously I know I moved a little closer to him and then he put his hand on mine. It was a little rough, but I didn't mind. It made me think he did real work not just computers.

"Plus, their citizenship notification came in the mail yesterday and somehow, I feel free and wanted to celebrate. I think it was God who put you in my path today. This is nice."

He gave God the glory. Have mercy Lord! Have mercy!

"It is nice."

He moved closer to me. Our thighs touched. He kept his hand on mine. We just sat there for a while in silence. Then he asked me about myself. Not about whether I was married or why not. He asked about me. What I dream. I told him about self-publishing Dinosaur Brains. He was impressed! I told him about the book on citizenship that I want to write. We got lost in the meaning of citizenship and if he felt different as an American or Cameroonian. It was so interesting and fun and hot because all the while we talked, we touched. Nothing disgusting but a rub of the cheek here a squeeze of the hand there and always either our thighs or hips abutted against each other.

Three drinks and 2 hours later the conversation ran down, and I said we should probably go. He paid the bill and we walked out of the bar with our pinkies locked. When we'd been walking a block in silence he stopped, turned to me and said, "I have a confession."

Crap! What?

"I don't remember your name. I've been hoping you'd say it all this time and I didn't know how to ask without offending you. And it's not because you're not memorable I just really stink at remembering names!"

I burst out laughing and sort of collapsed against his chest. It was rock hard. I can't tell you how comforting that was. Like he was a fortress—my fortress—and I was safe. He smelled clean and spicy like sandalwood and something warm—cinnamon? I guess he was relieved because he started laughing too and he put his arms around me. We just laughed in each other's arms. That's when I looked up and smiled at him and said my name

"God, you have a beautiful smile—Trina!"

And that's when he kissed me! YES! HE KISSED ME. Slightly open mouth but not wet and with moderate suction. It was Glorious. I don't know who pulled away first—I hope it was me. We walked to the bus stop in silence holding hands. The bus got there right after we arrived and, true to his word he paid my fare and we rode in silence-bus rules—joined at the hip, thigh and leg like Siamese twins. At our stop he helped me off of the bus and when the bus had pulled off, he kissed me again, this time just slightly more than a peck.

"Have a good evening," I said.

"Thank you," he said and watched me as I walked to my car.

Sweet right?

I know.

Wish it was real but it's pure fantasy.

I haven't seen LoKIE in months and he hasn't called so maybe he's not a ho. But this is sure better than talking/thinking about the election, Sandra Bland, Michael Brown, Keith Lamont Scott, Tamir Rice, Philando Castille and all the black folks killed by cops recently. Better than thinking about the stupid Heffa from IBF who cornered me in the grocery store and said Black Lives Matter is a hate group and "maybe Banner is God's choice for us."

I wanted to yell in her stupid face, "Yes, heffa, he is but have you never read Romans 1 where God says He'll give us the leaders we deserve? Y'all chose this!"

Instead, I did the Christian, *I hate you in Jesus' name* smile and said, "That's a heck of a scary thought," over my shoulder as I walked away.

I can't deal with it all so I'm retreating into romantic fantasy.

Yeeeessssuh! I know he's married so I shouldn't be fantasizing about LoKIE. I'm not really. It's the IDEA of him. Not him . . . sort of.

71

Dear Diary,

I'm feeling like crap. No energy. Joints feeling ooky which acupuncturist said is due to edema. I don't look swollen but something's up. Anyway, skipped work—I'm sure it's stress that's happening.

Couldn't get out of bed this morning. Could have probably pushed through but just no energy/desire. Research suggests low blood sugar is the cause. Need to eat protein before I go to bed. Maybe. Feel crappy. Went for massage.

Here's me being racist. I asked for this Chinese guy who, last time he saw me, zeroed in on pain centers. In my head it was like he had some special Chinese power that allowed him to see my blockages. I wanted him to just get in there and get my chi flow going. I was getting a little angry because he didn't seem to be intuiting the pain areas, but I was too embarrassed (also, maybe I was testing him?) to say what I wanted. Made myself laugh because I imagined him putting on a "super-Asian" act for stupid people like me. Then going out between massages and being like a hip-hop b-boy. Left disappointed but realized

I was shaky—blood sugar. Tried to get myself together but just no energy.

During massage (here's revelation) I realized that what I need for good health is sex. My doctor suggested CBD oil but I couldn't get a security clearance if I popped positive for weed so . . . sex.

I was laying there and imagined orgasm. I was not turned on by the touch or the thought but recognized that this was the missing ingredient. You know there are trigger points INSIDE the vagina and further up and the internal release of orgasm is healthy and, I imagine, like putting jumper cables on Chi.

Until I can figure out the sex cure, experimenting with a macrobiotic diet. Trying to get healthy. Was going to go shopping for food for a macrobiotic meal but no energy so I went to the KFC drive thru instead.

72

Dear Diary,

I figured out the sex cure.

I'm gonna have to have sex with LoKIE.

If I put my mind to it I think I can get him in bed.

The problem is I really think Jesus is coming back any day.

I can't allow my mind to linger on what if Jesus comes back while I'm fornicating with a married man who I have no desire to have a relationship with.

73

Dear Diary,

Saw LoKIE. Haven't seen him in a while. We rode home together. I looked busted, so I knew I had to postpone the seduction until I didn't look so frog-like and jowly (best to do it in the morning when I'm fresh and tight).

He still looks good, but the spell wasn't so strong. I noticed how tight his suit was—"I'm struggling" tight, not "I'm fashionable" tight. Saw a little ash between his thumb and pointer finger and then there's the fact that he outed himself as a bonafide idiot.

The driver, black woman, was a talker so Slug rules say the rider can talk back if you want to. There were four of us in the car—all women, except LoKIE.

"We all got to get out and vote y'all. Don't let that joker in!" the driver said. Dollars to donuts she's referring to Banner as the joker but there's a tense moment of guessing before the front passenger, who is obviously friends with the driver, chimes in.

"I know girl. It's so important. Y'all are going to vote right?" she says and turns to the back seat with a huge smile on her face which ignored me and landed smack dab on LoKIE even though she had to be a contortionist for him to see her because he was sitting directly behind her.

"Cuz I'mma tell you, if he gets in . . . you can hang up any kind of diversity programs or focus. Voting rights are on the line. We are looking at going straight back to the '50s." Passenger said.

"Yup his base will be empowered and no telling what them boys will do then." Driver said.

Driver and the passenger got into a volley of all the horrendous things the candidate has said and done then Driver said, "I don't know how anyone could NOT vote for Pamela."

"I don't think there's any way he wins" Passenger said, and I couldn't hold back any longer.

"There are loads of reasons not to like Pamela. I don't want her as President, but I could never vote for Banner. BUT, and I hope I'm wrong, I think Banner wins this thing and he's taking America down."

"NO! uh-uh!" Driver

"Folks are stupid but not that stupid!" Passenger

"That's why we have to vote!" Driver, Passenger and I repeated over and over in varying ways at fever pitch.

Then a whispered, deep, accented voice broke through the din

"You know your vote doesn't matter right? That's why I'm not voting. This system is stupid. I've been a citizen 8 years and I haven't voted once." LoKIE

It was like a deluge of cold water. I couldn't come up with anything to say. I'd heard this argument about the electoral college. I understood its merits and they were many, BUT this man CHOSE to be an American. He took a test to be an American! He gave up citizenship in a corrupt country where his vote TRULY is meaningless. He's Francophone Cameroonian so I assume he wasn't fleeing persecution. He wanted a better future. And he has one because folks who look like him but sound like me had bled, fought and died for the rights and opportunities he, his wife and his children have INCLUDING THE VOTE. Then I cooled and thought, they fought and bled and died so he could have the CHOICE to be an idiot who did not vote.

"But if I were to vote in this election" he said, and I know I wasn't the only one in the car happy that there was the hope of redemption for this fine man, "I'd most likely vote BANNER."

WTF!?

Lord! Is there no one else I can have sex with?

74

Dear Diary,

Trying to do gratitude journal.

Today I am grateful that at least I am NOT AT ALL conflicted about who to vote for in this election. I don't trust Lawton, but I hate Banner.

"Power, like a desolating pestilence, pollutes whate'er it touches."

—Percy Bysshe Shelley

75

Dear Diary,

Banner won. Lord help us. I expected it but I still had hope.

Perilous times doesn't even begin to capture where we are and I swear to goodness I don't know how I'm supposed to be. Pastor Daniel talked about Micah 6:8 yesterday

"He has shown you, O mortal, what is good. And what does the LORD require of you? To act justly and to love mercy and to walk humbly with your God."

What the heck does that mean in the Banner Age? Like exactly?

No clue.

76

Dear Diary,

For posterity to show how ridiculous (and real) this stuff is, I'm just gonna leave this right here . . .

Associated Press: Idaho Lawmaker suggests Otieno staged white supremacist march in bid to paint Banner as Racist

> Idaho State legislator, Byron Zalniger, doubled down on his suggestion that it is plausible that America's first black president is to blame for the white Supremacist march that left one-woman dead last weekend.
>
> Zalniger was referencing an article in American Thinker which speculates that Black Lives Matter, and the Virginia Governor planned the riot; and that Barasa Otieno has a war room in his home to plot against President Banner's legislative agenda.
>
> After receiving online backlash for the article, Zalniger doubled down by reposting the article.

"(Otieno) was a community organizer before he was President of the United States, so I still do think it's plausible."

AN ELECTED lawmaker. Welcome to the AGE OF BANNER.

77

Dear Diary,

Lord, you know I'm not worthy to teach the kids in IBF

I curse. I drink. I do yoga and meditation. I would have sex outside of marriage if there was someone to have sex with. In short Lord I'm rotten and I know I expect/rely on a "cheap grace"- sinning over and over again banking on the fact that you will accept me because I said (and truly believe) the prayer of salvation.

But Lord these kids . . .

Tonight, we were talking about Matthew 24 and Mark 13—The End Times. I am fascinated by these chapters because they read like a horror story. The moon turns to blood. There are evil spirits that fool the people. Natural disasters. Persecution. And there is a comeuppance. Man deserves the wrath of God and He is allowing it to fall heavy on the earth. I will have a front row seat for it. But I don't imagine that I'll *experience* it because believers/Christians are raptured up to heaven before it all goes totally tits up. Not that we are good or anything but because we have accepted the mercy of God (there goes that cheap grace notion).

I got carried away in my presentation of the end times and when I finished, I looked at the class—twelve 4th- 6th graders. Their faces were ashen and eyes wide.

Marty, who had tears rolling down his full brown cheeks took a shuddering sigh and said, "so that's it? God just kills us all? There's nothing we can do?"

I saw Karen, my co-leader who is as big a sinner as I am but in the opposite direction—she's self-righteous—shaking her head in a tight circle that at once said "NO . . . Yahhh! Everybody's screwed!"

I tried to speak before she said anything. She loves to teach but she's crazy. Once when we were going over how to share the Gospel, she gave the example of talking to a man who was crying because his aunt had just died. "I would ahsk him if he was cryin' becazz his deah aunti was bunning in hell," she said in her thick Bostonian accent.

I did not need her answering this question.

"What happened to 'God is Love'? This sounds like God is hate! Why should we follow a god like that?" Valerie said.

She is eleven and already has issues with God. Her dad is a preacher, but she and her mom fled Louisiana because he was abusive. We weren't supposed to know that but because of her animosity toward God and everyone else, Jennifer, our new leader told us the story. That knowledge hadn't helped her relationship with Karen who didn't like her at all. She gets on my nerves too, but I try to have compassion for her.

I saw Karen's eyes buck and her nostrils flare and again I tried to say something but what do I say to that? It is a hard truth that the Lord will one day leave earth and people to our own devices and the result will be *Super Urgly*.

"Ahh you sayin that you know bettah than Gawd, little gul? That kind of ahtitude is why Gawd will get tie-yad of this worldt. And when he does," Karen said and gestured as if to slit her throat, "it's ovah. Ya heah?"

Holy CRAP!

There was a collective wail from the kids. Karen sat back, crossed her arms over her chest and did the same satisfied circle shake of the head as before.

It took a full three minutes to calm them down. We were sitting on the floor in a circle. I had to pull the most severely affected close to me, stroking them and cooing. Marty and Greta crawled into my lap. When all was quiet, I had us take a deep breath and asked, what questions they had.

I called on Mary first and shot Karen a look that made her slouch back against the wall, lips pursed.

"What did we do to make God so mad?" she sniffled.

How to answer honestly and not make God into an angry junkyard dog ready to bite?

"We have angered God, that is true. We have disobeyed him from the very beginning. Remember Adam and Eve?" They all nodded their heads yes. "Have you ever disobeyed your parents? What happens?"

"They get mad" Mary said.

"They get mad, that's right. Is it because they are mean or because they don't like you?" All of the kids except Valerie shook their heads "no."

"No. Most parents try to do the right thing. They tell you to do the right thing because they want to protect you. God is the same way. He tells us right and wrong for our own good but a lot of times we don't listen, and we do it our own way. What happens when you disobey, and your parents get mad?"

There was silence then Jonah, who we all think is going to be a preacher, ventured a guess.

"We get in trouble?"

"Right." I said and made a note to congratulate Bridget, his mother on what a fine young man he is. "That's called consequences. If you don't do your homework or if you get smart with your mom what happens?"

"She takes my Ipad."

"No tv"

"can't play outside."

"Yeah. Those are consequences. There are consequences to disobeying God too." I knew it was an inadequate response, but their faces brightened in understanding, and I hoped the months we'd spent with them teaching the Bible and salvation had kicked in.

"Yeah, but why do you have to lose everything because you did something wrong?" Valerie.

Talk about a loaded question. Shit. Twelve sets of eyes bore into me, and my mouth went dry.

"Isn't that the whole point of Jesus?" Jonah said.

WOW—scripture comes to life. "Out of the mouths of babes"

"What do you mean?" Valerie said. Her body language said she was ready to beat poor Jonah, but her eyes seemed to plead for something.

"Well. The punishment is that we lose everything whether we like it or not, but Jesus came so we don't have to. He's like our 'I'm sorry' to God, right Miss Pardo?"

"Yeah. You're right Jonah."

"So, the earth and people who don't say 'I'm sorry' to God get the comicises"

"Consequences. Right, Jesus" I started but was interrupted by Paolo.

"So, we can save the world by getting everyone to accept Jesus?"

At least four of the girls smiled coyly at the pretty little Brazilian boy with thick curly locks and eyelashes that would cost at least $150 at the Lash Studio.

"We don't save the world but yes, if everyone accepted Jesus there would be . . . they would be saved from God's wrath . . . his anger" I said.

Just then, Ivy poked her head in the door and said the mothers were waiting for their children. Thank you, Lord. We were getting into some pretty sophisticated theological waters with that last point.

As they gathered up their belongings, I tried to put a pin in the discussion, so we didn't get angry phone calls from their mothers during the week.

"So, yes, the world is going to end. Yes, it is because of our disobedience and God's anger. But God sent a remedy in Jesus—we just have to accept him. We should share Him with everyone we know so they don't suffer. Make sense?"

They nodded their heads yes as they ran out to their moms, some giving me hugs as they left. When they were all gone, Valerie was left waiting for her mom. Karen and I shared a look of exhaustion and annoyance. Her mom usually stays long after the lecture getting encouragement and prayer from Jennifer and the other ladies who lead the women's portion of IBF. All well and good but that means we have to stay late too in uncomfortable silence with Valerie. Karen rolled her eyes and continued to pack up her things. I ventured over to Valerie who was sitting on the table, even though we told her not to every week.

"How you doing?" I asked.

She shrugged her shoulders—better than rolling her eyes, so I got closer.

"Did you understand the discussion earlier?"

She nodded her head yes but did not make eye contact.

"Do you have any questions?"

"No. It's what my dad believed too. He used to say it to us all the time." Valerie said and slowly looked up at me with the saddest eyes I've ever seen. As I tried to conjure up what to say she hopped off the table, gathered her belongings and walked to the door where her mother stood. She looked at me with the same sad eyes that Valerie had looked at me with.

78

Dear Diary,

I saw Ngoc again! I haven't seen him in years. His family moved away years ago. He is still cute but he's not the little boy who carried the rings down the aisle at my wedding. He's short but thick!

Mo and I were at Walmart, and we heard someone calling her name. When we turned around, Ngoc was standing at the end of the hair products aisle waving frantically while his mom struggled to hold him back.

As soon as she recognized him, Mo let out a squeal and went running down the aisle toward him. That was all she wrote. There was no way diminutive Mrs. Nguyen could hold him. He waddled surprisingly fast down the aisle and into my baby's arms.

OMG! It was the sweetest thing!

My svelt, beautiful 17-year-old baby girl was holding on to this short, squat man-looking child like he was her long-lost friend. He told her about school and how much he missed her. She got his information from Mrs. Nguyen and promised to keep in touch.

When they parted, all four of us were in tears.

There isn't much that gives me hope in the world today but that chance encounter and my little girl's love for this boy who most of her friends would be embarrassed to be seen with . . . that gives me hope.

79

Dear Diary,

The world feels like it's spinning out of control. If I thought Otieno had some Hitler-esque possibilities I don't know what to make of Banner. It's not Hitler-esque, it's pure-d fascism on a runaway train! Two words—Muslim Ban. Trying to manage my anxiety but I woke early this morning and couldn't rest until I had written this and it's still not a complete representation of my fears/predictions. God help us. I think he is truly evil.

The Reason I Left

@realresistance: First they came for the Socialists,

@USAPres: Muslim Terrorist Animal steals bus and kills people in Europe.

They should all be banned from public transportation until we know what the hell is going on #uwkwthigo

@realresistance: and I did not speak out—

@USAPres: @realHaedonBanner calls for a complete and total Muslim ban.

We can't take the risk folks.

@real resistance: Because I was not a Socialist.

@whatthehell: September 18, 1941—Jews may not use public transport anymore.

@realresistance: Then they came for the Trade Unionists,

@USAPres: If THEY disrespect OUR Flag and anthem, Strip the SOBs of citizenship or put them in jail.

@realresistance: and I did not speak out—

@USAPres: Constitution is FLEXIBLE folks. Born here doesn't equal welcome here. Pull up Anchors send boat people back to where they came from. #noanchorbaby

@whatthehell: July 14, 1933—"Undesired Persons" can be deprived of German Citizenship.

@realresistance: Because I was not a Trade Unionist.

@realresistance: Then they came for the Jews,

@USAPres: We are going to deport all illegals with a criminal history. We're rounding them up folks they're out of here.

@realresistance: and I did not speak out—

@USAPres: Fill up Guantanamo! Too many bad hambres out here!

@whatthehell: June 15, 1938—All previously convicted Jews (including those with traffic offenses and similar records) are arrested and brought to Concentration Camps.

@realresistance: Because I was not a Jew.

@realresistance: Then they came for me—

@USAPres: **UNTIL WE KNOW WHAT THE HELL IS GOING ON** #UWKWTHIGO

@USAPres: I hear you! Polls say you favor postponing elections #UWKWTHIGO

@USAPres: We will stop the Fake News—enemy of the People. Lock them up

@USAPres: Nidal, Bergdahl, McCain. Military needs true Americans not LOSERS who get captured.

@realresistance: —and there was no one left to speak for me.

@whatthehell: August 22, 1933—Jews are forbidden to use public beaches in numerous German cities, such as Berlin-Wannsee, Fulda, Beuthen, Speyer.

@whatthehell: May 21, 1935—"Wehrgesetz" (= Conscription Law). "Aryan Descent" is mandatory for being allowed to serve in the armed forces.

@whatthehell: July 23, 1938—Decree that Jews are required to have special
Identification cards with them from Jan. 1, 1939.

@whatthehell: July 27, 1938—All street names with any Jewish background are
Changed.

@whatthehell: November 7, 1938—Herschel Grynszpan, whose parents were afflicted by the expelling of Polish Jews, shoots the German Diplomat Ernst von Rath in Paris. As a result, the nationwide pogrom of November 9 is Arranged.

@whatthehell: November 11, 1938—Jews are not allowed to own neither to carry arms anymore.

@whatthehell: April 30, 1939—Eviction Protection is abolished: Landlords may cancel contracts of Jewish tenants anytime.

@whatthehell: No further restrictions were made after 1942, because there was not really anything left to restrict. Also, it was not regarded necessary by the German authorities: On January 20, 1942, a decision was made to step by step deport all German Jews to the Death Camps in the East.

80

Dear Diary,

Lord. This has to be a spiritual battle I'm watching. How do good people, regular Americans—largely Christians, support the things Banner is doing/wants to do?

- Deportation centers?
- Talk of rescinding/phasing out asylum status?
- Taking kids from parents at the border (God forbid. I can't believe this will happen.)
- Threats to end Gay marriage?
- Talk of capital punishment for women who have abortions?
- Banning all Muslims (even citizens) from entering/re-entering the country?
- Leaving NATO and the UN?
- Locking up drug addicts and homeless people for being drug addicts and homeless?
- Cutting funding to cities and states that didn't support his election?

And when did the President get this much autonomous authority? Where are all the leaders who, even if I didn't agree with, I trusted that they were trying to do the best thing for the country? Gone. They're all gone it seems.

Lord help us. This must be a spiritual battle. Nothing makes sense if it's just man acting.

Scared.

87

Dear Diary,

Started writing a story? Book? Something. I don't know what it will end up being. It's a take on the Gospels only it is the Gospel in an upside-down world. I'm calling it the Faux-spel (Faux Gospel) of Banner. Right now, it just helps me kind of make sense of the crazy that is the American government at this point. It's like what Romans 1 says, God taking his hand off of us as a nation and letting us have what we want.

A world without Him.

Scary.

82

Dear Diary,

So . . .

I *almost* didn't go to church today. Yeah, afraid of what they'd say or worse—not say. It also feels a little like a betrayal to go to a white church when I've been in such a vile mood, see all white people—especially white American Christians—as Down Low residents of Damnfoolistan (DFS), aka the Banner base. Also, were Fallu and Dana right? Am I not black enough? Am I fooling myself about my safety by going to a predominately white church?

Whatever. I had to go. Angela was going to meet me at church. She gave her life to Jesus doing a play I wrote last Summer so I kind of bought her. Oh, get off your high horse—I know that wasn't politically correct, but you know what I mean. And I want to see her grow and I want to be used by God. Blah blah blah . . .

Plus, it was my turn to be a greeter at church.

Surprisingly I was genuinely nice to people as they walked into church. I heard the questions in my head "could that Asian family have voted for Banner?" "Why is this white lady being so friendly?" "Are you a resident of Damnfoolistan?" But they were merely whispers in my reptilian brain, so my amygdala *felt* them. But the logical, prefrontal cortex of my brain was able to override the disdain and hate and threat. Shockingly I produced genuine smiles.

I walked into the auditorium looking for Angela but couldn't see her, so I just grabbed a seat. I was settling in when Pastor Daniel said, "Before we get started there are a couple of verses we need to look at." He proceeds to show how BIBLICALLY God speaks *against* white (or any human) supremacy. How this is not something that is *at all* consistent with the Bible and how we as Christians cannot espouse this. God is just and merciful and will not be mocked. God is not white or black or American. God is God of all. Above all.

That was all that I needed to hear. I still have a church and I really love Pastor Daniel Paige. He is not a Damn Foolistan (DFS) preacher. But Tom Markress with his shrine to Banner in his office; Paul Johnson who is training his followers in warfare to take the country by force in Banner's and Jesus' name; the Writz children, Dr. Hobson and the pastors who host Banner praise and worship services at the White House when the cameras are present, their churches are definitely DFS.

83

Dear Diary,

I haven't seen Low Key Idris Elba in a while—at least not to talk to. I saw him briefly from a far at the slugline. He seemed sheepish as he waved at me. Yeah foreigner, how you like your freedom not to vote now? Come talk to me when Banner rescinds your citizenship and ships you and yours back to Cameroon. There's no way I could have sex with him now.

But when one door closes, another opens.

A few weeks ago, a nice-looking man gave me the once over before getting into the slug line or as Fallu called it, Suburban hitchiking.

I was listening to music—preparing my Zumba playlist for class so I only noticed as he was just about past me. He was cute. Dark brown skin—red undertones. Sort of short. Square-ish stocky with thick hair which looked like it would be "good" (curly/soft/mulatto) hair if he let it grow out. Pressed blue pants and a pea coat—looked like a sailor. In a word—not my type at all but still handsome and had a nice smile. It gave me a lift because he obviously looked at me and smiled. I have been too embarrassed to say anything even to you, for a while. Just feels pathetic how happy it made me.

Today I saw him again. And he's nice! I walked up to the slugline. He turned in time to see me walk up and we both gave big smiles. He was on the phone so no conversation, but I was happy because my smile was automatic. When he saw me smile, his smile blossomed across his face—lots of teeth. I don't know, it felt like a connection.

Anyway, the line moved swiftly but we didn't talk. Then a car came. I walked behind him to get into the car. He turned and smiled at me, asked if I wanted to sit in the front seat (Slugline rule no. 1: the first person in line gets to decide which seat he/she wants).

"Ok, sure. Yes" I said—very eloquent.

And he held the door for me to get in! As I reached to close it so he could walk to the back door, he said, "no let me get it for you" and he *waited* for me to get situated and then closed the door.

He obviously didn't know the rules of Slugging. Slugline rule no. 2: Passengers must ride in silence unless the driver engages in conversation. He kept talking.

"What's that building?" "WOO! That sun is BRIGHT!" "So glad it's not raining though."

I half commented back to him because he's cute and it's rude not to comment when someone is talking. The driver stayed silent and turned up the radio.

When we got to the lot, he opened my door for me!

"I'm proud of myself. This is the second time I've slugged this week," he said out of the blue as we started walking to our cars.

"Good for you! It's easy and convenient." I wasn't sure if I should stop and talk or keep walking so, I just shifted the weight from one foot to the other so it looked like I was moving but I was still close.

"Yeah, I just haven't gotten the hang of getting here you know to get to work on time. But I need too, it's too expensive." (hmmm . . .

money conscious but willing to spend on himself and his perceived needs. I like that.)

"Are you driving the other days?" I said and couldn't keep the incredulity out of my voice. It sounded like I was saying "You're not dumb enough to DRIVE are you?" Yeah, we slugs are a snobbish bunch.

"Yeah" There was a little shade in his voice, so it sounded like "yeah dummy how else would I get to work?"

"umph, that gets expensive."

"But like what do you do when it's raining and you want to slug? I mean if it's raining and you're standing outside waiting for a car to show up . . . "

"I use an umbrella"

He understood the un-verbalized "IDIOT CHILD" at the end of my sentence and burst out laughing. Nice laugh like he was being tickled. It felt easy talking to him too. It was nice. Definitely fantasy-worthy.

84

Dear Diary,

The Devil went down to McAllen Bible, looking for a soul to steal.

Yup, that old devil Banner showed up at church today! I thought I was gonna die when he walked out on the pulpit/stage. I had fantasized that I, along with masses of others would walk out or turn our backs but there was just stunned silence replaced by a roar which after a moment I realized was my blood pounding in my ears. Everything was blurry and I thought I may have been having a stroke. After a moment I felt wetness on my hand and realized that I was crying and that is why my sight was blurry. In slow motion I saw the pastor raise the Bible with his right hand then touch demon Banner's shoulder with his left hand. Banner's attire was really casual—not even a tie. I almost didn't recognize him. He looked normal, not the caricature I see on the news. Even his mouth wasn't doing the weird thing that makes him look like a fish gasping for air. I had to shake my head to place myself back in the room and realize that it was true. I was in the same room as the evil king. I also was trying to get my head around what this likely meant: I had lost my church.

Then Pastor Daniel's voice filled the huge auditorium.

"Oh God, we praise You as the one universal King over all. You are our leader and our Lord, and we worship You. There is one God and one savior and it's You. Your name is Jesus and we exalt you, Jesus.

"And we know, we need Your mercy. We need Your grace, we need Your help, we need Your wisdom in our country. And so, we stand right now, on behalf of our president, and we pray for Your grace, and Your mercy, and Your wisdom upon him.

"God, we pray that he would know how much You love him. So much that You sent Jesus to die for his sins, our sins, so we pray that he would look to You. That he would trust in You. That he would lean on You. That he would govern and make decisions in ways that are good for justice, and good for righteousness, and good for equity, every good path.

"Lord we pray, we pray that You would give him all the grace he needs to govern in ways we just saw in 1 Timothy, chapter 2, that will lead to peaceful and quiet lives, Godly and dignified in every way.

"God, we pray for your blessing, in that way, upon his family. We pray that you would give them strength, we pray that you give them clarity, wisdom.

"Wisdom. The fear of the Lord is the beginning of wisdom. Fools despise wisdom and instruction. Please, oh God, give him wisdom. And help him to lead our country, alongside other leaders.

"We pray today for leaders in Congress. We pray for leaders in courts. We pray for leaders at national and state levels.

"Please, oh God, help us to look to You. Help us to trust in Your word. Help us to seek Your wisdom and live in ways that reflect Your love and Your grace, Your righteousness and Your justice. We pray for Your blessings on our president toward that end. In Jesus' name we pray. Amen."[2]

There was silence as Pastor Daniel motioned for the demon to exit, stage left. The demon hesitated but Daniel turned to look at us, the congregation, and then Banner started walking off the stage as we clapped politely. I clapped because the Holy Spirit had spoken and because Banner was leaving. I love Pastor Daniel. I love MacAllen Bible Church.

85

Dear Diary,

Today Banner said Pastor Daniel thanked God because "the country is winning with Banner, folks!"

I know that the Holy Spirit spoke in the sermon and the prayer. The Gospel was preached clearly in his presence. There is no excuse.

Still, I feel like vomiting and crying.

86

Dear Diary,

THE SEX CURE WORKED!

Don't tell anybody but . . . I did it. No, not Low Key Idris Elba (LoKIE) . . . Fallu (shhhh . . . .)

Took some sleuthing but I found his number—I'd hidden it from myself. It was a Thursday. Stupid Banner . . . and LoKIE! And the travel ban looked like it was going to go thru. I needed something really good, and a Pret a Manger harvest cookie was not gonna make it. I know, not my finest angels working.

Turns out Fallu is kind of with a white chick—not the same one. Not married but living together. "Not committed- committed honey!" he said. He has three kids. One with this chick.

If I'm honest I kind of felt righteous taking a black man back from one of them.

I know! I Know! I'm wrong but . . . whatever.

"Hey" I said, not knowing what to expect.

"Honey!? Is that you?" (I know. The Exclamation point was back. I was a gonner.)

"Yeah"

"Honey! I was just thinking about you!"

"I was thinking about you too."

"I'm so glad you called. Listen. That white girl . . . I'm sorry."

"No. We were divorced. You'd moved on . . . "

"But I hadn't. I still loved you . . . love you."

See I was toast. So, I said, "I still love you too."

"I want to see you."

"Me too."

And that was it. Trap was set. And now I'm so so so so Satisfied.

Damnit if white chicks didn't teach him something! He was Good! Really good!

87

Dear Diary,

I wish I could write a paper about this for a medical journal. Sex is FREAKING JUMPER FREAKING CABLES ON CHI! Even Kelly, my acupuncturist, commented.

"You don't really need me today. You seem really . . . balanced. What ya been doing?" he said and smirked.

"Nothin" I said and melted into the face cradle. But that's a lie! I been doing It and now . . .

I can concentrate!

I'm not cursing as much—cuz I'm FREAKING SATISFIED!

I feel happy!

Food tastes wonderful!

The sun is shining, and I don't need to hide from it because I haven't had a migraine since Jumper Freaking Cables!

I wake up before my alarm and go to the gym.

My Zumba class ladies are like WTF (much grinding/twerking and LOADS of energy?!)

Last night, class was so hot that I called him from the gym and told him to hurry over to the house. When he got there, I ambushed him. (Sooo . . . you're welcome husbands of Zumba ladies. I know I send them home ready for you.)

Thank ya Lord! Halle-Lu!

Ok, I know the Lord ain't got nothing to do with this.

Nobody knows, and I like it like that. Fallu's not trying to tell anybody, and neither am I.

88

Diary,

I saw Sailor at the Slugline again! The one I had the witty repartee about the umbrella with. Is it wrong that I kind of like him? I mean because of Fallu?

We were in the Slugline and this homeless guy comes crack-head bopping down the street. It looked like his legs were either too long or too short to walk and he didn't know when they really touched down on terra firma so he had to toe-heel tap tap twice to be sure with each step. He made a bopping b-line to us—in the middle of the line. Sailor looked at me and shook his head chuckling.

"Eh-eh! Eh –Bru. You uh you got a dollar? I'm hongrey. Uh what about uh a quarter and dime? Some . . . something so so I could get me something to eat?"

Yeah, it was Chicken Wing.

Sailor starts digging in his pocket. I was touched. I thought about warning him but then decided I had no right to block Wing's game.

While Sailor's digging, Chicken Wing pulls out a half-smoked cigarette and turns to me, half looking in my direction.

"Eh sis. You got a light?"

"Nah I'm sorry" I was disappointed. I didn't know Wing smoked and I wondered if the cigarettes had been a gateway back to the crack he obviously had fallen back in love with.

"That's alright" puts the unlit ciggy in his mouth and drags on it like it was lit. Sailor hands him a dollar and some change. Wing squints, counts it then frowns.

"Wish it was a five. I ain't mad at you though Bruh." Then he really looks at me and steps a little closer. "You married?"

When I nod yes, he shrugs his shoulders and toe-heel tap taps his way on down the line.

Sailor and I stared after him, mouths agape as if the extra rush of air would help make sense of what just happened. Then I hear Sailor say, "did he just..?" I turned to look at him and his face was a priceless replica of what I imagined my face to look like. Eyes squinted mouth pursed in a question, head cocked to the side. All I could do was nod yes and laugh. Once I started so did he. We were in peals of laughter holding our sides. His laugh made me laugh even harder. It was like he was in pain. His face was all contorted and he would go silent for a second then wheeze "AAAAAAAHHHHH! AAAAAAHHHH!" When he caught his breath he said, "you married?" and we were off to the races again crying laughing. I kept screaming WOO-OOW! As I bent in two trying to catch my breath. The whole line was looking at us and laughing.

By the time we got to the top of the line we were just giggling. No words just beautiful smiles, eyes rolling at the memory of the encounter and slight chuffing cough/laughs.

89

Dear Diary,

What is going on? I went to the delicatessen, Devon and Blakely for lunch today. You know how long it took me to get a freaking soup? 25 freaking minutes. The place was regular-packed, but they didn't have ANYBODY working. Just the Persian manager/owner and three little Latinas from what I could see. They looked more scared than usual. Hope all is ok. Nicole said I should slip them a note that says, "Blink once if you are ok; twice if you need help." It was funny at the time but now I'm thinking maybe it's a good idea.

My boss, Tim, said it was the same at the Subway. None of the Eritrean or Latinas who usually get your order wrong with a smile.

I tried to go to the Korean deli the other day, but it had a big "CLOSED" sign on the door. Even the Korean vendors who sell the Make America Great shit are gone.

I'm fighting against the conspiracy theories in my head but . . . Where they at tho?

90

Dear Diary,

The Age of the WASP (White Anglo-Saxon Protestant) is ending but, mark me, they ain't going out quietly.

Oh, it seems they will have no choice but even liberals are going to get tired of being called out for their shit. But for now, the onslaught continues, and I think the blacks and browns of the country (world?) are just watching and waiting– at least I am.

Went to a comedy club the other day. Muslim comic. Not really funny but he was going hard after white folks in general and men in particular. Can't even remember the jokes—they were true but not funny. I was one of only a couple of melaninated folks in the joint. Younger middle-aged crowd. Very liberal (joint was packed—Muslim comic is rarer than a Zebra). They laughed raucously for the first 25 minutes at jokes poking fun at "Becky" and "Zach". Stories of how they—as white people—bore the responsibility for the mean treatment the comic had suffered. But around minute 27 the laughter went from raucous to hearty to thoughtful giggles. Soon it went to the three then the two then the one-breath Ha! The last straw was when he said something about a Million Muslim March in NYC

"We'll dress in full regalia. Hijabs, kufis, beards. Muslim pride!"

This garnered cheers of approval from the crowd. "Yes! Muslims should be proud! We like that!"

Why did he wait for the cheers to die down and then say,

"We won't let anybody know we're coming! You'll know we're here when you hear us shouting Allahu Akbar!"

We few browns and blacks in the audience howled at that image. But I think the implication, given all of the Becky and Zach jokes, was a little too much for the non-melininated because the sold-out hall remained eerily quiet.

91

Dear Diary,

I kind of hinted about sleeping with Fallu to Lin. Of course, she, my sexiest friend, figured it out. I guess I was too effusive about the quiche at brunch—went there straight from Fallu (still smelling like sex) and I couldn't help it. That quiche was Ah-Mazing!

"Who are you fucking?" She just came out with it. Blammo! Nah, she ain't a Christian.

I tried to deny it but even I could tell that my smile was a mile wide!

I may however have led her to believe it was Low Key Idris Elba from the Slugline, which she thought was CRAZY because he's a Banner-ite, but for now she's accepting it.

92

Diary!

Sailor is a real gentleman.

City squirrel is back. With all the construction I hadn't seen him in a while but he back. Big and bold as shiznitz. And people are still dumb and acting like squirrels are Disney characters.

I was standing in the slugline, aka suburban hitchhiking line. And I saw City Squirrel circling this white family. They didn't have city stank on them and it is Spring, so I knew they were tourists. City stalks them in a cute way. It was as if he identified the little girl and knew she was a good target. He scampered next to her getting her attention. Then he stopped and stood on his hind legs—intriguing her but most importantly, separating her from her herd. She pulled out a cookie from somewhere and bent down and handed him a little piece—WHICH HE REACHED OUT AND TOOK! I shit you not! I'm telling you there is something evolutionary happening with City Squirrel.

Well, why did City do that? The little girl let out a shriek of joy and motioned for the rest of the herd to return and watch as City gets even closer to her and takes another piece of cookie. Everyone is elated except the daddy—smart man—who says "Becky! Don't play with him!" They all snapped to, which made me wonder if Daddy was also a little abusive. Well, City wasn't having it. Becky still had at least half a cookie left and he wanted it, so he chased them. Of course, Becky and the momma and brother thought this was the cutest thing and they skipped and bobbed and weaved and ran like idiots down the sidewalk of busy Pennsylvania Ave at 5 freaking 15 in the evening (TOURISTS!) like they're in a Disney park, filming a commercial. Finally, Abusive Daddy turned and saw the stupidity of his family and he yelled at them to come on and he clapped his hands loudly which made City stop, back up then boldly scamper back toward them. But Abusive Daddy wasn't playing, and City saw that, so he turned away from the family and looked directly at me. I had stopped at Pret a Manger for 3 cookies. It had been a bad day. I'm trying to give up calling Fallu on bad days, so I got cookies. I deserved my cookies. They were good.

City was scampering past when he must have gotten a whiff of the harvest cookie I had just snuck in my mouth and he stopped, zeroed in on me and I SHIT YOU NOT—smirked. I know he smelled my fear and he calculated that cute was not going to work with me, so he STALKED me. He crouched low and moved his left hind and front feet forward at the same time then slowly the right feet moved forward. Like a freaking Navy Seal! Left feet. Right feet. Left feet. All the time smirking at me and his eyes went from the cookie in my left hand frozen in front of my open mouth to the bag in my right hand which held the cookies. I swear he was reading my mind or at least my body because just as I started to move (don't ask me where I was going) he starts to sprint—SPRINT!—towards me.

Now there was a black guy standing behind me and he saw the whole thing. But he thought the shit was funny! And he starts to giggle when City starts sprinting and then he was full out cackle when I screamed "Oh Shit!" and ran into the street trying to get away from

City. And he kept on laughing while we had a standoff. City was too smart to run into the street, but I wasn't. I almost got hit and cars were honking but I'd be damned if I was going to go back to the sidewalk.

"Throw him your cookie" the laughing idiot yelled at me.

"Screw you!"

(No, I didn't say it, but you know I wanted to.)

That's when Sailor (who I hadn't noticed was a few people behind me in line) stomped up to City flailing his arms and screaming for him to leave me alone. City ran a little ways away and thankfully a tourist family walked by and he had another target.

Sailor came and got me from the street.

"It's ok. He's gone. You alright?"

The line clapped rewarding him for his chivalry. But Idiot Man was still laughing. Do you know what Sailor did? He said, "Man, don't you see she was scared? It's not funny." Dude stopped laughing but . . . I had to admit it was more than a little funny.

"No way was he getting my cookie!" I said and broke the tension. Sailor gave me a broad smile and the chuffing laugh I like and nodded a goodbye as he walked back to his space in line.

Kind of feeling him.

93

Dear Diary,

Oh Shit. They're going after White men. The WASP-swatting is getting real.

Every day there's another story of a white man harassing white women and today even white GAY men joined the fray. A white actor was accused of sexually harassing a BOY 30 years ago. Even when the actor tried to wave gay status it didn't get him off the hook. He was just another white man taking advantage of his privileged status. Dirty dealing even on the down low is, as Malcom X said, coming home to roost!

WASPs are going down.

But mark me, it won't be without a fight.

Watching and waiting.

94

Dear Diary,

Daily news had picture of one of the Swatted WASPs accused of sexual harassment and the headline read:

PERV-NADO!

HAHAHAHAHAHAHAHAHAHAHAHAHAHAHAHAHAHA HAH!

Wwwoooooooo!

HAHAHAHAHAHAHAHAHAHHAHAHAHAHA!

Yeah, Jumper Cables are working wonders on my mood.

95

Dear Diary,

I saw Fallu's kids—just pictures. They are adorable.

The café au lait-colored boy with curly hair, Solomon, and his female equal, Blessing. They were 4 and 2 in the picture. Solomon is on Fallu's back with Blessing pulling Fallu along by the finger.

His wallet fell out of his pants when I picked them up off of the floor. I wasn't snooping. It fell open to the pictures and I was looking at them when he came out of the bathroom. He has another little girl, Alicia Amal, the name we had planned to name our daughter if we'd had one. She's 3. He showed me a picture of him holding her when she was a newborn. I wanted to get mad at him for giving away our child's name, but I couldn't be. I have never seen Fallu as happy as he was in that picture holding what should have been our child.

Shit just got real.

96

Dear Diary,

Swat a WASP long enough and he'll start to sting. It didn't take long for the backlash to begin. Of course, he's not stinging the folks swatting him. He's stinging black folks. Fallu said, when elephants fight the grass gets trampled.

Chicago was federalized last night—National Guard went in, surrounded whole areas. Loads of arrests. I woke up to the breaking news alert on my phone. Can't say I condemn the act completely, but the implications are terrifying. There have been open gang wars across the city for a few months. Long gone are the good-ole-days of weekends with ONLY 82 shootings. It was ok when violence was contained to black and Latino gang areas but for the last two weeks there have been running gun battles down State Street. The Dan Ryan was shut down by car chases. A little white boy got caught in crossfire and was killed—on the Gold Coast. Two police killed in a car chase and gun battle. Of course, there were loads of black folks killed too but that's not news-worthy.

Chicago is a mess. Talked to Dana today. We haven't spoken since we went to the church service where Otieno was absolved by the black church. Oh to have Otieno in power (yikes—things really are bad). Anyway, her school—which is connected to her church—has closed for two weeks because the surrounding streets were in the hot zone for one of the wars. Cousin Tara has been crying for this since before the election. Apparently, the police and the Governor asked for it. Even the people . . . this black guy interviewed on the mainstream news said, "We need the police to get these little niggahs outta here. Protect us! Kill them!"

You know it's bad when. . .

Banner is crowing- he threatened to do this early on. Damnfoolistan is happy cuz it proves we need to be contained . . . like animals.

Rumblings that more cities need the same.

97

Dear Diary,

I lynched a teenage boy.

There was a video of this white boy staring down an elderly Native American man. The boy had this smirk. I know that smirk. It's a smirk that says I'm better than you and belies so much potential violence. It's mirth masking menace. When I saw it, I wanted to see that white boy bleed.

The headline said, "White Teen Disrespects Native American Man".

Without a second thought I reposted it with the message "find him!" I stopped myself from completing the thought, "kill him" but I definitely wanted that.

Even when the whole video was released and the boy gave his side of the story, I just saw a smug, entitled white boy threatening a grown man of color. I had to blink twice and shake my head to refocus my eyes to see how the boy may have been trying to defuse the situation, not incite it. It was like looking at those pictures where there's a pod of dolphins hidden under a flock of seagulls. Humanity was hidden under white supremacy, and I could only get glimpses of it and only if I looked really hard.

The scariest thing is that I didn't want to look hard. In my heart I said, "he may not be at fault THIS TIME, but he should pay anyway."

Everything is race first now. I thought we—I had gotten away from that.

WE had!

I had!

Now we're back there.

What happened?

What is happening?

98

Dear Diary,

I've been using the Fallu jumper cables like crazy lately. The world feels out of control. I just need to feel good, but I feel like crap. Not sleeping. Weepy. Chi sluggish. Feel sick.

99

Dear Diary,

Still feeling off . . . sickish.
Wait . . .
Pregnant?
Oh Shit!

100

Dear Diary,

Why shouldn't I have his baby? Nothing says he can't have another child named Alicia Amal—the real one. The one that was supposed to be. Maybe God will give us Sundiata Sitaffa, the son we were supposed to have.

Bought the test but afraid to take it.

101

Dear Diary,

What if God gives us the triplets we always dreamed of . . . until Fallu went fully bat shit crazy. After the shock, my family would help me raise them. The kids would love cousins. These babies would want for nothing.

What would I do about Fallu? I'd have to keep him at arm's length unless . . . maybe he's changed.

Will take the test this weekend. Until then, just getting used to the fact. Once it's real, I'll have to tell someone.

102

Dear Diary,

No. I couldn't let Fallu near the babies. What we have is about as much as we can stand. No real conversation just stolen quickies then he needs to go back to white chick.

Worry about that later Trina. Just focus on the babies.

Wow! Babies.

103

Dear Diary,

Period came last night.

104

Dear Diary,

I just re-read what I wrote. WTF! Who is that woman? Who is sleeping with a man who has a common-law wife and three babies by two women? Who was hoping to be baby mama number three?! Reading those entries cut the cables on my chi. No wonder I was sick. My thinking was sick.

I took the test just to be sure. I'm not pregnant.

I wish I was pregnant—who knows if I'll have another chance to have a child. But thank you Lord for protecting me from me.

105

Oh Shit, Diary!

They just televised the Cabinet meeting. All of these folks appointed by Banner supposed to be talking business. It was a Praise and Worship session! They went around and each praised him! Vice President Pinx, who is supposed to be the Christian rock in the White House, started it off.

"The greatest privilege of my life is to serve as vice president to the president who's keeping his word to the American people."

Senator Majority Leader Reince, rounded it out with, "We thank you for the opportunity and the blessing to serve your agenda."

WTF!

Even the media knew it was a Praise Party and they didn't know what to do.

I keep saying that this is a spiritual issue and people look at me like I'm crazy but what do you call it? The Faux-Gospel in full effect!

Banner fires people when they get too much attention.

Who does that sound like?

Satan. He wants all the attention. He's getting it through his pick to ruin the country. Haedon Banner. I'm telling you he's not the anti-Christ but he IS leading the world to be able to accept the real one when he comes.

Thank you again Lord for not letting me bring a child into these beginnings of the last days.

106

Dear Diary,

Ok. I know I'm supposed to be sharing the Gospel with folks especially now since apparently given the state of affairs with the Presidential cabinet holding a praise party to Banner in the Oval Office, Jesus is about to stand up and blow the shofar and call us all home any minute but . . . I don't want to share the Gospel with the fools God is placing in my path. Jonah much?

But come on! I keep running into the heffa who told me Black Lives Matter was a hate group. For some reason she wants to talk to me and although she claims to know the Lord, she doesn't sound like it. Her theology is Banner-Wacky.

The guy with the bull horn talking about Armageddon in one breath and "keep out the mongrel hordes" in the next. Why did he try to stop me on my way back to the office from Au Bon Pain? He asked if I believed in the Resurrection—perfect opening to have a dialog and give him a Word as he was giving his word, but I just wanted to eat my soup, so I pretended not to hear him and scurried on.

Then this super annoying guy at work who is hostile about Christians, literally asked, "what do Christians believe, like for real, believe anyway?" I told him but I know I was using Christianese on purpose to make him feel stupid and just leave me alone.

As I write this, little Paolo from IBF popped into my mind. "So we can save the world by getting everyone to believe in Jesus?" Ugh.

I have no defense. I just didn't want to share. Forgive me, Lord.

107

Dear Diary,

Fallu just left.

I called him. In my defense, Banner's head of National Security was just caught on tape throwing up a Nazi salute when he was in Argentina and the nation appears powerless to do anything but express outrage and indifference.

He came by, a little under duress. We haven't talked about Alicia Amal but he hasn't really been the same since he told me about her. I know he feels bad about what we are doing. So do I.

I met him at the door naked. He kissed me. I felt him through his clothes. And somehow, the guilt vanished.

I pushed him against the door and frantically undid his pants as he unbuttoned his shirt. I pulled his pants down and while I was there, I blew him for a moment then I felt his strong hands grip my locs and pull my head back, releasing himself from my lips with a pop. I looked up into his eyes and there was an animal staring back at me. I wasn't afraid but I did feel a little panicky. I turned to the left and started to scramble up the stairs. I got to the fourth step when I felt his hand on my left ankle then another on my right calf, effectively stopping any forward progression. With the expertise of a WWF fighter, he flipped me onto my back. My shoulder blades and lower back hit hard simultaneously. I screamed into his mouth which was devouring mine and choked on the air as it rushed back down my throat.

He was on top of me holding my hands above my head, grinding his pelvis into mine trying to get in but my legs were pinned shut under the weight of his legs. Something about the futility of the effort struck me and I began to cry. He saw my tears, covered my mouth with one hand as he began fondling me, bringing me back to him and to the act that I had initiated. I shut my eyes and opened wide for him anticipating the shock of coupling. When it didn't come, I opened my eyes to find him masturbating furiously between my legs. I looked between us, expecting to see his erection about to blow but it just flopped uselessly with the rhythm of his strokes. I reached out to help him and a tear fell from his eye landing on my belly. We both froze for a moment. I tried to look in his eyes to convey some message of solace, but he stomped naked and flaccid toward the bathroom and said "Nevah call me again!"

While he was in the bathroom, I snapped a picture of him and his kids with my phone. If I ever get the urge to see him again, I'll look at the picture and remember what it feels like to be the whore who ruined Alicia Amal's family and hopefully I'll do as he said: never call him again.

108

Dear Diary,

It starts in the heart but manifests itself in a slightly snarled lip and distended nostrils which seem to wish to block out an odor and take in the full measure of its stench in one in/ex- halation. The eyes are slightly squinted bringing to her realization that there is something wrong. She's off and annoyed for no particular discernible reason.

Breathe.

Nothing has happened. In fact the day is going well.

Breathe.

What is it?

Breathe.

It had become evident when she had to keep herself from rolling her eyes at the co-worker whose only fault was existing. The poor woman was bringing good news—"there's free lunch in the kitchen."

Why did she have to preface it with, "I was looking for you"? The interpretation (right or wrong) being: "you failed and are in trouble. I caught you! Everyone knows you aren't doing what is expected and we are all mad." That's what garnered the internal, unseen scowl.

Breathe.

Breathe. And that's when she felt it.

The niggling tightening of the skin above and to the side of her left eye. Not quite the temple.

Breathe.

Actually, it's the entire eye. Tight and slightly feverish skin stretching down to the cheek. It feels great to close the eyes.

Breathe.

Hmmm . . . the left ear . . . it's full.

Breathe.

The skin of her nose is burning.

Breathe.

Teeth itching and wanting to fall out of her head.

Breathe.

Reach up and turn off the desk lamp. Yes . . . that's nice.

Breathe.

Breathe.

"Oh, it's a migraine." She whispers softly in her head as she watches the dim fireworks silently popping behind her closed eyelids. "Just a migraine."

109

Dear Diary,

CRAP!

Alabama just passed a law, making abortion illegal—ever—unless (maybe) the mother's life is in danger.

I just got my heart and mind in the same place on the heartbeat laws. My party line has been that it is tough because women don't always know they're pregnant before the heart beats AND the heartbeat means proof of life SO . . . maybe an upshot is that we, women, will be more careful with birth control. (I never even thought about birth control with Fallu.) I also hoped that an upshot would be laws that made men more responsible/culpable for unintended pregnancy. Not sure how that would work but somehow. AND, the punishment for breaking that law was not clear.

But CRAP! Alabama!

They are talking life in prison for performing and "indulging" in an abortion (like abortion is an ice cream cone or a massage). It is like murder for hire and pre-freaking-meditated murder, they say! It's extreme and cold and mean and political and . . . the logic flows from my stated position on the issue.

CRAP!

I don't know what to think! I mean I know I don't want anyone dying for getting an abortion. I just don't want it to happen! I don't want people to want (need?) abortions! I do think it is murder. I do think it is a spiritual stain on our nation! But I've never lived in a world where abortion was illegal!

I asked Mommy what she thought. She is after all the one who started me on the prolife road. Do you know what she said?

"I don't know."

SHE DOESN'T KNOW!?

CRAP!

Banner's cronies are crowing about it! Their arguments are the same as mine.

Am I a Bannerite?

Oh, hell no! And yet . . .

FUUUUUUU@*%!

110

Dear Diary,

Good time to do this:

Rapture Nearness Checklist:

How close are we to the Rapture of the church? Where are we on the prophetic timeline?

"The granddaddy of all the signs—Jews back in Israel."

Check!

"Earthquakes, famines, disease and signs in the sky."

Check-ish? More Check than Ish. Big ones in California, Nepal, Alaska . . . Ebola rampant in DRC, Chad, Guinea and spreading . . . famine well all over Africa and parts of Asia. So ok, yeah . . . Check.

"Perilous times."

Definitely Check. Sure it could and will get worse but . . . the suicide rate is through the roof. Lately there have been a lot of people jumping out of windows or off roofs. Three in DC in the past two months. One even killed a man on the ground when he landed. I look up when I walk downtown now. Hoping I'll see them falling and be able to get out of the way. So . . . perilous times: Check.

"Wars and rumors of wars."

Nahhh, nothing is changing there I don't think.

"Violence and sexual immorality"

Even more so Check (Fallu). Sex yes AND the violence is really getting crazy. School shootings? Mall shootings. Church shootings. And oh yeah, the US locks up infants and toddlers in subhuman conditions after separating them from their parents at the border so definitely Check.

"False Christs."

Banner and DFS are bad but I still think that's a nahhh

"The whole world will turn against Israel."

Nahh.

Maranatha! Even So Come Quickly Lord Jesus!

777

Dear Diary,

Bad sign. I took a Xanax before leaving the house today. Brewing a migraine and just jumpy. Bad Chi. Environmental social stress? Running low on pills, have to ask Siti to get some more to "share." Her doctor prescribed them ever since she started having chronic debilitating back pain a few years back.

Beanie keeps telling me to go see a doctor. I don't want to say it to her because she wants to go to med school to be a doctor but, Doctors suck! All Dr. Jablonski is going to do is sniff like the air is bad and spit, "you'd feel better if you weren't so fat."

No thank you.

For a second, I thought about Fallu then I looked at the picture of Alicia Amal. It worked again. Thank you, Lord.

I'll stick with my acupuncturist who'll work on my chi even if it is fat chi.

112

Dear Diary,

Oh shit. News filtering out of Chicago is horrid. Turns out you kind of have to have a "permit" to leave the occupied areas, aka the hood. They're not calling it that but that's what it is. The internet is monitored and some are reporting that their access to Social Media is restricted or monitored. Ok, I got that information from a blog entry posted on Facebook but it is totally plausible.

The Governor had to admit that they are restricting access to and from certain parts of the city based on criminal history, known gang affiliation and residence.

Cousin Tara said a friend of hers had to show her class schedule as proof that she was taking a class at Loyola in order to get near campus. Guess who lives in that neighborhood! YUP very few people who look like Tara and her friend or me.

Tara still backs federalization. "The kids are in school, and the only shootings have been cops and guards keeping order."

WTF!

On a more upbeat note, still No Fallu and I saw Sailor from the Slugline again. He's cute and excitable like a little boy.

A Tesla stopped at the Slugline. He was sooo Geechy about it. Neither of us got into the car—we were further back in the line. He starts talking about the technology of the car and how it's blowing his mind. There were four of us talking (Sailor, me and two other girls—cute and young). He turned to the two yung'uns and said, "you probably are too young to remember this but this is straight out of the Jetsons! Before you know it, we are going to have flying cars!"

I love that his frame of reference is the Jetsons. Not so happy that I was excluded from the youth proviso statement he made. Do I look old? No! But I looked older than the others because I am—by a good 10-15 years. BUT that means so is he!

He seems smart too. He has good grammar without sounding like he was on a job interview—just natural. We were trying to remember who invented electricity (none of us dummies could think of Ben Franklin. I got stuck on Alexander Bell the other ladies just looked dumbfounded). He was like, "No but Tesla was the one who did the discoveries I'm pretty sure." He looked it up on his phone and everything.

You know I didn't know—I was still arguing that it was Bell . . .

It was nice to see a man get so excited about something and be conversant on it.

I didn't leave the situation sounding TOO dumb though. When there was a lull in the conversation I said "Dios mio que vengan los carros!"

The Spanish piqued his interest, and he asked me if I spoke Spanish. Well. Yes. I just spoke it (I didn't say that). I downplayed my abilities like any self-respecting passive aggressive self-deprecating woman would do. And, when he spoke choppy Spanish at me, I smiled and acted like I understood (actually I didn't understand—he DOES NOT speak Spanish) Still it was a nice exchange.

113

Dear Diary,

I'm doing a social media fast again. There're are too many awful stories, and I don't know where to let my mind rest. I'm overwhelmed because what do you do? How do you know the truth? Sounds like Pontius Pilate. "What is truth?" In the age of alternate facts, it's a good question.

The last straw this time was the caption under a picture of black clad men rounding up a group of homeless-looking people on the street at night:

US GOVERNMENT EXPERIMENTS WITH QUIETLY REMOVING HOMELESS PEOPLE FROM SIGHT! "PEOPLE WON'T EVEN MISS THEM, BELIEVE ME!" PRESIDENT SAYS IN SECRET BRIEFING.

That's a terrifyingly plausible headline but if you look closely the picture looks like it is set in somewhere like Nigeria based on the unpaved roads and a sign for AFRICEL Telecom sim cards (not that it's ok to happen in Nigeria but . . .)

114

Dear Diary,

Chicago is quiet for the most part—at least the running gun battles have stopped. Seems like they "cleaned up" the streets. Gang members in jail. Blogs say that there are a lot of sick crackheads who can't get drugs so they just lay on the sidewalks miserable. I saw pictures on Facebook. It's terrible.

The mayor of Chicago is asking for 100 million dollars for beds in treatment facilities. Looks like she'll get it. It's not clear if treatment will be mandatory.

Haven't seen Sailor in a while. Feeling crappy again. No sex drive so haven't even wanted to call Fallu. The news just gets worse and worser!

Sailor's cute just not my typical type. Actually, he's really cute. The few times we've talked he was really nice, got my sense of humor, and we have the same cultural references. But he's an American black man and they NEVER find me attractive—too many curves in the wrong place.

115

Dear Diary,

Banner's minions are at work.

The Senate just approved his nominee for a lifelong federal judgeship. No biggee right? Wrong. The guy was UNANIMOUSLY rated "NOT QUALIFIED" by the National Bar Association. He has never tried a case. He's made a number of highly partisan statements—in writing. But he LOVES his master. So, the servants of Damnfoolistan approved him.

116

Dear Diary,

Is this the resistance?

A guy was arrested at the White House for wearing a Malcom X t-shirt. They are investigating him for "suspected terrorist ties" but they picked him out of the line of visitors because his t-shirt pictured Malcom in the window holding a gun. Homeland Security said, "the shirt threatened armed resistance." I have the exact same shirt.

Businesses in DC are being encouraged to encourage tele-work. There are marches against the occupation of Chicago. The courts have upheld the forced treatment of addicts and the administration is looking at expanding it to all mentally ill. Too expensive to have hospital beds so they're talking about prisons (for now) until they can build special barracks or something to house them in.

Ladies and Gentlemen, a direct quote from the President of Damnfoolistan:

"These folks it's crazy they live in a neighborhood, and we wouldn't want that so you gotta clean it's like hell and no investors so we gotta do. Banner is gonna do the hard, nobody wants to but we all know. You know. I know. The lying media and the elites in Washington . . . I tell you they are snobs. Wow. With their tight suits and colorful socks. My daughter, the really hot one, says I shouldn't say that because it's the fashion but they don't know. So, we are gonna help you folks Believe me. You're FINALLY gonna get the help you have been looking for, for you and them. Ok? No more crazies shooting up churches and good people. Alright? Only good people."

Translation from National Alliance on Mental Health. "He's going to incarcerate the homeless the mentally ill and drug addicts like criminals."

And there's real support for it! Ever since the guy killed 26 people in that church in Texas and it was clear that he had at least "anger issues" that were equated with mental illness, the rumble for locking up the mentally ill "until they are *healed*" has grown louder. They may just do it. But not before the protests run their course.

I'm going to bed. It's only noon.

117

Dear Diary,

I probably should stop watching the news but I'm afraid to.

There's something new every day. Sometimes a couple of times a day and that's not even taking into account international news. It's like a firehose of information and if you don't watch, stuff happens and then gets replaced by something new happening. Things are happening too fast.

They say you know when your body shifts into active labor because your contractions suddenly require more, then *all*, of your attention. Is the world in active labor . . . prophetically?

Who knew it would feel like this? Ok, dumb question. Jesus said the end of the age would be like birth pangs. I just thought it would feel different or I wouldn't be here for it or . . . it was just a myth.

118

Dear Diary,

The Chicago model is a thing now and so far 5 cities and states have filed for intervention.

The Chicago Model starts with isolating the dangerous elements of an area. So far, they've used the National Guard but there's talk of developing a special force specifically for the isolation and intervention stage. It's quarantining poor and drug blighted areas like they are contagious and deadly. Once the dealers and gangs are locked up, phase 2 starts. They let the drug addicts die or get sick enough to come out of hiding and then round them up and force them into treatment. So far there's no clear plan of how to keep them off drugs except to not allow access to them. No drug dealers—no drugs. It's not clear how long the Guard stays put but for now parts of Chicago are still under curfew and quarantine. You have to show cause for leaving and returning to the area. A job is due cause but going out with friends to enjoy the city/state/country/world, is not. That sounds like a recipe for disaster but folks like Tara and Cousin Abraham who were afraid to leave the house for years say it's *nice*.

Even some civil rights leaders and organizations are hopeful that it will result in a resurgence of a healthy, prosperous black middle class in neighborhoods that have been destroyed by drugs and violence.

So far, Baltimore, Detroit, Delaware, Kermit WV, and Espanola, NM have petitioned for intervention.

Baltimore and Detroit may have been coerced if you ask me.

I hope Jesus comes back soon. This sounds like Nazi Ghettos.

119

Dear Diary,

I spoke to Cousin Tara today. She's officially part of Damnfoolistan. And I'm officially really freaked out.

"Tara don't you see this is just what happened with the Nazis? Don't you see that they are quarantining the ghetto?"

"AND can't you see that this is the safest my neighborhood has been since I was 16?"

"Yes, but safety at what cost?

"At the cost of not being afraid to let my daughter play in the playground across the street because it is infested with drug addicts and drug dealers?"

"Yes, I get that it was bad."

"Do you? Really? See I think you boil my life and my neighborhood down to a tv episode."

"What?"

"You can feel bad about the situation but hopeful for the characters who are doing something you think is worthwhile and when it all goes to hell you can feel super self-righteous but at the end of an hour-long episode you get to think about something else."

"That's ridiculous! I care about what is happening in Chicago. I grew up there!"

"And you left!"

"You could have left too. You had the same opportunities I did."

"And I squandered them, right? So, I deserve to live in a warzone because I decided to stay?"

"You said that. Not me."

"See this is why Abraham and I supported Banner!"

"I can't with you!"

"And that's why I'll vote for him again. You and your self-righteous attitude. Your elite status. You think you're all high and mighty because you live in some lily-white suburb. You're a suburban black now and you look down your nose on us who are still here. Well guess what, 93rd and Cottage Grove is the suburbs here. I own my house and so do my neighbors, but our kids still can't play outside. You live like that for even a week and then tell me how I shouldn't rejoice that the National Guard has taken over and instituted calm and law and order.

"But you're in a militarized state."

"And in this militarized state the running gun battles in front of my house are over! The little monster who shot my godson because he was wearing the wrong color hat, is dead. The demon who turned my best friend from high school into a crack whore is in jail—for good!"

"They'll never leave. Banner will never recall the Guard. You are going to be under occupation from now on!"

"Who wants them to leave? As soon as they go what do you think will happen? The fools will be back!"

"Yes! Because there are no jobs for them! Do I really have to tell you that the reason for the drugs in the community is poverty? Lack of opportunities?"

"Yes, you do, I suppose because I had the same lack of opportunities and the same education they had and I'm working a legit job, not selling crack or my ass. So, if I can do it these little niggahs can too. You all always want to blame something other than us."

"So, you agree that there is an uneven playing field? An unequal access to money, opportunities and power?"

"Hell yes but I'm also saying that that's not a good enough reason for why my 10 year old child knows the difference between the sound of a .357 magnum and a 45."

"And you're ok with being locked in? Not being able to get out without a pass or a REASON to leave your neighborhood?"

"That'll change."

"Huh! When?"

"As soon as everything is calm, and we know who the good people are. We'll be able to leave and mingle with everybody else."

"What is good and who defines it? Does it extend to traffic violations? Do they take into consideration missing or late bill payments? If you are unemployed, will you still be considered good?"

"You know that's not what I meant! If you are not a troublemaker, you won't have a problem."

"You're brainwashed"

"And you're paranoid."

"This is the Nazi Ghetto"

"NO. This is the Chicago Ghetto and for once it feels safe the way the rest of America, the way you, always feel."

120

Dear Diary,

I had a full week of migraines last month. I really fear I'm becoming bi-polar sometimes because my mind just keeps chattering like a demented monkey. I've decided to try some alternative healing *stuffs* (as Fallu would say). I need to quiet my mind. This past weekend it was a flotation chamber.

It didn't work. The monkey just chattered away underwater.

Good news! Still Fallu-free.

121

Dear Diary,

So this happened last week when I was on my way to the Banner hotel:

Associated Press: Hordes of rats stampede through DC

Officials estimate that upwards of 30,000 rats ran amuck through the streets of downtown DC, snarling traffic and terrifying pedestrians. Rats were seen flooding Lafayette park, in front of the White House as well as the White House lawn and foyer.

"Aerial footage suggests that the small colony of rats emanated from the 16th street corridor where there are multiple construction projects. The rats are seen running down 16th street to Pensylvania Ave then inexplicably turning left. They then ran down Pa. Ave and entered the Banner hotel sending hundreds of guests fleeing into the street," Rand Spicer of the Department of Public Works said.

One-hundred Animal welfare officers were dispatched to buildings between the White House and the Banner Hotel to manage the onslaught of vermin.

"We are testing the rats that we catch but it does not appear that rabies is an issue. At this point our assumption is that construction crews dislodged a small rat nest disorienting the colony and sending the rats above ground in search of safety." Spicer said.

Rat colonies can contain hundreds of thousands of rats. The estimated 30,000 in this incident is relatively small. Spicer estimated the cost of the apprehension, disposal and clean-up of the rat stampede could exceed one million dollars and take two days to complete. OPM has announced that the Ronald Reagan Federal building as well as the DC government offices will remain closed for the rest of the week to facilitate the clean-up.

I thought I was going to die! May still die of embarrassment. Thankfully I was able to escape the stampede and wonder of wonders— Sailor was on his way to the Slugline when he saw me running like a crazy woman down the middle of Penn Ave screaming and crying. He ran toward me and got me to safety, but I peed on myself. So . . . that was wonderful. He is such a nice guy. He got us an UBER to the lot. I was a wreck, so he got my phone and called Siti (my Emergency contact) to get the address to the house (yeah, I was a bit incoherent – so I've been told. I don't have much recollection except for the terrifying bits).

My family loves Sailor. I'm still a wreck. Can't sleep or eat. Surviving on Xanax and Valium.

Apparently, Sailor's name is David Cook.

122

Dear Diary,

Sailor—I mean David—is nice.

He called to offer me a ride to work today. I didn't talk to him. Mom told me. Apparently, since the rat stampede, they talk to him a lot about me. I heard mom say something to him about therapy. I can't deal with all that right now.

I can't go back downtown yet. My boss, Tim, is understanding. Lots of people freaked out. Telework at an all-time high. They're still saying it was a function of all the construction. I think it was deliberate, but nobody has claimed it, and they are trying to limit the news of it because the . . . things got into the Banner hotel and wrought havoc. One good outcome is that Banner's embarrassed.

123

Dear Diary,

Had to try to go to work today. It's been more than a week. I haven't slept much. Still on Xanax and valium but everybody says I need to get back on the horse.

I wasn't feeling it when I got up but—I had to mount the horse—so I got dressed and packed the essentials—Xanax and Valium.

I tried to eat a couple of crackers to settle my stomach but for some reason holding the crackers sent me into tears. I wasn't hungry anyway.

Got it together and fixed my make-up. Swallowed the bile and walked to the door. I couldn't open it. I just stood there shaking. Mom came in to get me (she was going to take me to the slugline). She opened the door and stepped out. When I didn't move she sighed loudly.

"Honey, are you going to be able to do this?"

I could hear the concern in her voice as well as the annoyance. It's how she sounded after the divorce when I'd hyperventilate at the thought of going out with friends. It was like, "I love you but . . . come on, get over it already."

"I'll be ok. Gotta get on the horse." I mumbled.

Then there was a twitch on the ground behind her in my peripheral vision and I got just a glimpse of a tail. Squirrel, but a rodent none-the-less.

The horse bucked. I fell off and went running and screaming to the bedroom.

I'll try again tomorrow.

124

Dear Diary,

I had my first EMDR session. Eye Movement Desensitization Reprocessing. It's a trauma treatment that "reprocesses the memory of the trauma" by "stimulating both hemispheres of the brain." That's what the pamphlet said that the doctor gave me. Whatever, it was hard.

I didn't get too far. I kept needing to "ground" myself. Interesting process though—if I weren't the one experiencing it. The therapist said I should go over the memories in my head if I wanted to. I don't know that I want to, so much as it won't leave me alone, especially when I sleep.

The memory starts with me walking to the meeting that day.

I didn't want to go. Not only was it going to be a lot of Blahblah blah it was at the Old Post Office Pavilion on Pennsylvania Avenue, aka the Banner Hotel.

I hated that building since the Deserved One took it over and converted it into a hotel. During construction I used to walk by it and spit unless the ACLU had the giant inflatable rat on the sidewalk in front. Then I'd smile as I averted my eyes—even the non-sentient rodent *gave me the heebee jeebees* to look at it. But since the election, Banner has lost money on that hotel because people hate him and won't hold functions there. So, it was the nicest/gaudiest place you could hold a meeting and get a REALLY good deal.

I was late to the meeting, but I wasn't rushing. I couldn't get over the hypocrisy of hosting an immigrants rights meeting at Banner DC Plaza. The only thing that made me go was that the logo for the conference was a disguised raised middle finger—my idea, given for free—to the designer who I had drinks with one night.

I had a bad feeling about this whole thing. Actually, today I'm not sure if it was a bad feeling or if I was just being a bitch and didn't want to go. Whatever it was, I was late, but I wasn't rushing.

It was a nice day, warm and clear so the walk was nice but it smelled like phlegm all around me. It usually only smells like that by the CVS but today it smells like phlegm (salty, thick, slightly nauseating—under-stench of piss/funk/dirt. Like a man who doesn't wash his hands after going to the bathroom. It brings to mind the gunk under your nails when you are dirty, have been sweating and then scratch the creases of your thigh. Nasty and private.) I noticed and curled my lip to protect my nose as if to block the access to my smell receptors and taste buds. It didn't work.

With the therapist, Dr. Judy, that smell was over-powering and I actually had to run from the room and vomit. Nothing came up because I haven't been able to eat anything since it happened. Well almost nothing. I got really hungry one day and, mom, anxious to feed me (lest her obese daughter whittle away to nothing) made me a peanut butter and jelly sandwich. I gobbled it down, but the last bite of the sandwich had a pocket of jelly and it squirted into my mouth. It felt like fat. I started to scream. I ran to the bathroom, stuck my finger down my throat and vomited which freaked me out even more because I imagined the scene in the movie <u>Ben</u> when the rat comes through the toilet. I ran to the bedroom and cowered under the covers crying until I could Manage to put two Xanax in my mouth and swallow.

The therapist says vomiting is perfectly normal.

She's a fool but I like her. Sailor referred me to her.

Phlegm.

Right.

It smelled like phlegm but there were no homeless people around—where I always assumed the smell emanated from.

I walked down Penn Ave and saw the kids playing in front of the day care center that the higher-level Government workers send their children to. I hear it costs like $1500/month—for the under 4 y.o. crowd! You better find Maria or Shontwella and pay $750 like the rest of the world. These kids are cute and clean. No snotty noses, full diapers and Timberland's for them. This is the Gymboree set. Clown clothes for kids, thin blond ponytails and brown/black caregivers. So I guess they got Maria and Shontwella after all. There's even a Dayquan, complete with long cornrows, acrylic nails and perfect makeup. I wonder if the parents are happy when Billy says, "Yaasssss Queen!" and snaps his fingers in a perfect imitation of Mr. Dayquan.

Billy, Becky, Zach, Yonas et. al were out in the front with Maria, Shontwella and Dayquan playing *duck, duck goose* and *I'm a pretty pony*. It was the cutest, most normal scene.

And then I heard Fallu and he was REALLY pissed.

I heard his long, drawn-out tooth suck. Sort of a high-pitched squeak. I've never had a flashback that I know of but today, thinking about it, I think it was a flashback. I remember this terror that I never wanted to admit to when I was married to Fallu.

The memory switched to Ireland on one of the visits I made there when I believed Mrs. Fitzgerald to be an agent of Satan who was hell bent on keeping me and Fallu, God's couple, apart. We were at a pub and I could tell Fallu was supremely uncomfortable because he was doing the African man acting like a cultured little girl, "company's

251

present" voice. I was a little tipsy and feeling SUPREMELY turned off by his affectation. A good old Limey came over trying to make conversation and he was more interesting than the inhibited love of my life at that moment, so I talked to him.

Maybe I was flirting but I called it "just being conversant and not freaking afraid of the man!" And that's what I said—loudly—when we left the pub and Fallu accused me of flirting.

Then I heard Fallu's tooth suck from behind me: low, loud and high-pitched. I turned, and everything slowed down. I remember blinking a blink that felt like it took five minutes. When I opened my eyes, Fallu was towering above me (6'3" over 5'4") and all I saw was his mouth. It was in a tight upside-down triangle and the gleam of his teeth shone in the dark through his lips which were pursed. The screech of his sucking was loud like that of a giant bird. His eyes were slits of rage. His fists were clenched. His torso was at an angle. In this position and with his height, a small amount of energy flinging a back-handed fist to my jaw would have left me sprawled on the ground, jaw likely broken, eyes definitely blackened.

A normal person would have backed down. The emotionally battered woman I eventually became would have backed down. Hell, she never would have dared to do . . . anything. But, I hadn't been trained—yet. Plus, there were white people on the street watching so I knew he wouldn't do anything.

Thus, untrained, tipsy, American, Trina said, "you gonna hit me? Forget you!"

"Let's go." He rumbled.

I didn't fight. I was stupid enough to think I'd dominated him. I laughed. A sneering, breathy "huh!"

He put his arm around my waist and deftly propelled me forward.

From behind, I'm sure it looked like we were about to go home and get busy, but he looked down at me and I knew we were anything but good. I refused to let him see my fear. I was scared enough not to move though—not sure what waited for me when we got back to the Irish hovel I was paying for and which he called home.

Encountering my resistance, he smirked and gripped the fat, flesh and muscle of my upper left arm; squeezed and twisted leaving me no choice but to walk and pray that he didn't kill me when we got "home".

That's as far as we got today before I dissolved into tears and literally begged Dr. Judy to let me leave.

Next appointment in two days.

"I can't wait," I said dripping with sarcasm.

125

Dear Diary,

It wasn't really protocol, Dr. Judy said, but we did "process" the incident with Fallu. I had buried that memory I guess and hadn't thought of it again—even when he pinched me toward the end of our marriage. But thinking about it between sessions I realized I held myself responsible for a lot of unnecessary pain. If I had read the signs correctly back then I would have dumped his ass in Ireland and saved a lot of money and heartache. Maybe I would have met someone else. Gotten and stayed married. Had a kid or two with someone who loved me. Who knows.

But I wanted him. I wanted to be married. And as detrimental as it has been, I'm actually glad that I had the experience of being married even if it was to a crazy, HOT as hell African man who as recently as this year I wanted to have a child with.

I chose him. Proof that, the heart wants what it wants but the heart truly is freaking stupid.

So, I have to say Thank you Lord, for the experience and (most especially) for the dodged bullet(s). After all I could still be married to him or, God forbid, have gotten pregnant which would have locked me into some God-forsaken relationship until death.

Thank you, Jesus for the gift of divorce and a second (and third) chance.

Jesus the God of the Mulligan!

Amen.

126

Dear Diary,

Third session started with me across the street from the Devil's tower, aka Banner hotel, aka the Old Post Office Pavillion.

But before we got started, Judy asked if I was angry with myself for having agreed to go to the Devil's tower. She's astute.

The answer is yes. It felt like a betrayal of everything I believed or at least that I ranted about. I had been there the day before the stampede happened. One of the conferees invited me. He was cute and smart. He is an immigration attorney. There's a strong resemblance between him and Fallu. Same big bald head. Same Pretty teeth. Same swagger. Same way of undressing you with their eyes and silently promising a freaky good time.

By the second drink I knew that I wasn't going to risk an AIDS infection and/or unintended pregnancy and the guilt of spreading for a guy who, after you scratched the conversational surface, was boring. I just couldn't square what that would look like if Jesus came back in the middle of it. BUT, the hotel was BEAUTIFUL! Gaudy in the way I like. All gold and marble. It just looked GILDED. OPPULENT.

AMAZING and that was just the hotel bar. The place for commoners. I felt special. Important. Whorish! Jean, my companion, had a room and do you know what I did? I risked leading him on and getting into a dangerous situation to see upstairs. WHORE OF BABYLON! Do you know what was even more embarrassing and awful? He turned me down! I couldn't even be a whore in the Devil's lair. He paid for his drink and left me to slink from the bar like a 10$ street hooker in a call girl's environment.

So thankful Judy is a Christian. We talked of redemption and salvation from an AWFUL and DANGEROUS situation. We looked at pictures of the hotel. It is beautiful dammit! Its beauty is not evil. I was able to just call it the Banner Hotel. Not the Devil's lair. Not even the Old Post Office Pavilion. The Banner mofo hotel. I'm not completely healed yet. Smile.

We left the session on another note of gratitude.

I don't know when we'll get back to EMDR. Maybe next session.

127

Dear Diary,

We did it today.

We started the memory in front of the day care. I didn't get stuck on Fallu or the Banner mofo Hotel—progress.

I remembered hearing the screech. But before that, I felt something from behind me—a chill. The screech came from the left. I was standing on the curb, back to the hotel, looking at the kids. When I turned toward the sound, I spotted something low to the ground moving like a wave down the street coming toward Del Friscos and Elephant and Castle. Both establishments had patrons seated outside enjoying a late lunch/early happy hour. Some of them stood and turned in the same direction as the screech. Then there was chaos as tables were overturned and people went running, some tripping and falling on the wave that had reached them and was now moving underfoot. By the time the wave reached 12th street I began to realize that the screech was coming from the wave and the wave was alive.

Again, I felt the chill and there was another collective screech from the wave before it crossed the street heading toward Billy, Suzie, Zack, Yonas and all the kids at the daycare.

Here's where it got surreal. Everything slowed down and blurred but there are certain things I see clearly and, try as I might, I can't stop seeing them.

It was as if the wave, which now I could see was a wave of rats: stopped at the curb waiting for the light to change. Several in the front of the wave stood on their hind legs. They sniffed the air, twisting left and right as if getting directions and then they crossed 12th street, en masse, moving toward the kids.

In their wake there were people scurrying away, but some had tripped and were now serving as ramps for rats to jump on as they propelled themselves forward or, for some, upward onto the tables which held uneaten lunches and appetizers.

My attention shifted to the right as one of the little ones squealed "PETS!" before being trampled by the stampeding rats. I hadn't noticed before, most of the kids had graham crackers or juice boxes or goldfish crackers. Of course, this was afternoon snack time, after lunch and nap so they would be able to hold out until their parents could get dinner on the table.

I hadn't noticed but the rats had. I saw a rat jump into one of the strollers holding a sleepy toddler. She woke up screaming. I couldn't tell if it was a scream of pain or anger at having her cracker taken from her.

The daycare workers, Maria, Shontwella and Dayquan grabbed as many kids as they could and shooed the rats away until a rat bit Dayquan's finger and others climbed up his thin frame and into his pockets. Apparently, he was holding snacks. I heard his screams and the rats' squeals but had to look away as he twirled in terror, rats dangling from his fingers, pockets, one latched onto his lip, two swinging from the ends of his two long, perfectly symmetrical cornrows and another perched atop his head. He looked like a playground spinning swing but instead of kids hanging from him there were rats.

Then the herd pivoted right and made a b-line across Pennsylvania Avenue toward me!

That was as far as I could go.

Judy says it was an abreaction. All I know is I was crawling around her office screaming and crying and I felt a tail slither across my bare foot. I lost my shoe in my attempt to exit the room.

I don't know how long it took to get me back to the present safety of her office, but I was shaking like I was in Antarctica wearing shorts for about 30 minutes. The same as I did that day.

No gratitude today.

Just "you're safe. You're safe. It already happened. This is just a memory."

I guess that is something to be grateful for, but I don't feel safe.

128

Dear Diary,

I finally feel like I have a LITTLE handle on this thing.

Today I was able to see and experience that the rats were not coming for me. They were moving PAST me.

After I saw Dayquan spinning with the rats, I felt something graze my foot. I looked down and saw the tip of a bald gray/black tail as it passed over my foot. That's when everything sped up to double time. I started running across the street toward the hotel and I looked down and all around me were huge rats going in the same direction. There were so many of them that they were running over each other. I think at one point they were three or four deep. I remember screaming. Something told me to run to the left down the middle of the street and I did. I stepped on a couple of rats as I did. It was squishy and unstable like stepping on a half-inflated rolling ball. My foot went all the way to the ground then sprang up and propelled me forward. I remember hearing a loud squeak and clicking sound and thinking "Please God don't let it bite me!" I almost lost my balance but thank God, I didn't.

That's as far as I've ever been able to get in the memory before losing it. Today the memory continued, and I remembered being carried into a building and then into my house.

I know what happened. I've been told but I couldn't remember.

The second time we went back into the memory, I saw Dayquan and I felt the rat tail. But this time I heard someone yelling. I turned to the left and there was a guy—Sailor—running toward me yelling. I ran toward him. Somehow, I knew I'd be safe. Then it's weird. The scene changed to 20 years ago.

I was at the high school track with Mogo, Mom and Siti. Mo was about 3. There were all these people out enjoying the evening, getting exercise. Something made me stop walking around the track and turn toward the circle of turf in the middle of the track. And again, time slowed down as I looked at Mogo who was in the middle. Siti had run to get the ball they had been playing with and mom was at the other end of the track. Mo looked at me and then we both looked behind her. There was a huge, white, wolf-looking dog barreling toward her from the outer edge of the circle. Mogo took off running and I bent toward her arms open wide just as she flew at me wrapping arms around my neck and legs around my waist. "You're ok. I got you. I won't let anything happen to you." I said, and I meant it with all of my being. I would have killed that dog had he tried to hurt my niece. Then it hit me. That's how safe I felt in Sailor's arms that day, and I was.

Judy had me stay there in the memory of safety and protection for a bit. I was safe. I was saved. She tried to make the connection to God and safety, but I got stuck on the reality of a human, skin-clad man saving me, and it felt good.

After the session I was exhausted and when I dreamed of the rats underfoot, they turned into that giant inflatable ACLU rat. The rat that spoke of power and calling out evil practices and what I want to stand for. I'm still creeped out by the feel of the rat underfoot and Dayquan as a rat swing, but I'm not debilitated by those memories anymore.

More than anything I'm flooded with the memory of Sailor running toward danger to save me.

Grateful and more than a little smitten.

129

Dear Diary,

Christmas was nice.

Because of my nervous breakdown around the Rat Stampede, everyone was trying to make me feel good so my family surprised me with a caroling party like I used to host. Everyone still hates caroling and feels it is corny, but they did it with a smile because they wanted to make me happy. The kids invited their friends, and we even did it at Siti's house because it is bigger than my townhouse. Sailor couldn't come—he went to visit his dad. There were about 30 of us which made it really fun and funny because half of the group was so busy talking that they joined in the songs halfway through the first verse, so every song was sung as kind of a round. After the second or third song like that, I stopped being annoyed and just laughed at the absurdity of it all.

On Christmas eve Beanie came to church with me, even though she doesn't like Pastor Daniel's voice and his "dry cry" when imploring people to accept Christ.

I didn't realize how alone I've felt. It was really nice to feel kind of in the center of things.

God!
God!
Stay away!
Come Again Some
OTHER Day!

130

Dear Diary,

Never again will I go to a meditation conference! It was something Judy suggested as part of my therapy. NEVER AGAIN!

Meditators (at least the ones who are into therapeutic meditation) are some crazy, uptight folks. The energy was just too much. This one guy kept referencing his time in the service and training as an interrogator. Others were anxious, almost panicky, to tell how zen they have become from the many trainings they've been to. A man who looked like a dirty Santa Claus asked me out. He was nice—getting over a divorce, God bless him— but I had visions of being locked in the basement-turned-torture chamber, of the house he kept telling me he was fixing up. The whole thing just shut me down. I came home took a Xanax and sat in silence in front of the tv.

Mom gave the conference to me as a Christmas present, so I had to go for the second day. The second day was the worst. There were too many people there and the anxious energy made the technology go haywire. The mics weren't working, the wifi was spotty, and everybody was zen pissed which looks like regular pissed, but everyone ends their catty remarks with a tight, "that's ok though."

By lunchtime, folks had had it and it started to get a little scary. Loads of skinny, uptight women. I realized that the hypoglycemia struggle was real cuz these skinny heffas were rolling up on us fat heffas without fear in the lunch lines which were way too long.

I was standing in line minding my own damn business and this really dried out lady who was probably younger than me says, "Do they have sandwiches here?"

"Yeah" I said.

"Is that what everyone in this line is here for? A sandwich?"

"Uhhh . . . Yeah, probably." I said, trying to get the "I don't know heffa, but it's a safe bet," tone out of my voice.

"So, they'll have sandwiches?"

I wasn't looking at her or I might have noticed the franticness in her eyes. If I had, I probably wouldn't have said what I said next. But I didn't so I did.

"Yeah . . . unless they run out before we get up there."

What did I go and do that for!? It was like I had announced that there was plague at the top of the line. At least 4 people turned to me in terror.

"What? You think they'll run out?!"

"I don't know, I mean maybe. I'm just *inviting* us to set expectations correctly," I joked trying to use the vernacular of the conference.

Nobody laughed. The little lady in back of me was actually wringing her hands and looking toward the front of the line, on tippy toes, trying to see how many sandwiches were left. When the line moved, she kept herding me out of the way, so she could get closer to the food. My higher self said, "Let her get in front of you, Trina," but we know that didn't happen. In the end they put out more sandwiches and salads and a hypoglycemia crisis was averted—barely.

I left early and went to a Starbucks and got a triple grande vanilla latte with caramel drizzle and whipped cream. It felt dirty and anti-zen and wonderful.

131

Oh Shit, Diary!

Is this what it felt like to be a Gentile in Nazi Germany or the middle class in Pinochet's Chile?

I almost don't want to write this down because I feel so bad that I didn't do anything but what could I have done? What good would come of me going . . . away?

I stayed at work really late. It's quiet after 7 down here because happy hour is over.

There's a homeless man who has a dog. They live in front of the Starbucks on the corner of 13 and F. Gray pit bull/bulldog mix it looks like. He's a pretty dog and well cared for—healthy and menacing if he weren't so sweet and docile. I can't help but wonder what twist of fate led him to this homeless life rather than fighting in some underground dog fighting ring. He looks like in the right (or wrong) setting he could take out a fair share of opponents. He's really calm though so I don't imagine that he was rescued from that kind of fate. Maybe Dogman (his master) once had a home and a family and the Puppy was all that was left of his old life. Sad.

270

I'd never heard the Puppy bark before. Folks love the Puppy, and the Dogman is rather engaging—not scary. People MUST bring him dog food because the Puppy looks really healthy. The Puppy has a little house—it's a baby trailer hitched to a bike—Dogman's transportation. Another holdover from a different life? On hot days the Puppy sits in there to keep cool. He's always well-groomed and clean. He's an old dog but he's sweet.

Dogman doesn't look like he stinks but he seems a little dusty. It's almost like he's invisible, ghost like. He's wiry, dark skinned and has a deep, loud raspy voice but he doesn't use the full force of his voice, so he doesn't scare anyone. But you kind of know not to mess with him from the way he carries himself. Homeless, yes, but a man nonetheless. I like him although I've never spoken to him other than to say "no" when he asks for money or food.

So, I stayed late to get some writing done and left the office around 9. It was a clear night, nicely cool but not cold so I decided to walk to a metro station farther away from the office. I was proud of myself for being able to do that without allowing the memory of the screech, or Dayquan prevent me from living my life.

I heard the commotion before I turned the corner. It sounded like a scuffle. Voices—muted but definitely charged. My first thought was to turn and walk the other way, but something said just keep walking. So, I did. When I was at the corner in front of T.J. Maxx I saw Dogman scuffling with two big black guys who were dressed in black shirts and pants stuffed in black ankle boots. They were clean and pressed. This wasn't a street crime, it was official. One guy, the smaller of the two, had Dogman backed up against a shiny black van. It looked like he was trying to cuff him. The other guy seemed to be trying to block the scene. There were a couple of folks walking quickly by with their heads down trying to be invisible, like I was.

Dogman was fighting against being cuffed. I heard him say " . . . did I do?!" before he broke loose from the smaller guy. He ran a couple of steps away from him.

"Just get in the van, man."

"Hell no man! What did I do?"

"Loitering. We can't have you sitting here."

"Fine I'll leave, damn. That's all you had to say." Dogman raised his hands in the universal "don't shoot" stance. He backed away, packed his stuff up, got on his bike and started to pedal away. The Puppy seemed to acquiesce too, and they began to move down the street; Dogman on the bike, the Puppy trotting alongside leash lashed to the bike.

They'd gotten about five feet away when the bigger guy sideswiped Dogman and he went down. The puppy started barking. I'd never heard him bark before. It sounded almost like his vocal cords had been cut. It was raspy and low and bespoke of constrained power, like Dogman's. His body language certainly wasn't confined. Even from my distance I could see his neck thicken and his powerful chest expand.

The big guy pulled out his gun and Dogman sprang up from the ground to stand in front of the Puppy.

"Naw. Man. Naw. Come on I'm just gonna leave, you don't gotta do all that now." Dogman grabbed the puppy's leash and backed away.

Too late, Dogman and I realized that the smaller guy had been making his way behind him, so the officers had formed a sort of pincer around Dogman and the Puppy. The small guy rushed from the side so silently I didn't know anything had happened until I heard him scream and saw that the Puppy had lunged and was now dragging him down. His arm was firmly locked in the Puppy's jaw.

"No! Baby no!" Dogman screamed at the Puppy. "Please man! Don't shoot. I'll get him off. I'll do what you want. Just please! PLEASE!"

BANG!

Dogman was covered in the puppy's blood and brain spatter. There was an instant of silence then this sound. I can't even describe it. It was a cross between a wail and a scream, strangled in the throat. Dogman had dropped to his knees and was rocking the Puppy's body, there was no real head left.

"You didn't have to do that Man! He was just scared! He was just a old dog. A good old dog."

The guy the Puppy had bitten, tenderly helped Dogman to his feet.

"Let's just let him go man. The van is almost full anyway," he said to his partner.

"Hell no!" the big guy said.

"Come on man!"

"Almost is NOT Full! Have that niggah throw that shit in the garbage and then put his ass in the van with the rest of the trash," the big guy said.

I heard a roar and suddenly Dogman was on top of the big guy but only for a second. The smaller guy was on his heels pulling him off of his partner almost before they hit the ground. The bigger one rolled and recovered, getting to his feet quick. Then both of them were kicking Dogman until he rolled onto his side in fetal position protecting his head. The small guy pulled his hands behind his back and cuffed him. They kept kicking him for a couple of seconds after he was cuffed and then the big one dragged a limp Dogman by his hoodie to the van. The smaller one opened the door and that's when I saw the others. I recognized Chicken Wing among the crowd. As the door slammed shut, I turned around and ran to the nearest metro station to get to the safety of my home.

Great job acting justly, loving mercy and walking humbly with your God Trina. Great job.

273

132

Diary,

I came home sick today.

I haven't told anyone what I saw with Dogman and the puppy.

Today the lady who sits in the folding chair at the corner with the sign that says "Homeless. God Bless You" wasn't there. I tried to convince myself that she just took the day off—I'm convinced she's not homeless in the conventional sense of the word. Maybe she lives in a shelter or something.

Tim and I were headed to Pete's for coffee (I don't go to that Starbucks anymore) and he commented that all the vacant eyed 20-something street urchins who usually roam aimlessly were gone.

"Even the lady with the speaker and mic who sings off key hasn't been here in a while. She was annoying but I kind of miss her," Tim said.

When he pointed it out, I couldn't deny what I knew was happening.

"Maybe they're being rounded up," he said softly, conspiratorially and with mock humor.

The bile rose in my throat filling my mouth with the frothy, juicy precursor of vomit and I stopped walking. After a couple of paces Tim noticed and turned back to me.

"Trina? You're green. Are you ok?!" and then I let go of everything I had in me.

I still haven't told what I saw.

133

Dear Diary,

CrapCrapCrapCrapCrapCrapCRAP!
JESUS JESUS JESUS JESUS JESUS!
They say the rats were infected!
This was in my news feed today.

Associated Press: CDC Confirms Medical Brigades Sent to Treat Homeless Infected by Potentially Fatal Bacteria, Unleashed by Rat Stampede

Officials from the Centers for Disease Control confirmed that three men found dead in an Alexandria, VA motel three months ago died of Spirillum Minus, commonly known as, Rat Bite Fever.

CRAP!

It is estimated that the 30,000 rats that poured into the streets of DC carried the potentially fatal bacterium. The risk of infection is highest in the homeless population. Medical brigades are mobilizing to test and treat scores of homeless in the DC area.

"Look the good and decent people of DC if they got sick were going to go to the doctor and get treated. The three guys who died were probably homeless and we're looking into if they were bad guys. We think they may have been really bad guys," President Banner said.

SHIT!

Could that have been a medical van that picked up Dogman, and Chicken Wing?

134

Dear Diary,

Sailor, aka David, doesn't think it was a medical van that picked up Dogman and Chicken Wing. We've been riding to work together. I took him up on his offer after Dogman. I just don't feel safe, and I had to walk past the Starbucks every day. He drops me at my building. Today I was really jumpy and asked him to go up 13th instead of down F. That way I wouldn't have to look at the corner. I just feel sick and can hear Dogman weeping over the headless puppy. Yesterday I had to hide my tears when we rode past it.

When I asked him to avoid the corner, he looked at me kind of weird and then asked, "Flashback?"

"Yeah" I said really softly. I knew he was thinking about the rat stampede and I hoped he would just leave it at that.

"You saw them this far up?"

"No" I whispered. I wanted to yell 'can't you just do this one stupid thing without asking a million questions?' but I knew that wouldn't be fair. He does ask a lot of questions though. It's usually cute but today I didn't want to have to answer because I couldn't fix my mouth around a lie. I was dying to share what I'd seen but I was terrified to share what I had seen. Not to mention being embarrassed and horrified that I didn't do anything to help. Siti would have helped. She takes action, stands against wrong. Apparently, I just think and talk but when the shit hits the fan I just watch.

"Is there something triggering you?"

I just shook my head no.

"What do you think it is?"

Again, head shake.

"Have you talked to Judy? Maybe you should talk about it? Did something happen?"

Something about the way he asked made me look at him. I know I looked terrified. It's how I felt. Then, damnit tears started rolling down my cheeks.

"Oh my God. What happened?" He pulled behind a row of illegally parked cars on 14th street and turned off the engine. Then he just waited for me. My mouth was working but there was no sound coming out. He reached out and held my hand in both of his. "It's ok. I won't let anything happen to you and if you want, I'll turn the car around and take you home if you need me to. Just tell me what happened."

So, I did.

Eyes shut. Seeing the whole thing as if it was a movie. When it was all out, I opened my eyes. I hoped to find him staring lovingly at me— my protector, firm and strong. What I saw was my terror mirrored back at me in his face. I felt sorry and ashamed for spewing my fear onto him. Infecting him.

"But I think it wasn't what . . . I . . . I . . . they say they are picking up the homeless to test them and offer treatment. Maybe?"

Sailor shook his head no.

"No seriously! Maybe Dogman and Chicken Wing were just gonna be treated" I said full of poorly manufactured hope.

"Yeah maybe" he lied to me then turned on the engine and swung into traffic and dropped me at my door—avoiding Starbucks.

135

Dear Diary,

We haven't talked about Dogman and Wing since that day, but he won't let me slug and he doesn't take me past Starbucks—EVER. I really like him.

136

Dear Diary,

I shouldn't be jealous but I am. For the past 3 days Sailor has been picking up all these women and driving them to work and back to the slugline. Young black and brown women. He picks me up then swings by to get them. No word about why. He just started signaling for specific women to get in his car at the slugline and then those same women (or similar ones) were in the car when he picked me up from work. It's the way of the slugline. If you see someone you know you can pick them out of the line. It sucks but it is understood and accepted.

I don't like this new thing he's doing. In fact, I'm pissed.

I want to say something but what do I say? He hasn't been inappropriate or flirtatious with any of them—or with me either for that matter. It's his car but this was my time. I want to cry but I would be stupid and wrong to cry.

137

Dear Diary,

On the 5th day of the second week of having to share the car, and him, with these cute but somewhat vapid other women I was pretty salty. When he picked me up from work that afternoon, there was this girl already in the front seat where I usually sit. I had to get in the back and the rest of the little heffas piled in as he made 2 more stops. When he dropped them off at the lot I stayed in the backseat for the ride to my house and listened to my ipod. He kept looking in the rearview mirror trying to get my attention. NOPE. When he pulled up to the house he jumped out and got in the backseat with me and just laughed.

I wanted to chop him in his throat. I just gave him a tight-lipped smile and raised my eyebrows.

Translation: What niggah?

He laughed harder. Then he grabbed my hand.

"You mad cuz you had to ride in the back seat?"

"What? No." Dumb ass! What the hell do you think?

"She called and her building is next door to mine. She jumped in and I didn't know how to tell her to get in the back seat. I'm sorry."

"What are you sorry for? It's your car. I'm just grateful to get a ride. Especially since so many . . . people . . . are riding with you now."

"OOOOHHH! You do know why right?"

Silence.

"Something's coming and it's not good. They're rounding folks up."

He saw the terror in my eyes and placed a hand on mine.

"Whatever is happening, it's not safe for black folks. You know that right?"

I nodded a reluctant agreement.

"It's especially not safe for young black women to be out on the street slugging. I can't let you all be out there alone and not do something to protect you. It's what my Daddy would tell me to do. What he would do."

"Oh"

"You understand?"

"You really think there's danger?"

"Dogman and Chicken Wing"

"Ok! Ok!"

"Good." Then he kissed me. Just a peck but he smiled and looked me deep in the eyes and opened the car door for me and watched as I walked to the door.

I don't know what is more powerful. The kiss or the fact that he is scared.

Mixed feelings.

138

Dear Diary,

Us kiss all the time now! Seems like our lips are magnets and whenever we near, we kissing.

It's been so long since I felt this way. Actually, I don't know that I've ever felt this way. It's beautiful but not feverish. I'm, dare I say it? Secure. Weird being with a man who doesn't need saving.

We spend a lot of time together relative to our schedules. I'm still teaching IBF and Zumba two nights a week and yoga twice on the weekend. He has his stuff too, but we find a lot of time for each other. He introduced me to this microbrewery called Water's End, right in our neighborhood. We go there most Saturday evenings. He reads. I write. We talk. It's a cool place, now that I'm used to it. The only thing that would make it better is if it were a wine bar and had a higher bougie-quotient.

They don't serve food, but you can have food delivered or bring it in yourself. Last week Sailor brought Adobo. Right. I had no idea either but it's a popular Filipino dish and . . . he made it.

YAAAASSSSSSS MY Sailor COOKS!

The Adobo was A-delicious! Hahahaha (sorry I'm happy and that equals dumb jokes). It's stewed chicken in this tasty but different, vinegar-based sauce. Delish!

While we were eating, this little girl (around 4), pointed at our food and said, "ummmm. Mommy that smells good!" I smiled, opened my mouth wide and shoved a forkful in.

Then the mama said. "It does smell good little Becky. Why don't you ask if you can have some?"

WTF?!

Becky looked at me as I again ostentatiously shoveled in a heaping forkful. She wisely thought better of asking me for some and then locked her eyes on Sailor.

"Kahavesome?"

Mama: "May you have some what?"

Becky: "PEAS?"

Sailor put his hand on mine. I loved this because he knew I was about to channel Sophia from the Color Purple and say "hey-yal naw!"

Instead, my kind, good cooking Sailor said, "sure," picked little Becky up, sat her next to him and made a plate for her. In an inside joke he pretended like he was about to take some food off MY plate then laughed at me when I put a protecting arm around it.

Guess what color Becky and Mamma were. Wrong. They were black—well Becky was mixed. Something evolutionary happening, that is not so good, but it is happening. Back in the day, no black woman would let her child ask a stranger for some food and then let her eat it. NEVAH!

And yes, it's a brewery which means beer and little Becky is a child. At a bar. With her mama. Again, E-VO-LU-SHUN.

139

Dear Diary,

So, The Water's End Brewery is basically a bar. All they serve is beer and coffee. I don't even know if you can get a coke. There's filtered water from a tap on the wall that you can have for free—they don't even SELL bottled water. So, I would not call it a family place, but all of these 20/30-somethings roll up with their kids. I mean from on-the-breast to about 10 years old. The kids are roaming and running around like it's freaking Chuck-E-Cheese and the parents are gabbing like they're at a PTA meeting. Some folks I've told about this are all cheered by the multi-generational aspect (again, guess what color and how old they are—wrong! Evolution! I'm telling you.)

I judge these parents to be wrong. IT'S A BAR! Granted nobody gets tore up from the floor up, the floors aren't sticky from puke and beer but still. Plus, ok this is probably my biggest hang-up, these are free range kids. They're not sit quietly at a table kids.

It reminds me of when I was in an airport in Burkina Faso. It must have been about midnight. The lines for customs were not that long, they just weren't moving. Plenty of men in white shirts and blue pants who theoretically could/should have been checking papers, but it must have been teatime cuz nobody was doing nuthin'. There was this African mother in line to the right of me with 3 little boys and a babe on hip. Even after a long flight and at midnight, she was still coifed and perfumed. Round and confident in her Muslim femininity swathed in gauzy breast-cancer- awareness-pink colored fabric with sparkly appliques all around. Her sparkly pink mule shoes looked too small and uncomfortable on her fat feet which were covered in old, fading henna tattoos. She slid across the floor so her feet (at least part of them) remained in her shoe.

She had that confident, unfazed air of African women. I'm sure she knew where her kids were at all times, but I'm not sure she cared as they ran and jumped and yuk-yuked like the Three Stooges, around and through the lines of passengers. They even played hide and seek behind the customs officials' booths. The blue pants men showed more concern than the mama. It was like they were playing with the boys and made sure they didn't hurt themselves all the while my pink, hennaed sister smiled and slid around the room, slinging the baby from one hip to the other by his upper arm, not sure what she was supposed to do but obviously never considering that she should stand behind the white line on the floor and wait silently with her children in tow until the tea break was over and the blue pants could morosely demand her documents and stamp them without making eye-contact—like the rest of us were doing.

So, I judged poor parenting equally. Shoot me.

Sailor laughed at me the first time we went to Water's End because he said the judgement was DRIPPING off of me. "You look like something stinks but you're trying to smile your way through it," he said. The truthful, accurate and poetic description made me laugh too and I settled down. Thank God, he recognized that drinking in a bar surrounded by kids was . . . odd.

"I'd have never brought my son here," he said.

Oh yeah, Sailor has a kid.

140

Diary,

Sailor is much kinder than I am. It's nice to be with him. Maybe I'll be kinder too . . . Nah. lol

We went to this thing called Pub Theology at the brewery. It's basically a seeker friendly/non-churchy way to talk about God. You go to a pub, drink and talk about God-light stuff. Heavy on pub, light on theology. There were about 20 people there. Sailor and I were the only ones who had Bibles. The speaker never pulled out a Bible or scripture—not once. I was pretty disgusted, but Sailor is a good time guy and can have an interesting conversation with a rock so, it was fun.

We met this guy and his wife. They were about our age. The wife seemed normal. She looked Native American-ish and seemed a little embarrassed by her husband, who seemed somewhat dimwitted. I felt bad for her and grateful for Sailor. The guy spoke like his tongue was too thick for his mouth, it was annoying. And, he never outright confirmed it, but I surmise he was at least DFS affiliated if not an outright Bannerite. I tried to ignore him, but Sailor engaged him in conversation.

Somehow Sailor got the guy going and he tells this story about how he wanted to be a California Highway Patrol like Erik Estrada in the 80s tv show CHiPs. I started to look down my nose at him but remembered that I went to the University of Miami BECAUSE I wanted to meet and marry Phillip Michael Thomas from the tv show, Miami Vice. So, we all have reasons for the choices we make.

Anyway, the guy says he went through the training and passed all the courses, but he didn't get placed as an officer because he didn't speak Spanish. He went on a low-key rant that he was a victim of reverse racism because he wasn't Hispanic. Just as I was about to launch into a full-blown rant, his wife said, "You could have learned Spanish and gotten the job. You weren't qualified without it."

Enough said in my book so I smiled at her and went to the bathroom. When I came back Sailor and the poor, downtrodden white guy were conversing. The wife was talking to some other people.

"Did you ever consider learning Spanish?" Sailor was asking when I slid clumsily onto the stool next to him.

"It was hard enough for me to pass English in high school. Spanish wasn't going to happen" the guy said around his thick tongue. I felt a little sorry for him.

"What did you end up doing?" Sailor asked.

"Being a CHiP was my dream for years. Having it ripped away . . . it broke up my marriage. I had to leave California. I just couldn't stand it anymore. That's how I found my way to the east coast. Got married. Things are ok but I'm still angry about it," he said and took a swig of his beer.

"I get that, man." Sailor said and patted him on the back.

On the way home, Sailor recited Langston Hughes' poem.

"What happens to a dream deferred?
Does it dry up
like a raisin in the sun?

291

Or fester like a sore—
And then run?
Does it stink like rotten meat?
Or crust and sugar over—
like a syrupy sweet?

Maybe it just sags
like a heavy load.

Or does it explode?"

Woo Jesus! I like that man.

141

Dear Diary,

I finally got the nerve to ask about Sailor's son. Danilo.

He's 27 and lives with his mom in the Philippines. He was born when Sailor was posted there.

Sailor never married Danilo's mother, Honorata. "She was just someone to hang out with. I didn't love her."

WTF?!

So yeah, that made me question all the kissing we've been doing. Sounds like he just threw her away. She married a few years later so I guess no harm no foul. It is what it is. On the bright side he says he always took care of them. Danilo stayed with his mother when Sailor left. He was a little over a year old at the time. I guess Sailor could see the distress on my face because he kept trying to reassure me.

"I never lost touch with him. Money went to them automatically every time I got paid."

But he didn't visit.

When Danilo turned 14 Sailor brought him to the US for high school thinking he could go to college here. He sent him to South

Dakota to live with his father and stepmother. What the HECK was he thinking? Philippines to South Dakota with family he didn't even know?! Sailor was still on active Duty in the Navy, on a ship in the Persian Gulf by then. When Danilo graduated from high school the only gift he asked for was a one-way ticket back home, which he got.

Sailor says Danillo's doing well. He was able to study nursing and he works in a hospital in Manilla. Has a 4-year-old son. Felipe David. Named after Danilo's stepdad and Sailor. Adorable kid!

Yes, I asked.

Sailor married a girl he met when he was stationed briefly in Seattle, but it didn't survive his long months on a ship. No kids. "I never wanted to be an absent father. It just happened with Danilo. I didn't want to be untrustworthy again."

A number of go-nowhere relationships. Nothing serious in a while.

I didn't ask if we were serious.

142

Dear Diary,

It's been a while, and I haven't seen or thought of Dogman and Chicken Wing. I hope they're ok. The news said there have been a couple of deaths attributed to the Spirulina thingie the rats had. The lady with the God Bless You sign came back but she doesn't sit in the same spot every day like before.

Sailor says I'm fooling myself but maybe it really was a medical van.

"Then why kill the puppy?" he asked me. I didn't have an answer, but my friend Sandra said maybe they wouldn't have been able to manage him. Maybe.

I've told a couple of people now but not Siti. She would freak all the way out and I can't handle that.

143

Dear Diary,

Sailor moved here for a job—engineering (blahblahblah) but really, he's a historian at heart! He loves to read and we have talked about writing his family history together. Of course, my specialty is fiction, so he'd have to be ok with a bit of creative license. We'll see. It's a fascinating story. Here's what I know so far.

His first known ancestor on his maternal side was Peter "Little Pap" Mitchell. The first record mentioning him is on a list of slaves owned by James Mitchell in 1827. Then in 1860 this notice was found.

> *Ranaway* from the subscriber living near Liberty Hill, in Iredell County, N.C., a Negro man named
>
> *Peter aka Little Pap*
>
> Formerly owned by James Mitchell. He is 33 years old; of a yellowish complexion—round face and small eyes. He is marked with a scar in one of his ears, which has not grown together; also with a scar on the underside of his heel; which has not healed; he has also a small scar

on one of his cheeks and is about five feet, five or six inches in height.

Anyone taking up this Negro and lodging him in jail or delivering him to me, shall be reasonably compensated.

At some point Peter made it to Kansas City, Mo. The next mention of Little Pap seems to be on the Certificate of Live Birth of a girl in Kansas City, Mo. In 1879. The child is Louise Mitchell. The child's mother is listed as Louella McGee age 15. (Peter was a pedophile). The last mention found of Peter was a news article in 1892.

Kansas City Star—an African American Newspaper

The peace and calm of a Saturday afternoon shopping was disrupted by a knife fight leaving two dead in the middle of busy Ward Street. Peter 'Little Pap' Mitchell killed James Cunningham the son and heir to Cunningham's Grocery and Feed, in front of the family's popular establishment. Mitchell, an ice delivery man, took a switchblade to the young Cunningham after his daughter gave birth and named Cunningham as the father. Louise Mitchell, 13, gave birth to a daughter Friday night. Overcome with rage Mr. Mitchell confronted Cunningham, 27, accused him of rape and demanded reparations to which Cunningham accused the Mitchell girl of prostitution. A knife fight commenced. Both Mitchell and Cunningham died of their injuries.

A Birth Certificate lists Louise's daughter as Mary Mitchell.

There is no official mention of Louella, Louise's mother, until her death in 1912 in Sioux Falls, South Dakota.

Louise (Louella's daughter) is listed on one of the class rosters for Madame C.J. Walker in 1905 in Denver, Co.! (How'd she get there?!) We next find her in Sioux Falls, South Dakota opening the California School of Beauty and Culture, training others to do hair (Again, how'd she get there?) in 1910.

Louise's daughter, Mary, married a Native American man, according to Sailor's recollection.

Transcript of Sailor's account:

Sailor: My mother, Mary's daughter, was Yankton Sioux. She grew up on a reservation. Her name was Anpona but everybody called her Ana, except my dad. He called her Anpona when she was sad, and it would make her smile. She said it meant "experiencing the Sunshine".

Me: Did she speak Sioux to you?

Sailor: Only a little. Mama wouldn't teach me because she said she didn't want me to be marked as Sioux. There was a lot of hostility still when she was growing up and it hurt her. She was born and raised on the reservation in 1930. She said her father was a good Man and tribal leader. He met Mary Mitchell, when she was 18. Unci (it means grandma) Mary's grandmother, my great-great-grandmother Louella, died the same year. Unci's mother, Louise, was busy with the salon and school. Unci Mary didn't have much to do as a young woman, my mom said. She finished elementary school but didn't go further. Sounded like she just kind of hung around the house cleaning and cooking for Unci Louise.

Me: Did you meet . . . Unci Louise?

Sailor: No, she died before I was born. I only saw Unci Mary a couple of times when mama would take me to see her and then at her funeral.

Me: Do you know how Mary and your grandfather met? What was his name? Did you know him?

Sailor: I'm not sure how they met. Mom didn't like to talk about them that much. She said nobody wanted them to get married. Unci Louise forbade it but Unci Mary was insistent and she ran to the reservation with my grandfather, Enapay. They were married in the Sioux way, but people didn't accept Unci and by extension my mom. They were always foreign. Sapa. I hated to hear her talk about it because she would get so sad. But there it is. Her mother fought to be accepted in the community and she fought to get away. She ran when she was 18. Went to a white school then to a teacher's college and taught elementary school for native kids in Sioux Falls. She met my father, James Cook in 1959. They married in 1961 and I was born in 1963.

Me: So, you're an only child?

Sailor: Yeah. My mom was 33 when she had me. She's 9 years older than my father.

Me: Cougar?

Sailor: (Chuckle)

Me: I bet you were spoiled! Mama's little Baby.

Sailor: I was but she died when I was 16.

Me: Oh. Sorry. How?

Sailor: Cervical cancer. It ripped me and my dad apart. She was the center of our world and we forgot how to communicate with each other. He re-married the year after she died, and I had to leave.

Me: A year after?

Sailor: Yeah, she was one of my Aunties.

Me: Opportunist?

Sailor: No. She's lovely actually and she loves him. I just couldn't get my head around it. I was so mad that my mom was gone but I was even more hurt because I was glad that she was gone. She was in so much pain and back then we didn't really talk about what was happening to her. It was kind of shameful.

(long pause.)

Me: Did you get a native name?

Sailor: "I always asked her for one. She would just say, 'I'm waiting for your name to reveal itself to me.' When I was 10, I'd been skipping a lot and the school called her at work and said I was going to fail if I missed any more school. She was so angry! After my dad beat the daylights out of me, she came to my room and said, 'Son, your behavior seems to be revealing a name for you, but I don't want to give it to you.' I begged her to tell me. 'I'm afraid if I give it to you, you will live up to it, so I won't make it final—yet.' I begged and begged her to tell me until she finally did. 'Stoyela. Untrustworthy' she said.

I never asked for my native name again and I never lied to her again.

Me: DAG!

Sailor: Yup. Live with that.

Me: So, is that your name? Stoyela?

Sailor: I thought it was but one day before I knew how sick she was, I was watching Carol Burnett with her. It was our thing. We would watch tv together because she couldn't do too much else. Carol Burnett was her absolute favorite. I knew she was sick, but I didn't know what was wrong. I just knew she couldn't do the stuff she used to do but we'd watch Carol Burnett and it was like old times.

One day, Carol and the little, short guy . . . I can't think of his name. Anyway, they were doing a skit where Carol is the clueless secretary.

Me: Mrs. Sue Higgins!

Sailor: Yeah, yeah! That one! Mom loved that one and she started laughing and laughing. She had an infectious laugh, so I started laughing too and we were rolling. Then she hugged me and said, 'I finally know your name! Ohanzee!'

Me: What does it mean?

Sailor: Shadow. Comfort.

Me: That's beautiful.

Sailor: I hope it was true. I hope I gave her comfort.

I love this man, David Cook aka Sailor, aka Ohanzee more and more!

144

Dear Diary,

Conspiracy theories abound! Three Supreme Court Justices dead in the course of 2 weeks! All liberals. Granted two were old as Methuselah but the other was in a car crash. It's sad but more than that it's terrifying.

The Congress is packed with Damnfoolistan minions. They have a super majority and they all have woodies for Banner! Three of them were caught in the halls of Congress and asked how they were going to vote on the proposal to nullify all of the citizenship naturalizations from the past five years. Do you know what they said (almost in unison)?

"I'll vote with the President."

When the reporter asked, "what does the President want?" They all said some version of, "He hasn't told us yet."

This is who will be confirming the three new Justices.

Good Job Satan.

145

Dear Diary

<u>Rapture Nearness Assessment:</u>

How close are we to the Rapture of the church? Where are we on the prophetic timeline?

"The granddaddy of all the signs—Jews back in Israel."

Check!

"Earthquakes, famines, disease and signs in the sky."

Check-ish? More Check than Ish.

"Perilous times."

Check.

"Wars and rumors of wars."

Ish.

"Violence and sexual immorality"

Damnit! Check.

"False Christs."

Not yet—thank you, Lord

"The whole world will turn against Israel."

Thank you No!

Maranatha! Even so come . . . NO!

Please God stay away. I've only just found Sailor! I know I should want you to come but God help me I want to live in his arms and have him love me here, on earth, not in heaven. At least for a little while. Lord Please don't come soon.

146

Dear Diary,

Sailor and Mark built Siti a greenhouse in her backyard. Why?

"Their house is the biggest. You will shelter there and have access to food when the shit hits the fan," Sailor said.

He bought me a safe to put all important papers and extra cash. Why?

"For when the shit hits the fan."

He's insisting that we all learn how to shoot a gun. Why?

"So, you can protect yourself when the shit hits the fan."

I swear he and Siti should be dating! They think alike.

Beanie and I tried to get into the apocalyptic survival mindset and made some beef jerky. It was really tasty, but I don't know how helpful this skillset will be "when the shit hits the fan." We used a lot of store-bought ingredients, chief among which was BEEF. And it was expensive.

One thing we're all in agreement on—we need God. We've been doing a family Bible Study on the book of Revelation.

147

Dear Diary,

Being loved gives you confidence.

I let Sailor read the Fauxpel—The Faux Gospel. It's my take on what is happening spiritually around us. How Satan plots and rejoices in the happenings of the day. He loved it! He loves my writing! He wants me to publish the Fauxpel and the history of his family. We need to take a trip to South Dakota and the reservation to do more research for that one, but I have to admit, what I've written is pretty good.

As soon as I write that accolade about myself, I hear Fallu in my head.

"Honey! You need to wait for someone to say that about you!"

And Fallu never would have said that about me. I know in my bones that he didn't think I was a good writer. I don't think he ever read anything I wrote.

"It's not interesting Honey! The stuffs you write are too American. Nobody cares about those stuffs"

Even writing that now makes me have to go to the bathroom. It's like ice shards running through my intestines and resting in my colon.

I'm not ready to publish the Fauxpel yet I don't think. The last time I published was Dinosaur Brains, and it was completely out of malice. I wanted to show Fallu. I remember having long arguments with him in my head. Showing him that I was a "real writer" and that I had a book. With each sale I imagined waving the ten dollar check in his face and yelling.

"Who's the real writer now bitch? And the word is stuff not stuffS, you ignorant asshole!"

148

Dear Diary,

Sailor and I have been going to church together. He loves Daniel Paige and MacAllen Bible as much as I do. Especially because Daniel is putting our times in Biblical context and the church is really trying to do stuff to affect the world before it's too late.

We both joined the food pantry ministry. More and more folks are in need especially because of the draconian cuts in assistance being enacted. There was a report in the NY Times that poor parents are abandoning their children at hospitals because they will get food—even though they know eventually the kids will be kept at jails because there aren't enough foster families or other facilities to hold the onslaught of kids in need. That's how bad things are getting.

Last night the pantry ran out of food and there were still 20 families standing in line in need. What do you do? Those families were just desperate—not affiliated with the church. In fact, they were unchurched but they saw us all pull money from our pockets, fall to our knees and ask God to give us a way to feed His people. We had collected $100 (nobody carries cash anymore), barely enough to pay for food for one family. After we prayed, we were planning to give each family $5 when the comptroller walked in and told us that the Board had given us permission to use emergency cash and give each family $100. God provided $2000 on the spot. We saw it. The Families saw it. We ALL gave honor to Jesus and when it was done three of the little kids and one mom asked to receive Jesus as Savior.

149

Dear Diary,

Sailor told me he loves me yesterday and he said it in front of my whole family.

I was excited about the newest chapter of the Faux-spel. We were at Siti's house, and I got up my courage to say,

"I wrote something that I want you to read. I think it's really good!"

In unison, Siti, Mom, Beanie, Mogo, the Twins and I said, "HONEY! YOU NEED TO WAIT FOR SOMEONE TO SAY THAT ABOUT YOU!" and we laughed. Some of Fallu's Fallu-isms have become part of our family vocabulary.

"Babe!" (Sailor calls me Babe—yes, exclamation point) "What is all that 'waiting for someone to say something' about?" he asked after my family had agreed to read the Faux-spel.

"It's just a Fallu-ism"

"Uhm!" he grumbled and I could tell he was on the verge of pissed. He knew about Fallu. I didn't talk about him much because Sailor was livid about the pinches.

"It's just one of the stupid things he used to say that stuck, like 'cook it before you cook it' or 'no suh, she is my wife'."

"What does it mean?" he said cocking his head to the right, bucking his eyes and biting the inside right corner of his bottom lip.

"When I would complement myself, he would always say 'Honey! You need to wait for someone to say that about you!'"

"So why is that a 'Fallu-ism' that stuck?" This time I saw his tongue roll up and down the inside of his cheek.

"It was funny cuz . . . I realized that I do kind of think highly of myself—maybe sometimes too highly undeservedly. . . It's just funny."

"Umph" he said. There was a beat as he nodded his head and gripped the marble top of the island we were all standing around. Eyes about to pop out of his head. Then he said, "I don't think it's funny." Barely contained pissed-ness in his voice.

I could feel the collective backs of my family rising behind me and knew if I didn't shut this shit down quick it was fixing to get *'urgly'* (another Fallu-ism) up in this camp.

"You know it's not really about what you think though, right?" Yes, I did say that.

"Oh! Yes, it is. I love you and as much as you try to act like it's funny, you say it all the time and it stifles you. So that niggah's been gone for years and he's still putting you down. I won't have it. So, from now on when you get ready to fix your mouth to say that shit, know this, IF you really need someone to say it . . . I already said it's good. I love you. And I love what you do because you have done it! Sorry for cursing Miss Lovey. But Babe I'm serious. Don't say that mess again. You hear me?"

All I could do was kiss him right in front of everybody. Then Mom, Siti, Beans, Mogo and the Twins hugged and kissed him. Mark even shook his hand as he left the room—conversation overload. Dear God I love me some Sailor!

150

Dear Diary,

My Sailor was right.

Shit - hitting - fan.

Riots and protests in several major cities. Videos of the so-called Chicago Model, hit the airwaves. It looked like the Nazi Ghettos. People could only get out if they had work papers. Cars are searched going in and out. Several kids tried to sneak out and they were gunned down—on camera. Apparently, this is something that happens not infrequently, but it has been hushed or believed to be fake news until the video.

Protests in DC are still peaceful, but loud. We're still working but it's tense. The rest of the country is not so lucky.

Chicago is burning. The National Guard got mowed down. Liberal resistance outside the wire hooked up with the Resistance inside and they met in the middle.

Detroit and Flint and the rest of Michigan are up in arms- they'll probably be Chicago modeled soon. Running battles in the street. Guard and civilian deaths.

Baltimore has been a powder keg since Donny Moore was killed by the white cop and his body was left in the street. They never took to the Chicago Model. They burned down the ghetto and hordes of angry folks with nothing to lose are spilling into the areas of the *Gente decente*, invading homes, taking over hotels and killing cops and guards. The scary thing is, some of the cops and guards are changing sides and fighting with the Resistance, so it is becoming an organized fighting unit.

Civil War much?

151

Dear Diary,

It wasn't grandiose but it was perfect.

We were having a family dinner last night at Sailor's house. Sailor and I cooked and invited everyone over—his idea. All there except my baby boy, Manny. He was working, of course. After dinner Sailor stands up and starts talking about how he always follows his gut and how it saved him more than once when he was deployed to the Persian Gulf.

"This time my gut is telling me that if I don't do what I'm about to do, I'm going to die a very unhappy man. So," he gets on his knee in front of my chair, "Trina Pardo Joseph, will you marry me?"

I have to admit I wasn't paying that much attention to what he was saying. He likes to talk. He especially likes to make speeches. I have a bad habit of tuning him out. But when he got on his knee, I had laser focus. When I said "yes" my whole family roared their approval.

He had asked everyone for their approval and had gotten a unanimous yes! They all knew what was going to happen. It couldn't have been more perfect.

152

Dear Diary,

Soooo . . . .I submitted the Fauxspel to a friend of a friend who is a publisher. In essence he hated it. Said it was Cartoonish and Caricatured. Preachy! They "represent a cliched, archaic and perhaps (per-freaking-HAPS) inaccurate representation of the heavenly realms." Said reading it made him IMPATIENT! I bet he would've said the same to Frank Peretti. His writing is similar to The Fauxspel. And his book <u>This Present Darkness</u> sold over 2.5 million copies!

Uncircumcised fool! I bet he is a Banner-ite. A freaking POD—Publisher of Damn Foolistan. I bet he is a pundit for or at least a follower of FOX news and I stepped on his master's freaking toes. PREACHY!????! The Word seems like folly to those who are perishing. He must be perishing. If I were so preachy and holier than thou as he seems to say I am I would pray for him but I'm calling down wrath—MY wrath. Who the f . . . I got your preachy!

Cartoonish? Cartoonish would say Satan was walking around in a red suit. The Fauxspel is just putting feet to what the Bible says about Satan. He's a deceiver. He's searching for ways to trip us up. He has followers. He's not omnipotent but he has power. God allows him to do what he does. He and his followers are watching and waiting just like the angels, for Jesus to stand and re-invade the earth.

Preachy!

153

Dear Diary,

We gonna need a bigger fan cuz all this shit is going to cover this little lottie-dottie sized fan.

Parts of California demanding the state secede from the nation. The Governor and the Mayors of L.A. and San Francisco disbanded the Guard and police, confiscated all of the official weaponry, then started a voluntary fighting unit of "CALEXIT" to fight Banner's America.

Banner's National Guard and police Patriots took as much firepower as they could steal and have regrouped in the rural and more conservative areas of the State and there are freaking BATTLES to hold/gain territory. Parts of Oregon and Washington State are talking of joining the Resistance too.

Banner troops are being amassed in cities and towns to fight the Calexit troops. Their battle cry?

"You will not replace us!" Just like in the white Supremacist, Tiki Torch March a couple of years ago.

It's like the Fauxpel come to life.

Preachy my behind! Umph.

154

Dear Diary,

I had to watch Mack Lewis's sermon online again to make sure what I thought happened today in church really happened:

"My text today is from 2 Samuel chapter 12. It's a well-known story, oft repeated. David is king and he got tired of war so he stayed home and got bored there too. He had six wives and who knows how many concubines, but he went on his roof and saw a woman and decided to rape her. Yes, rape. He was KING DAVID not some hoodrat. Who was Bathsheba to say no to the king? Nobody, that's who. I know the thought is that David was fine so who wouldn't want to be with him but even if she did want to, she didn't REALLY have a choice so sounds like a rape to me. Anyway. He rapes her she gets pregnant can't get rid of the kid, so David conspires to trick her husband to sleep with her and then when that didn't work, he had the man killed, and in a magnanimous gesture marries Bathsheba. Nowhere in that whole thing did anybody ever say what Bathsheba wanted.

But anyway . . .

"In chapter 12, God sends the Prophet Nathan to King David and he tells him a story:

> There were two men in a certain town, one rich and the other poor. The rich man had a very large number of sheep and cattle, but the poor man had nothing except one little ewe lamb he had bought. He raised it, and it grew up with him and his children. It shared his food, drank from his cup and even slept in his arms. It was like a daughter to him. Now a traveler came to the rich man, but the rich man refrained from taking one of his own sheep or cattle to prepare a meal for the traveler who had come to him. Instead, he took the ewe lamb that belonged to the poor man and prepared it for the one who had come to him.
>
> David burned with anger against the man and said to Nathan, "As surely as the LORD lives, the man who did this must die! He must pay for that lamb four times over, because he did such a thing and had no pity."

"David had really poor impulse control but I ain't mad at him for this decision. Would that we, the people of America, had someone or somehow to chasten and punish those who steal from the poor and give to the rich! Who take children from their mother's breast and lock them up or give them away to God only knows who. Worse yet we see the sinners of the nation claim that the wrong they do is right and pleases God! How our anger should burn against those who bastardize the name of our Lord and make the little children suffer and call it right. Those who use scripture to defend the right of the tyrant. For the tyrant does not pretend to know God but his followers do. What will we do? What should we do? Can we stay silent? Is that what God meant when he said Obey the government? No! Never! Jesus, the one we love and revere, would never have us remain silent as tyrants run roughshod over the poor and vulnerable.

"Our wrath should burn a hole in the earth as we see the injustice done supposedly in His holy name! The spirit of Bonhoeffer should be ablaze in us. Not with violence but with indignation and like Peter and the disciples we should be unable and unwilling to stanch the flow of words that speak truth to evil—and what we are seeing today is undoubtedly evil! Banner-ism is a malevolent scourge on our country and the Christians who misguidedly support him do NOT represent The Lord!"

The congregation around me sat silent for a heartbeat then one person, maybe it was me, maybe it was Sailor or Beans. Maybe it was someone else, began clapping. Then another. And another and suddenly the church was on its feet! For a full five minutes there were hoots and hollers the likes of which I have never heard at MacAllen. For a second, I was transported to Fellowship Baptist church in Chicago. I looked around expecting to see black bodies dancing like they were at a Heavenly night club.

Beans caught my eye and asked if I was ok, my confusion of place and time obvious to my sweetheart baby girl. I nodded that I was ok and then caught a glimpse of my Beautiful Sailor who was lost in the moment, screaming at the top of his lungs, and pumping his fist in the air. Assured that I was ok, Beans went back to her own place of ecstatic approbation for what this bespeckled, nerdy yet strangely cool, young black man had just said. I smiled, filled with love and contentment for my family—the small group and the larger family of MacAllen-ites who love Christ and obviously felt the same as I did; that it was about time that our spiritual leaders took a side and said the truth that we all had been grappling with alone, wondering if we were hearing God correctly or if, God-forbid, the COD were.

In that moment I gave thanks and scanned the crowd of my brothers and sisters in Christ. The Asian family with two little ones. The white grandparents are surrounded by their children and grandchildren. The entire deaf section. The young wheelchair-bound woman who screamed her love for Jesus and the Word being preached with unabashed abandon at least five times every service. The Hispanic family with the tell-tale earphones which piped in the simultaneous translation of the sermon. The African, white, black, God-knows what other ethnicity, families and individuals on their feet! I shouted a loud "thank you!" as tears escaped my closed eyes and rolled down my cheeks.

When I opened my eyes, they landed on a woman who was seated amidst a sea of standing, praising people. Her arms were folded across her chest and her lips were tight. In slow motion she leaned and turned her head to the right. My eyes followed as her mouth worked out words into the ear of an equally tight-faced, seated man, her husband(?), who nodded exasperated acquiescence to whatever she had said. I blinked and my eyes fell on another island of seated, tight people. And another. And another. There was a large archipelago of seated tight islanders that rivaled the sea of praising standees.

A cold wind seemed to blast through the crowd and we, who had been standing, sat, blending land and water such that you didn't know where one began and the other ended.

Pastor Mack, who had been standing through the conflagration of praise that ripped through the house cleared his throat and continued.

"Verse 7 continues:

> Then Nathan said to David, "You are the Man! This is
> what the LORD, the God of Israel, says: 'I anointed you
> king over Israel, and I delivered you from the hand of
> Saul. I gave your master's house to you, and your
> master's wives into your arms. I gave you all Israel and

Judah. And if all this had been too little, I would have given you even more. Why did you despise the word of the LORD by doing what is evil in his eyes?

"I know you are wondering, 'Mack, what does this have to do with the Tyrant in the White House and those who slavishly follow him.'"

A hoot rose from the crowd and was followed by others. The division of land and sea in the crowd was again evident for a moment. Mack held up his hand to quiet us.

"We are the Man" he said, and his voice broke.

"We, the Church in America, have been given everything but we, not those who follow the evil master, WE who hoot and holler about the injustice we see today, WE are the Man. Have we not embraced greed and made it so normal that we've allowed a new Gospel based on prosperity to flourish? Have we not entertained ourselves into oblivion? Have we not turned a blind eye on the suffering and pain of the white poor because white poor people have a larger piece of the pie than others who share the paltry pie that the poor are allowed? Have we not turned a blind eye to the poor, to the foreigner, to the widow and the orphan? Have we not softened and changed and blended the Word of God to be more palatable to the masses?"

The seated islands hooted, but their jubilation was swallowed by the utter silence of the sea!

And this is why I love this Man of God and all the others God has clearly chosen to serve Him. He continued.

"Verse 11 says,

> This is what the LORD says: "Out of your own household I am going to bring calamity on you. Before your very eyes I will take your wives and give them to one who is close to you, and he will sleep with your

323

wives in broad daylight. You did it in secret, but I will do this thing in broad daylight before all Israel."

"Surely, We are the Man! For without the groundwork laid by us, the tyrant could not flourish." He said and his voice broke again.

The islands and the sea held their breath. Mack continued

"Verse 13:

> Then David said to Nathan, "I have sinned against the LORD." Nathan replied, "The LORD has taken away your sin. You are not going to die. But because by doing this you have shown utter contempt for the LORD, the son born to you will die."

Mack wept openly as he told the age-old story and some of the Islands and part of the Sea wept with him.

"David repented because he was wrong. He did not blame anyone for the wrong and pain and death. He accepted the responsibility for his sin. Will we be the same? Will we repent, openly unabashedly for our many, many sins against God and the resultant evil that is being visited on our country? Will we repent? Will we repent?"

He kept repeating the phrase softly and as he did, it was like warm drops of water dripping onto ice. Melting my heart one drop at a time until there was a crack.

There is a phrase in Spanish, "me parto el alma" it rent/split my soul. As he repeated "will we repent" me parto el alma and I fell to my knees and screamed in such a soul-deep agony that I didn't know if I could survive it. My scream seemed to echo around me, but I didn't care who heard. I didn't care if I was captured on camera and my image of despair transmitted around the globe on the internet. I deserved to be humiliated by the depths of my depravity. I felt it acutely and yet there was such gratitude and love for God because even in the midst of my pain, I knew beyond a shadow of a doubt, He loved me and accepted me and forgave me. King David would not die, and neither would I. This assurance calmed my cries, and I slowly climbed to my seat. As I did, I realized that a good many people were still on their knees mirroring the cries that had emanated from me seconds earlier. Two times the number of those who were seated in the pews watching, were on their knees repenting before the Lord. Mack Lewis lay prostrate on the pulpit. I prayed silently for him as he slowly regained his footing.

He cleared his throat as he wiped his eyes and nose, then said, "Verse 15:

> After Nathan had gone home, the LORD struck the child that Uriah's wife—Bathsheba- had borne to David, and he became ill. David pleaded with God for the child. He fasted and spent the nights lying in sackcloth on the ground. The elders of his household stood beside him to get him up from the ground, but he refused, and he would not eat any food with them.

"Verse 19:

> David noticed that his attendants were whispering among themselves, and he realized the child was dead. "Is the child dead?" he asked.
> "Yes," they replied, "he is dead."
> Then David got up from the ground. After he had washed, put on lotions and changed his clothes, he went into the house of the LORD and worshiped. Then he went to his own house, and at his request they served him food, and he ate.

His attendants asked him, "Why are you acting this way? While the child was alive, you fasted and wept, but now that the child is dead, you get up and eat!"

He answered, "While the child was still alive, I fasted and wept. I thought, 'Who knows? The LORD may be gracious to me and let the child live.'"

"Like David, I don't know what the Lord will do to us and our country. Maybe we will see the Rapture in our lifetime. Maybe we are just experiencing the birth pangs of the tribulation. Maybe things will get worse. What I do know is that God is Good and He is not the one doing this to us. Perhaps His grace will allow us to see His words of prophecy come to pass. Whatever, God is Good. Will we stand firm in that and in His Word and in His wisdom? Will we have the courage to go to Him even though we sin over and over again? Will we represent Him well even if it costs us everything? Will we stand against tyranny and turn away from apathy? Will we continue to repent? Will we repent?"

My heart was pounding through my chest. I felt a combination of nausea and excitement, terror and elation. It was like the air was on cold fire around me. If I allowed myself to look, I was sure there would be ice blue flames licking my skin. I shut my eyes and tried to calm my breathing.

"But now that he is dead, why should I go on fasting? Can I bring him back again? I will go to him, but he will not return to me." Mack said, breaking into my calculations about what people would think if I ran screaming from the sanctuary.

"King David, the rapist, the murderer, the big time sinner, knew he was going to heaven. He knew that he would see his son again. He knew that he would see the Lord. He knew that because he knew the Lord. He didn't just know the scriptures—he knew the AUTHOR. David and Israel faced perilous times because of David's sin but his assurance in who God is never failed. Do you have that assurance? Our country and our world are passing away. The only thing that is sure and eternal and good, is God. He offers us citizenship in His kingdom through the shed blood of Jesus Christ. Offered freely to sinners like King David and Mack Lewis, and you. If you want Jesus today, just come forward, right now and be baptized today don't hesitate . . ."

Yup. So, that just happened. People were running to the altar to get baptized. No idea how many.

God, please protect Mack Lewis. That kind of preaching will never stand in Banner's America.

155

Dear Diary,

How can I be this happy when the world is falling apart? CNN is only online now. They broadcast but very few carriers are showing them. BBC has been banned since the ambassador and then the Prime Minister went on record calling Banner a fool and a scourge. Most of the MSNBC folks are either in jail, missing or in hiding. Fox and the other propaganda stations are running 24/7! Too late to talk of impeachment because the government is full of Banner's minions. Internationally, despots love him. It's all going to shit as Mommy says. So, I should be miserable right? But Sailor . . .

I'm just so freaking happy it doesn't make sense. And it's not like we DO a whole lot. There's not much we can do so we watch tv, read, talk, dance (he loves to dance)! We see each other every night. He doesn't stay over but he watches to make sure we are all ok. He's like family and he's mine. And I'm HIS. Thank you, Lord.

156

Dear Diary,

Just re-read the Faux-spel. I see some of the points. Especially in light of Mack's sermon. I still like it though and more important, Sailor likes it and he loves me like nobody's business so . . . ok, there's work to be done but even if I don't change it, Sailor likes it and he loves me.

157

Dear Diary,

Good Lord what have I done to deserve this?

My family, led by Beans, Siti and Sailor, "published" the Fauxpel for me. They sent it to a printer and designed a cover for it. It's a hardback book (one of a kind, single edition—that's on the cover). They even wrote reviews—glowing, of course- and put a "number one international best seller" sticker on it. Gave it to me for my birthday. Lord I know things are bad but really, the world could burn around me and I would be so satisfied to have lived to see this day full of love.

Thank you, Father.

158

Dear Diary,

Half of the anti-Banner states are calling to separate from the US. They aren't contiguous so some states would not be able to sustain themselves. Shit show.

Family is tense. Half are in favor of secession; half want to be Americans. Siti, Carma, Milga—secessionists which is to say democratic, not the fascism of Banner's America. Mark, Beanie, Mogo—Americans, meaning they think the political craziness will stop soon. Not sure where Manny stands. Mom and I, as usual, are in the middle. We are firmly purple. Banner and his minions scare the shit out of me, and I don't see them stopping the roll toward fascism. I want the America of yore which is more in line with the secessionist States— but the secessionists have an incredibly hyper-liberal base which I don't agree with.

Mark and the girls don't like Damnfoolistan but they don't agree with secession.

"This is our country. We can't just leave it," they say.

Siti is a firm Screw America! (the sanitized version of the unofficial secessionist battle cry) of course. She'd fight with Mdlexit (the Maryland branch of Calexit) if she could. And she's kind of pissed that nobody, except Carma, wants to fight. I always thought Carma would be more of a talker than a fighter. I imagined her writing incredible anti-Banner poetry, not picking up a gun but there's an anger in her now that I never saw when she was little

Milga is for secession but she's not thinking about fighting. Terrifyingly, she said she doesn't have the will to fight for the country. "If things get Nazi-ish like the secessionists warn, I'd rather die," she said. I get it but . . .

Sailor is more in line with secession, but he fought for the country so it's hard for him to say Screw America.

It's all so confusing and fraught!

We can't talk about it.

159

Dear Diary,

What you doing God?!

At church today, Pastor Page said Seven Thousand people publicly repented of their sin by getting baptized after Mack spoke. They've set up special services to baptize folks throughout the week and at the different campuses and microsites. Another Five Thousand have been baptized just since last Sunday. Today they were baptizing people in the fountain outside during church service and when he opened the doors of the church it was like people were being chased down the aisles asking for baptism.

It took us 20 minutes to park—there were so many cars and part of the bottom level parking lot was taken over by the line of people waiting to be baptized. It was chilly but folks were happy and when someone would get dunked a loud cheer would rise up. We watched for about 30 minutes—it was amazing.

160

Dear Diary,

Sad and happy day.

Last day of my Zumba class. It's been one of the few things that I leave the house for other than work. Thank God I still have IBF and yoga with the ladies in the neighborhood. Maybe we can do some Zumba too?

The recreation center is closing. Too much of a liability. This stupid war is crazy. Yes, I called it a war. Two weeks ago, there was almost a battle in front of the Center after a lady called her husband from her car in the parking lot and said she was afraid to go to her class because there were men, she assumed were part of the Resistance, blocking the entrance to the building. (Go home then, shit.) Her husband called a few dozen of his Damnfoolistan Patriot friends and they called friends and so on and so on. The MEN who were allegedly part of the RESISTANCE were teen-age boys. Guess what color they were. Yeah, black and brown—coincidence huh? So, the good old Patriots come out and start to shove the boys around telling them to "git!" The patrons inside were just watching, not sure what to do but some of the fathers of the boys rolled up to pick up their sons and it starts to get *urgly*. A Patriot got one of the boys in a headlock and then all hell broke loose. Cops came and broke it up before anyone was killed thank God.

The next day, the Patriots were standing guard in front of the Center.

The following day, the Resistance showed up too.

No violence, just really tense. When I went to teach my class, they each had formed lines in front of a door, so you had to choose when you walked in: Patriot door or Resistance door. There was a crowd of people, nobody wanting to choose. Some brave soul shouted, "Where is the door for Americans?!" and everybody who was confused about how to enter and not make a declaration, cheered. We all stood there and finally Mike, big black guy who is a Teddy bear but looks scary, came out wearing a badge (don't ask me where he got it from, I've never known him to be a cop but he looked the part) and said, "You can be here but you gotta clear away from the doors. It's a fire hazard. There was a HUGE cheer when they started to clear out. When I came out after class, they were still there, just on opposite sides of the parking lot. Stupid. They've been there every day since then—a simmering menace. Either Sailor or Mark takes me to class and picks me up. The women don't leave the house alone—especially Siti. That's more for public safety than for hers. She's always packing now that Sailor taught us how to shoot and she's got a hair trigger so, You're welcome good old Patriot boys.

So, the Center is closing.

My class was packed! My whole family came (even Mommy and Siti—they watched and wiggled from the sidelines). The Muslim ladies were there! I hugged and hugged them. Talk about guts. They wear hijab so that was a HUGE risk. I played America the Beautiful for the cool down and people were sobbing as they stretched. I couldn't let the class end on that note, so I just let the next song and the next song and the next song play. It was real high energy stuff and some gospel songs

I would usually feel strange about playing in my secular class. I kept dancing and so did they. We danced for another 30 minutes, and we didn't want to stop but Big Mike came in and said the Center was closing so we had to.

It was the second time Sailor had been in my class. Can I say I love that man?! He was wiggling and sweating and singing and smiling. I looked up once and he was LOST in Jidenna's *Long Live the Chief* just doing his own thing.

The last last song was the Wobble. I wish I'd had a strobe light and some mist cuz it looked like we were straight up in a club.

I'm gonna miss my class.

161

Dear Diary,

I'm trying to hold on to the repentant spirit that Mack's sermon engendered but the fastest growing "KKKristian" church in the US belongs to Ronald Wilkes. Here is a smattering of his recent sermon topics:

- Abortionists will be repeatedly aborted in hell.
- LGBTQ will turn into werewolves in the End Times
- God blesses the killing of Muslims and other Non-American Mongrels

He has 25 thousand people come to his "Church" every weekend. Boasts more than a million followers on Twitter and Facebook.

162

Dear Diary,

Mack Lewis was arrested for his sermon! Yes, that is where we are in this country. Pastor Daniel sent out an email this week informing of Mack's arrest and affirming MacAllen's stance that Christians are to resist tyranny. He didn't say that we should support armed revolt, but he was clear that we are NOT to be quiet in the face of evil and tyranny is evil!

I reminded Liz of when she laughed at the idea of America being hard hit by the Rapture. She didn't remember it but we both agreed she may have been prophetic.

163

Dear Diary,

Thank you LORD! Mack Lewis was released today! We had a prayer vigil outside the jail and at the courthouse. We were 5000 strong! Plus, the online campus folks flooded social media and the airwaves. Public opinion still matters. Trumped up charges of sedition leveled at Mack were dropped. On the courthouse steps Mack said this was just a first salvo to see what the public would bare. Daniel said this:

"What we are experiencing is not new. Jesus said the world would hate us because they hated Him. He also said there will be times of tribulation but His elect will not turn away from Him. MacAllen, we are His and we will never turn from Him! No one, not even tyrants, can take us from His righteous hand. We count it a privilege to preach His Gospel and we will preach it faithfully as long as He gives us breath. These are bleak times, but we know that the only savior is Jesus and Him crucified. Stand strong in the Lord, Christian. He has not forsaken us and He never will. Stand strong because we live in a world that is dying and we are called to share the message that God so loved the world that He gave His one and only Son, that everyone who believes in Him shall not perish but have eternal life.

"That is God's message for you, for the jailors who held Mack, for President Banner and for those who blindly follow him. It is the message that we will boldly preach until God sees fit to take our breath away!"

Dear Lord please protect these men and your church. In Jesus' name. Amen.

164

Dear Diary,

Guess who was the spark that resulted in the closure of the Recreation Center? Betty from IBF. Yup. A freaking group leader was so afraid of black male children that she called her husband to bring his gun and help her. We were in Fellowship, and she fessed up to it. All tearful and shit. Said she felt bad for all that happened and wonders what God is doing in our country. She never said she was wrong. I couldn't say anything. None of the black folks did. The white women threw biblical platitudes her way. The tension was THICK. Poor Jennifer tried to manage it and keep the conversation flowing but nobody said anything else, so she prayed and then all of the black leaders, except Iris, got up and silently left. We hadn't planned it. I'm not surprised.

If I wasn't responsible for teaching the kids, I wouldn't go back. The only hope is to teach scripture truthfully. I wonder how Betty is with her group of women some of whom are not white. I'm so glad she's not a children's leader. I know one thing, some of our members may not leave silently if they find out. I hope this isn't indicative of IBF, if so, the membership is definitely gonna trickle down to nothing.

Church still feels ok, thank God. The baptisms have slowed down a bit but still impressive numbers. I notice the Christians Of Damnfoolistan (COD) in the service now. There's a significant gaggle of them who sit on the left side of the auditorium but there are others sprinkled throughout. They are generally tight lipped and sit with arms folded, rolling their eyes whenever something said sounds like it refers to Banner. Daniel doesn't talk about Banner a lot but even when he isn't referenced outright, Banner's actions are so antithetical to Christ that talking about Christ highlights the deficiency. It takes effort for me not to watch the COD without looking like something stinks but I'm generally able to ignore them after about ten minutes. I don't know why they still come.

165

Dear Diary,

Nationwide state of emergency. No work for the past week. Streets on fire. Mom and I moved to Siti's. Sailor's there most of the time—guarding the house.

I'm going stir crazy. And it's tight in the house. Thank God the stores still have food and we can usually go out and get stuff when we really need it. Turns out none of us know the first thing about gardening so the greenhouse is just a sunny room with lots of dirt.

Kids are back home—except Manny. He wouldn't come said he was too busy. Apparently, all of this turmoil is good for the financial sector so somehow his job is flourishing. "The only thing now is for us to have a real war then I'm cashing in and we're all set," he said.

I don't have the foggiest idea what he means but it feels wrong. I hate that he works in finance and I'm afraid of what it has done to him morally. He's actually rooting for real war so he can make money off of it. Somehow, war means money. Don't ask me. He is making a lot of money and he is helping his family—and me—out immensely. Moral conundrum number 53,724: need his help/don't understand and fear where the money is coming from and what the money is doing to my little boy.

Mark and Sailor agree with Manny! WTF! Sailor and I had our first really big argument over that bullshit. Money is not everything—in spite of what I just wrote! So angry with Sailor I told him to leave but there was shooting a block over just after he left so he came rushing back. I was never so happy to see anyone in my life.

It's hard for the babies to be back home. Schools are closed. They tried to stay open, but the unrest was particularly bad on campuses and after the student militias started attacking each other, they had to close. They won't say, but I wonder if Carma was involved with the militia at the University. Her dad had to drag her back home. I can see her plotting to leave and she's secretive. Her sisters won't tell us anything.

166

Dear Diary,

We set the date! In two months, come hell or high water, we are going to get married. I doubt Sailor's dad and stepmom will come. They don't leave S. Dakota. We spoke to Pastor Dale at MacAllen about marrying us but with all that's going on with the church, extra services—except for baptisms—are suspended. Ideally, I would ask Pastor Farmer because I came to Christ under him, but I think he's in hiding. He hasn't returned any calls or emails, and his church hasn't posted any services on Youtube since the occupation. Atlanta—where he is—is an enclave of Resistance in the middle of Damnfoolistan strongholds. I hope he and Rosemary are alright.

167

Dear Diary,

Dolly Parton's cleavage ain't got nothing on the cleavage in the American "church."

Viral tweet from the heretic pastor @Ronald Wilkes: "Jesus said don't give food to dogs. Muslims, Resisters, those opposed to the real America are the dogs Jesus referred to. Starve the dogs or they will bite US."

Approved and re-tweeted by 345.7M and counting including @USAPres—President of Damnfoolistan: 489.8 M followers, @RevPaula—head of a megachurch in Tulsa: 8.7M followers, @Steenengion—Lead pastor at a megachurch in Cleveland 32.6M followers, @FamilyFocus—Conservative Christian NGO 3.8M followers, @BennyFox—Christian evangelist 4M followers, @Jrcracker—Head of international Christian charity and Banner's pastor 36M followers, @Jeffreeze—Head of a megachurch in Texas with satellite congregations in five states and a national tv broadcast 82M followers.

Retweeted with revulsion by 249M.

168

Oh Shit, Diary!

Carma and Beanie are gone. Milga said that Beanie saw Carma leaving in the dead of night and wouldn't let her go alone. They're headed to the Resistance—whatever that means. Siti is losing her mind, but I think in part she's proud of them. Carma for the fighting spirit and Beanie for not letting her sister go alone. Or maybe that's just me feeling that way.

I always thought I'd have that fighting spirit but at almost 50 I don't. It's hard to know what/who to fight against/for. The Resistance is just as bad now as the Patriots of DFS. Last week some idiot got hold of an RPG and sent it into a Patriot stronghold. Hit a heavily populated suburb. 50 killed, mostly children. It was in retaliation for a Patriot missile hitting Johnston Square in Baltimore, a Resistance stronghold—112 killed, mainly poor seniors.

About the 112 dead, Banner said "We got the thug sons of bitches who made lives miserable. We're winning folks!"

169

Oh well, Diary,

Our IBF chapter is going to close after this year. Too dangerous and too fractured. Apparently, Betty's foolishness was indicative of IBF. Hard to have a non-denominational, non-church affiliated international Bible Study that doesn't get corrupted by the craziness of the day. Guess the End Times shenanigans are too much for this 70-year-old Bible teaching institution with chapters in 90 countries. So far America is the only country canceling classes but to be fair, most of the classes in Europe had already closed—lack of attendance.

There have been a couple of shouting matches in the parking lot. There's a dividing line in the sanctuary for the lecture. DFS on one side; Resisters on the other. I had to get a student in line when she said she prayed for the Resistance to be killed because her pastor said that was what God wanted. There is no unity in Christ where DFS and Resisters are concerned. Different Christs.

I'm relieved because, God help me, more and more I hated my supposed "sisters" in Christ.

170

WTF Diary!

Associate Press: White House, Congress and Supreme Court agree; Presidential Election to be Postponed

Flanked by Chief Justice Riley and leaders of the Congress and Senate, President Banner announced the agreement between the three branches of Government to Postpone the Presidential election until calm returns.

"The Congress took a vote last night. The Senate and Supreme Court ratified it this morning. With so many threats foreign and domestic, particularly domestic, to our safety and way of life, we can't risk it folks." The president said.

The President did not take any questions but left the Chief Justice along with the Senate and House Majority leaders to answer how exactly this move is legal under the Constitution.

Senate Majority leader Stewart (R-Kentucky) said that the Congress has the Constitutional authority to postpone elections in the event of emergency. "Our Democratic colleagues have abandoned their elected posts in favor of this ridiculous 'Resistance' and the actions of these rebellious, unrepentant traitors have left the country in a state of emergency for the past 3 months with no end in sight. I call that an Emergency."

Rep. Stewart (R-VA) also cited the inability to have safe and free elections when citizens are under threat of RPG attacks, referencing the recent Resistance attack on a suburb of Alabama which left 50 dead as rationale for the unprecedented action.

The presence and apparent concurrence of the Supreme Court is significant as it signals that a constitutional appeal to the High Court is useless.

Resistance spokeswoman Sen. Hilaria Sanders, who now goes by her Native American name, Fierce Warrior, said the move was the expected next step in what she called the President's headlong rush toward dictatorship.

"We will continue to fight for our country, or we will form a new one," Fierce Warrior said.

171

Dear Diary,

Country not going to survive. State of Emergency means no work. No work means no money. No money means looting. Violence. So grateful Sailor talked me into following through on getting gold coins but it's not like I got a whole lot of them. Thank God, so far, I haven't needed to dip into them—dollars are still valid, for now. Government shut down so mom's social security checks are not coming. We're pooling our money but it's tight.

Every day I'm grateful though. We finally got the plants to grow so we have potatoes and onions and cabbage in the greenhouse. We won't starve. Mark has a friend who is selling chickens so he and Sailor and Manny (yeah, he had to come home) are going to build a coop. You know it's bad when Mark is willing to put a chicken coop in his backyard.

Scared as I am of birds, if I go into the coop with live chickens, it is officially the End.

172

Dear Diary,

Sailor and I have been good. Trying to hold off doing the whole Magillicuty until after we're married but it's hard especially since every day looks like it could be the last day of life as we've known it. Last night we almost broke but he stopped us before we went too far. After this bit of news my attitude was, "let's just do it." But Sailor kept us pure.

Associated Press: Country defenses on DefCon 1 as Pyong-Yang amasses troops at the DMZ and points missiles toward California after thwarted coup attempt. Pentagon confirms six navy seals killed in failed attempt to assassinate the N. Korean president.

> President Banner threatens to leave the declared independent state of California to defend itself if it is attacked. Last month North Korea successfully launched a missile with a range of 7000 miles. Los Angeles is less than 6,000 miles from N. Korea.

173

Dear Diary,

Married. Pastor Zulu did it at the house. Feels wrong to celebrate.

Babies are still fighting with the Resistance.

North Korea hit S. Korea and just offshore of Hawaii. War machine in full effect. Countless dead. Sailor's dad is ok but refuses to come here. I've met him via Skype. Crotchety. At 85 he signed up to bear arms against the N. Koreans. Sailor hasn't been able to reach his son and baby-mama, Danilo and Honorata. Wedding was just family—not really safe to have parties so we didn't invite friends.

Sailor thinks his Reserves unit may get called to Active Duty again. I don't see how. He's old. 54.

Lord, is this really happening?

174

Dear Diary,

Sailor ships out tomorrow.

I've come to terms with it. We all have. The whole country has since the missiles hit just off the coast of California. Suddenly the idea of Calexit (Mdexit, Massexit, Ilexit, etc.) didn't make sense. The enemy of my enemy . . . at the end of the day, We are America.

I won't cry. I know my tears will break him. Instead, I'm determined to give him something to FIGHT for, to come back to.

A sex tape.

I've made my famous paella. I won't eat too much—I don't want any errant, unintended sounds escaping onto the video. You have to think of these things. Like how do you make sure that it's not just a picture of moving covers? Ensuring that booty, if featured, does not look like a proctological exam; which would really defeat the purpose of the tape.

Straddled or standing will be the best positions according to DIYPorn.com. No props. Music is good but select the volume wisely, according to taste. Slightly uncomfortably bright lights, preferable.

Two cameras to get both reactions better than one camera. Check. Check. Check and check.

After dinner I will lead us into the living room (it is the room with the best lighting). I'll put on the sexiest song ever recorded: International Lover by Prince and our bodies will do the rest.

Part II

Opn.

Yu.

FCKN.

Ics!!!

175

Wow! This is one hell of a migraine. I can't open my eyes even if I wanted to. Best to just sleep it off.

176

I hear Sailor's voice. He sounds so sad. He is talking to someone I don't know. A woman! Who is she and what is she to you, my love? Whoever she is I don't like her. Whatever she is saying seems to be making my Baby cry. I'll kill her if she hurts him. I don't like this dream.

177

There's so much pain. It's like fire and wind all at once rushing down my throat and through my lungs. I tried to cough but it was like the coughing part of me wasn't there and as hard as I coughed in my head nothing happened in my body. Then something happened and my throat was clear. I feel dizzy. I think I'm on an incline but I'm laying down. What the hell? My eyes are closed so I must still be dreaming.

178

Shit. I'm trying to sleep! Why is everyone crying and calling my name?

Here I come, damn! Just a minute let me open my eyes!

Wait!

Why can't I open my eyes?

Why the Hell can't I open my eyes!

MOMMY???!

SITI!

DAVID!

HELP ME!

WHY THE HELL CAN'T I OPEN MY EYES! SHIT! HELP!

179

SHIT! OK. OK. BREATHE. YOU CAN'T PASS OUT AGAIN.
BREATHE.

BREATHE. Pranayama breathing. Ok. You can do this. You're laying down. Good. Now place your hand on your belly.

Come on Trina. Place your hand on your belly.

PLACE YOUR HAND ON YOUR BELLY! SHIT. WHY CAN'T I PLACE MY HAND ON BY BELLY? WHAT THE HELL IS HAPPENING? GOD HELP ME. WHY CAN'T I MOVE MY HAND? WHY CAN'T I FEEL MY HAND? OH GOD OH GOD OH GOD!

180

OK. You are not going to freak out this time. Ok?

Breathe. Pranayama breathing. Take a deep breath in. It doesn't matter that your hand is not on your stomach. The pranayama is not about your hand. It is about the breath. So, we are going to just breathe. In. out. Good. That was good. Just breathe. In and out. This is great. You can feel it in your lungs, and you can feel it leave your lungs through your . . . is that my mouth? It doesn't feel like my mouth. It feels like my throat. WTF? What the fuck!? Oh God what is . . . ok, ok, ok. Just breathe in and out. It doesn't matter if it's your mouth. You just need to breathe and concentrate! Breathe. Good. Breathe. Now open your eyes.

Open your eyes!

OPEN your EYES!

OPEN YOUR FUCKING EYES!

Oh God please. Let me open my eyes. Jesus please. God please!

181

" . . . breathing without the respirator but we are keeping the Trach tube in to be able to clear her lungs. So, life support is not needed. The only support we have in place now is the feeding tube."

It was the same heffa from my dream who made Sailor cry.

"What does that mean Doctor?"

Sailor! There you are! I thought I smelled you! Help me Baby!

" . . . nothing more we can do."

I don't like this heffa.

"So what? She just stays like this?" That's right Siti we don't like this dumb heffa.

"Unfortunately, yes."

What?!

"What?"

"No, no, no, no, no,no!"

Yes family! Fight for me. Oh Hell no!

"Doctor there has to be something, some experimental treatment? Something."

Mommy! Don't cry!

"I know this is hard to hear but she's not going to get better. It's been a month with no response. You need to decide the best course of action. I'm sorry. The nurse will come by and discuss your options"

This Bitch!

What kind of doctor sets off a bomb and just leaves a whole room sobbing?! Siti, take Mommy out and let her get some air. Mark . . . Mogo . . . Milga help your mom. Somebody help My Sailor! Where're Manny, Carma and Beans?

Jesus let me open my eyes. Let me help them! Please!

182

Almost everyone is here. I can hear and smell them. Sailor is far away but I smell him the clearest. Sandalwood, Basil, Frankincense. I can also hear his rubber soled shoes squeaking on the floor. He's pacing. It's what he does. Says it helps him think.

Milga. That must be her curled up with me. I can smell her hair—coconut and shea butter. I bet my chin is greasy. God, I wish I could massage her back like I used to.

Mo is running in and out of the room getting stuff for her mom and Mommy. My Sweet girl. I just hear her handing around coffee and water and tissue.

If I could, I'd smile because the air is full of my sister, a perfectly coifed bundle of ire. She smells like black pepper and thunder. I hear the unmistakable click click click of her nails flicking each other—a warning that she is trying not to blow up. If I could open my *fucking eyes* I know I'd see her leg bouncing up and down in barely contained rage. I think that's Mark I hear trying to calm her or maybe he's trying to give her an excuse to explode. I just hear his, "huh?" followed by more softly spoken calm questioning words and then, "y'know?" Watch out mark I'm in a coma and I can tell she's about to go HAM on you (as the kids say).

369

On top of it all I smell the gardenia of mom's perfume. She's silent but I know that means she's praying. Yes, Mommy pray for me! Pray that God heals me.

" . . . nursing home."

That must be the nurse. Uh-oh. This is not going to be good. She sounds white and young like a Trishann. Not Trisha Ann. Tri-shann, said quickly. Annoyingly. Siti's not going to hear anything she says. Hopefully Mark, Sailor and Mommy can hold her together.

"Or you can decide to let her go peacefully" Nurse Trishann said.

"Go peacefully! What the hell are you saying? You want me to kill my wife?!" Sailor? Uh-oh. I've never heard that tone before. Just listen baby. It's gonna be ok. Please don't hurt Trishann. Did someone just run out of the room?

"No sir. I just meant that some people don't want to see their loved ones suffer"

"You said she couldn't feel anything that she's not suffering. Is she in pain?!" No Siti. I'm not in pain. I wish I was. Well maybe I do. I don't know what's worse.

"No ma'am. I meant suffer not being who they used to be. She doesn't feel anything, but she could be like this for years and for some that's just as painful as real physical pain."

Yes. Trishann's right.

"How would we let her go peacefully? I thought that's what was supposed to have happened when she was taken off the ventilator."

Wait! What?! Y'all already tried to kill me? WTF! Sailor, what are you so mad about now? You must have already said your goodbyes to me. Oh my God. Lord, they tried to kill me.

"Well, in cases like these we would stop the nutrients . . . take out the feeding tube."

"So, she'd starve?!" Milga. I know that is the worst thing you can imagine my little Love.

"Well, yes, technically but"

"That's different from the respirator."

Is it though, Mom? The goal is still that I'd be dead.

"She always said she didn't want to be a vegetable on a respirator—heroic measures she called it, but I don't know about this."

Damn Mommy. I did say that didn't I? It's just REALLY different on this side of the rhetoric.

"In this case a feeding tube is considered a form of heroic measure. It is only prolonging life. She is not going to die as a result of the stroke but as a result of the stroke, she won't live."

So, it was a stroke. That's why I can't move? But why can I hear and smell and taste? Those are automatic things. But I can think too. Thinking is not automatic. Has anyone done an eeg to see that I'm still in here?!

"Her Glasgow scale is 3. That's as low as it goes. There is no response to stimuli of any kind."

But there is! I'm responding to you Trishann! I can hear you and I'm responding to you. You can't hear me. But I'm in here! Sailor. I know you can feel me. WE have the same heart can't you feel me in here?! Mommy? Siti? Anybody?!

"What is the procedure like?" Mark the pragmatist.

"It's easy and painless like having an IV removed."

Sobs all around. YES! Cry. Don't do this. I'm here! You already tried to kill me, and God wouldn't let you! Stop.

"Will it take long?"

WTF Mark?! You got somewhere else to be? You want this thing done quickly?

"Generally, around 10 days or so. She was pretty healthy before . . . so maybe 15 days."

15 days of starving to death?

"She won't feel anything?"

No! SAILOR don't do this baby, please. Feel me! I'm here. Don't give up on me.

"She doesn't feel anything now so no, she won't feel it."

Bitch! I am HERE!

"I'll give you some time to think. If you have any questions don't hesitate to ask."

I have a question! Why are you doing this? God? Why is this happening?

"Mom we can't do this!"

Thank you Milga! Don't kill your Poohpie!

"She's already gone sweetheart."

Shut up Mark!

"How do we know? How do we know she can't hear us? That she won't get better."

Yes baby! Fight for Poohpie.

Wait! What happened? Why did you all just scream? What's going on?

"I cut her! She didn't move. She's not there. My wife is gone! She would hate this."

Sailor! You just cut me? I didn't feel anything. So, this is real? I'm stuck here in a shell with just me? I could stay like this for 20-30 years! Shit!

183

I don't know how long it's been since they decided to kill me.

I guess I agree with the decision. I'm already absent from my body, it would be better to be present with the Lord.

I'm sleeping a lot now. Maybe that's the dying process. Trishann was right, I'm not in pain.

184

Pastor Zulu came by. I could only stay awake for part of it. He prayed for my family and reminded them that I was going home to be with the Lord if I wasn't already there. We never talked about it but I imagine he's not big on euthanasia. I'm glad he came.

185

Death must be close.

They've been taking turns saying goodbye. Manny, Beanie and Carma are home to see me too. It has been the worst experience of my life.

It's nice to hear how much they love me. I love them too. But there's never been any question of that. Fallu used to say that we said I love you too much.

"Honey! Nobody needs to hear that all the time. It sounds fake!" Yeah, that was reason number 723 why I could never have had a child with him.

I hate it because all I want is to hold them all and be held by them. I want to feel their kisses, kiss them back, wipe their tears. Do you know how helpless it feels to hear your loved ones cry and not be able to even cry with them let alone hold and comfort them? I know the spiritual thing is to say I feel their kisses in my soul, but I don't. I still need skin.

Sailor was the worst. "You were supposed to be the rest of my life." He said that to me. He even got in bed with me. I know because I heard his heart beating in my ear, and I heard him cry. He must have kissed me because I tasted the sweetness of his mouth and then the salt of his tears just before Mommy prayed for us. Then everyone said he needed to get some rest and his heartbeat was gone.

186

They talked about organ donation before the last time I fell asleep.

187

I had an awful thought. They'll read my diaries when I'm gone. They may know me even more intimately when I'm dead than when I was alive. I hope they forgive me and still love me after reading my thoughts . . .

I wish I could feel a pen in my hand one last time and write them notes to tell them all how much I love them.

188

I hear the door of the room open. There is a lot of commotion. People doing stuff—very busy, rubber shoes squeaking on the floor. There are no distinctive smells, and nobody is speaking, at least not in tones that I can hear. I call out but of course nobody hears. There's the sound of fabric rustling, and I feel like I'm in a small boat on high waves—rolling from side to side. Am I moving forward? I feel the air going in my nostrils fast. It's not the air of breath.

There are all of these new foreign sounds around me. Heavy swooshing sounds. Beeps and air pressure even the buzz of high voltage lights. I think of a mechanic's shop for some reason, but it smells clean—antiseptic.

I hear a voice. It's familiar and disconcerting. The voice makes me angry. No, rageful and I want to fight. In fact, I am fighting and suddenly my body works! So does my voice! I'm screaming and fighting and I'm almost out of bed when suddenly my legs and arms are weighted down again.

"Scalpel!" the rage producing voice says and my eyes pop open. That's when I see him. The surgeon is standing over me. My body is exposed and when he sees that I'm awake he smiles.

"NO! Get away from me you DEMON!" I scream as he removes his surgical mask and I realize where I know the voice from. It is Banner. I screamed and then there was a flash of light and pain but I'm out of the operating room.

Am I at home? The room is so bright that it hurts. I look around. If this is a dream, I don't want it to end! I can see my babies! It must be a dream, but it feels so real! Milga is sitting on the bed beside me. I can only see her beautiful skinny little arms and legs stretched out beside me. I know it's her because of the shoes—high heels and painted toes. Carm is sitting snuggled up with Beans in an ugly brown leather recliner-like chair. They're looking at their phones. Mogo is in an uncomfortable looking stiff-backed chair also looking at her phone. Manny, my baby boy, is sitting on the edge of the bed, watching Bloomberg news on the tv overhead.

I must be dead or at least in the throes of dying.

Oh! I can smell the Burger King in the bag in front of me on the tray.

Thank you, Lord for this last sight of my babies before you take me. I'm so happy! I imagine the smile on my face is the smile I love. The one that spreads and lights up my whole face. Fallu said it was what made him fall in love with me. Sailor says it gives him life. I'm so happy it's the smile I'll die with.

"Poohpie?" It's my Mogo. I look at her and smile! One last smile for my first baby before I die.

"Poohpie?! Poohpie!" They're all crying and screaming now.

"Shhh. It's ok babies," I whisper to the loves of my life. "I'll see you when you join me in heaven." They don't hear my words but it's ok. It's enough that they are here with me.

Suddenly the room is filled with nurses and doctors. The babies, I notice, are on their knees praying.

Through the commotion I hear Nurse Trishann.

"Can you hear me? Mrs. Cook! Can you hear me? Blink if you can hear me!"

I blink.

The room erupts in shouts of joy.

189

After my eyes opened, things went fast. They started "feeding" me again and soon Trishann started talking about discharge planning. They wanted to get rid of me fast because nobody had informed my family that there had likely been brain activity all along. They relied on the Glasgow score thing and didn't bother with an EEG. Whatever. I think my family was pretty ready to have me gone. I get it. I'm just not sure how I feel about it.

I'm expensive. I heard Mommy and Siti talking about the cost and the fact that insurance only covers a piece of it. Luckily, I had a little left from the sale of the house, so it hasn't broken us—yet.

I'm taxing. Somebody seems to be here most of the time. At least most of the time I'm "awake" someone is here. Not Sailor, anymore. He hasn't been here since he said goodbye. I get it. He had to report for duty. There is a war going on after all. I don't know how long I've been like this—months for sure. I don't think I could watch him die either. Bottom line, this is taxing.

Trishann says I have to be discharged. There is no more treatment. So, I can go to a nursing home, or I can go home.

HOME PLEASE!

190

I've been home for a little while now.

It was hard at first, but I think we have a handle on it now.

I wake up before everyone else. I take advantage of the time to do an energy medicine treatment. I start out with a scudder technique and end with a chakra cleansing. Just visualizing smoothing the energy around my body and getting my chakras spinning in the right direction. Lucrezia, the healer, came by soon after I got home to do a treatment on me and prescribed the movements for me to think through. Beanie still calls this voodoo but at the very least it gives me a way to order my day. So, I meditate on the energy in my mental hands and then go to work smoothing and holding and re-ordering the energy fields around my body.

By the time I'm done, Carma is up, and we do the yoga class we designed the night before. She does it physically, and I do it mentally, talking my way through possible adjustments and visualizing myself in the different poses. My favorite is still pigeon pose. In my new state I'm able to bend my arm back to grab the toe of my upraised foot. The flexibility of my imaginary back is beautiful.

By the end of yoga class, it's time for my diaper change. I "eat" with Siti and Mom after my feeding apparatus has been cleaned and prepped. Mark and the older kids go off to work while the twins study. Like most of their peers who are not serving in the armed forces, the twins are taking on-line classes as it's not clear how safe traditional campuses are. While they study, I "write" in my diary. I would kill to hold a pen or type on a computer—see my thoughts transformed into words but I make do writing them on my heart. Dr. Progoff would be proud—I Am the journal.

At mid-day mom turns on a Zumba, African dance or other cardio video and we watch it together. I prefer the African dance videos because I don't feel like I can out-do the teachers. The Zumba classes frustrate me because I know my classes were infinitely more fun.

I'm parked in front of the tv for the rest of the day while Siti and Mom do their things. Milga will sometimes watch a documentary or something with me. Mom reads the Bible to me daily. The rest of the time the family comes by periodically to change my diaper or the channel, check on my feeding tube and iv, clear my mouth of saliva, do physical therapy with me and to ask me if I'm ok.

Yeah, I can communicate now.

191

At first, I was limited to yes/no questions.

"Are you ok"

No, not at all. But I always answered with two blinks—"YES"

"Can I get you anything?"

A dirty martini, FILTHY, with extra olives, no blue cheese. Bombay gin. Oh, and a healthy side of crispy bacon! One blink—"NO"

"Are you in any pain?"

Yes. My heart is broken. I need to see my husband.

One blink—"NO"

In the hospital they taught us to use the letter board where someone flips through cards and I reject them one by one until they get to the letter I need to spell out the words I want to say. That takes dedication and sleuthing because I have some processing issues so although I can think clearly, spelling out my thoughts is a challenge. Luckily, before the stroke I had atrocious texting and they had learned to decipher my writing. Maybe I was brain damaged before the stroke cuz my spelling is about the same now as it was then.

So, the stroke.

Trishann said it was a brain stem stroke—rare. I have "locked-in syndrome." Prognosis: this is probably as good as it gets. Total paralysis except for my eyes. I'm lucky. I can smell and taste and breathe on my own. Siti's research says that means I may (MAY) one day be able to form sounds, even words but it's a loooooong shot.

Still my family takes really good care of me, especially since we are still in a war—two wars if you listen to Carma. According to her the resistance is still active and, although she hasn't said it outright, I think she's still fighting somehow. I'm proud of her.

192

One other blessing—I can cry.

I used to hate crying, but it is such a useful skill. Tears express sadness and joy. My family can distinguish between my happy tears and my sad tears. That's a blessing and a curse.

I tried to keep my sad tears to myself. I think everyone went along with the charade except Beanie. She came home from work one night and gave me a kiss goodnight. She caught me crying.

"What's wrong Poohpie?"

I looked at her like she was stupid

"I mean what else?"

We have worked out a couple of signs for everyday stuff. A flutter of my eyes means "nothing" "Hi Baby" and other inconsequential random statements. Three blinks means "I love you."

"Talk to me. What's wrong?"

I looked around the room and tried to look lost.

"Book?"

One blink—"no"

"Turn the channel?"

"no"

"You want Mommy?"

"No"

I looked around the room and sighed then the tears just rolled down my cheeks into my mouth—salt!

"Uncle David?" she whispered.

Two blinks—"YES!"

"We thought you were mad at him."

"NO"

Well, I was but I was mad at everyone and everything. I just couldn't be mad at people who were sacrificing everything for me to survive. He wasn't here so, yes, I was mad at him because I couldn't be mad at the rest of them for trying to kill me.

"He would love to know that."

Questioning look translated: how do you know?

"He emails all the time and asks about you. He's a mess because he feels guilty about the stroke and he thinks you hate him for leaving."

One slow blink "I don't"

"Do you want to email him?"

Two blinks and a flood of salty tears—"Yes please!"

Right then and there, my baby took dictation.

"Mx Saler.

I love you. IJm sprry. Ijm npt mbd. I love you. Pklledse colf hnme uo me. Ijm sp spory. Plearf ferhgiwe me. I love you.

U lowjng wife

Trina

I have always hated to be edited, especially now, so Beans sent it exactly as I'd dictated but she added:

Dear Uncle David.

I'm not exactly sure what Poohpie is trying to say here but I think it is that she's not mad and she needs you. I hope you're ok. Please come home soon. Love Beans.

Then she checked my feeding tube, changed my diaper and we watched reruns of Bob's Burger until I fell asleep.

193

It has been several days since Beans sent the email. I try not to be too eager but each day she says he has not written back. And each day I pray and cry myself to sleep after the family goes to bed.

194

It's been a while. I guess I can't blame David. But blaming him is easier than blaming myself.

This morning, I did a second yoga class after Carma went to study. The second class was full of heart and root chakra poses—opening me up to new beginnings and acceptance. Open heart; Cat/cow, melting heart, cobra, camel; bridge; squat; folded; deep lunge; the warrior series; wide leg forward fold.

I never do corpse pose.

I ended in mountain pose, standing strong; even if Sailor didn't want me anymore.

Even so, I was low.

Mom saw and put on a new video Teryn had sent of her African dance class. I loved this dance. The Lamba, a healing dance for the soul. For a minute I was lost in the drum and even happy, imagining myself in Guinea but also submerged in an ocean where my limbs were weightless, and I could float and move effortlessly. Then she read to me from the Psalms—my favorite one about God breaking the teeth of the enemy.

After lunch and my midday changing, there was a knock at my bedroom door.

I tried to stop crying or at least look like I was laughing-crying as I said, "come in" remembering the thrill of autonomy and privacy. Siti quickly rushed in and began fixing me. Straightening my clothes, smoothing my hair, wiping my ever-drooling mouth and rubbing my teeth and tongue with "sweet breath," a mixture of spearmint, cardamom and wild orange essential oils and coconut oil Pam, my DoTerra representative, had concocted to make my mouth taste and smell fresh. In the absence of the ability to slap Siti's hands away, I looked at her like she was crazy and endured the coifing. When she was done, she looked at me and smiled a strangely ecstatic and sad smile then left the room.

I smelled him before I saw him.

Sandalwood, Basil and Frankinsence.

195

Sometimes there are no words . . .

He stopped at the threshold of the door. Our eyes locked and as I registered that I was neither asleep nor dead but truly looking into the eyes of My Sailor, my eyes smiled brightly even as I began to cry. When he took the first step toward me, my heart beat so wildly I thought it would come out of my chest. My breath was shallow and rapid, and I screamed "I LOVE YOU!" over and over again, with my eyes.

The forcefulness of my reaction startled him. He halted his approach and looked behind him toward Siti.

"What did I do? Is she ok?"

"She's great. One blink means no. Two blinks mean yes. Three rapid blinks mean 'I love you'." She said and then I heard the door close as she left us alone together.

He smiled at me and with a purposeful stride reached my bedside. My strong protector, partner, friend, lover—husband was here. He kissed my sloppy, saliva-overflowing, slack, twisted mouth as if it was the most rapturous mouth God had ever created. And, in my mind, I kissed him back with more fervor than I'd ever possessed.

Even though I couldn't feel anything as he kissed my neck, the flat of my chest and then down to the space between my breasts, I remembered the past sweetness of his lips on my skin and inwardly I shuddered with the memory of pleasure.

The outward rigidity of my body and absence of physical cues that intimacy was desired gave Sailor pause. He stopped kissing me and looked at me apologetically. I silently plead with him not to stop and blinked three times trying to convey the depths of my love and my desire.

"Is this ok?" he said.

Two slow blinks "yes"

As he began to unbutton his shirt, he never took his eyes off mine.

I tried to calm my breathing, but it was no use.

Naked he stood before me and allowed me to caress him with my eyes.

Slowly he pulled back the covers revealing my flaccid, heavy body but he never looked away from my eyes. I began to panic and cry. I knew what my body looked like, and I couldn't blame him if he was horrified. Everything sagged and was formless. Try as my family did, it was hard to keep me completely clean. And, there was the diaper.

My Sailor looked down at my body and then back in my eyes. His eyes were dreamy—a look I had often dreamed of. He smiled at me and looked down at his own body. I looked too and was blessed by another sight that I had dreamed of. The thing that would make me whole as it joined me to him; two puzzle pieces finally locked in union to form the best thing God had ever created—Us.

My Sailor made love to me, and it didn't matter that I couldn't join his movements. We were connected. Our eyes only lost contact for seconds when he lost the battle with pleasure to keep them open. My professions of love, silent and blinked though they were, matched his audible whispers. When he collapsed on top of me, I reveled in the memory of his weight and thanked God for my life with him—even this life.

196

Sailor is only here for the long weekend. He was able to finagle a pass before he ships out to the Pacific—the battlefield. I can't bear the thought of it, so I don't think about it. Our visit, I decide, will be what we had planned our last night to be—wonderful memories to spur him to return to me. My family leaves us alone for the most part only interrupting us to tend to my feeding tube, bathe and change me. I refuse to have Sailor do it. Plenty of time for him to do that when he returns for good. Plus, I couldn't bear the humiliation of being that helpless before him.

On his second day I asked him about the sex tape.

"Ware is? Hoo c e? Sexy? I c?

"You don't want to see it." He said.

"Do."

"Everything's on it Babe."

"I No. s ok. C"

"Really? You sure?"

Two blinks—YES!

Sailor pulled out his Ipad and cued up the video from both camera angles. There I was! Firm! Mobile! Verbal! Whole! I am beautiful!

He held me and kissed me just as he always does in my memory of that night. There I am undressing him! God he's beautiful! Now he's holding me up as I call on heaven to witness and help me. Damn this is hot!

Then we go down to the floor—out of the frame of either camera! We were supposed to go to the couch. For the next 8 minutes there was nothing but the extended version of Prince singing and an occasional exclamation. This was incredibly funny to me, and tears of hilarity rolled down my cheeks into my open mouth.

"C nufin." I spelled out quickly and smiled with my eyes. Then there it was! That chuffing, breathless laugh that makes my heart soar!

"So much planning and we didn't get any of it!"

The sound of banging on the video broke into our moment.

"Alexa . . . un . . . lock . . . the . . . front . . . door!" It was Sailor on the video. There was still no picture of what was happening but from the cadence of his speech, I could tell he was doing CPR on me.

Then the video frame was flooded with strange faces and commotion.

"Clear!" The sound of the defibrillator starting my heart again.

"Babe don't die! Please don't leave me!" The panic in his voice is terrible.

"Sir, can you tell me what happened?" The paramedic said. A young woman. She's officious but she looks uncomfortable.

"We were making love. I thought she was ok. Then I kissed her, and she was rigid."

"Is she on any medication?"

"I don't think so. No. Yes! Birth control. Iron. Is she ok? Tell me she's going to be ok!"

"She's breathing sir. We're going to take her to the hospital."

The other paramedics have me on the stretcher and they're rolling me past Sailor and the young woman.

"Can I go with her? I can't leave her alone!" Sailor doesn't wait for the response. He's moving toward the door behind the stretcher. When he gets to the door, it's clear why the paramedic is uncomfortable. My Sailor is butt naked, Manhood just a swinging in the wind!

One of the other paramedics, a young white guy, stops him before he steps outside. Holding out a pair of pants he says, "Hey Man, put these on first. We won't leave without you. I promise."

Kindness. It takes but a moment.

Sailor put on the pants and the young man helps him with his shirt as Sailor puts on his shoes. The door closes and the video ends.

We sat in silence for a while.

I know the video should have made me sad—and it did—but I was happy too. The love of my life, once again, acting quickly in the face of an emergency, had saved my life with no thought to himself. He was so focused on my well-being that he flashed that poor little paramedic, and no doubt would have walked into the emergency room butt naked so that I wasn't alone in my time of need. What's not to be happy about? I am loved!

"But nakid" I spelled out and eye-smiled brightly.

It's times like this that I truly miss the ability to laugh.

197

I haven't really watched the news since the stroke. My life was trouble enough on its own I didn't need to borrow from the world. But with Sailor in harm's way, you can't pry my eyes away from the news. What a shit show!

Banner has a hard on to nuke N. Korea in a bid to end this war once and for all. The Congress full of his minions won't stop him. They still think he pisses gold and wiz-dom. Hahahah. See what I did there? Wiz-dom. S. Korea has taken a beating. Possibly a million dead. No telling what is happening inside N. Korea but we've been pummeling them with missiles. There's video that says they are resorting to cannibalism in some parts of the country. It's too horrific to imagine.

Here at home, we're no less of a shit show. There are all these rumblings about detaining Korean-Americans (all Asians really because China and Japan haven't exactly been full allies or something like that). Loads of protests nationwide, especially out west. The peace was already tenuous but now skirmishes are breaking out again. They're talking about rescinding the amnesty given to the National Guardsmen who defected before the war. If they do that, they have nothing to lose because they're facing court martial for treason which could be the death penalty. Some have started to defect again.

Strongholds springing up across the country. As part of the amnesty, all of the political leaders who led/participated in the resistance were stripped of their public offices and replaced by Banner loyalists—but at least they weren't executed.

There's so much going on it makes my head spin. Manny and Camille have been getting me up to speed with all the ins and outs of the political situation. The whole family, even the kids, watch the news now: the State news; the resistance news; CNN, BBC and Al Jazeera. You have to watch all of them then cobble together what you think is true.

Pontius Pilate was prophetic: What is truth?

198

Sailor is in the Pacific Ocean, manning a missile defense system. The Western shores of the US are the most vulnerable to N. Korea's missiles. Those that could, fled to the interior or south of the country. All that's left are the poor: residents of Damnfoolistan and residents of the ghetto. California is almost bereft of Mexicans as they were the only ones allowed to exit through The Wall. It's not funny but seems like Banner's south-western border wall is serving to keep us in rather than keeping anyone out. There was a massacre at the Wall last week when some DFOBs (Damn Fool Old Boys) and their families were not allowed to leave. Never ones to take no for an answer, they whipped out guns and forced the border guards to let them through. The Mexican authorities let the convoy of 10 trucks pass then surrounded them on a deserted road and told them to turn back. The DFOBs pulled their guns. The Federales pulled their guns. Somebody shot and after 15 minutes, there were 25 DFOBs including 5 kids (who were photographed holding their guns) and 8 Federales killed. Now armed folks on both sides of the Wall.

Shit show.

199

I don't know what's worse. Being trapped in my body, unable to fight or being trapped out there not knowing how to fight.

The kids have been talking to me a lot lately—mainly because I can't talk back, I guess. I hear the arguments they have with their parents, and I know it's hard for all of them.

Yesterday, after yoga, Carma whispered in my ear, "I'm going to leave tonight Poohpie. Don't tell Mommy please. She'll try to talk me out of it."

"Ware go?"

"Maryland for now. They're training people to fight."

"hoq u fite?"

"How?"

Two blinks—yes, how?

"I don't know yet. Whatever they need me to do. Last time, Beanie and I were just cooking and feeding the fighters. Maybe that's what they'll have me do this time too. I won't know until I get there."

"gun"

"If that's what is needed, yes."

"Y u fite"

"Poohpie you watch the news. You know what's going on."

"we saf tho"

"We're safe for now. But you all didn't raise us to sit back and watch others suffer. Asians in jail for being Asians? Poohpie? You think that's ok?"

"war ova soon Saler say so."

"And do you think they won't come after us? We have to stop them. The problems from before the war are still problems. Banner's crazy and now he has the Congress, Senate and the Supreme Court full of crazies!"

"k"

"You understand? Will you help Mommy and daddy accept it?"

Two blinks yes. She hugged me and, in my mind, I hugged and squeezed her back holding on hoping she wouldn't go.

"By self?" I asked when she let go.

"Arthur's going too." She gave me this sheepish smile.

Arthur. The little skinny boy with a big head and admittedly a big heart who rightly thought she was the sun and the moon. I wish I could blame him for her desire to fight but I knew she was the driving force here. He was most likely following her.

Three blinks—I love you.

"I love you more."

200

I thought she would be happy and proud that Carma's fighting. I thought it would be something good between us, but all Siti keeps saying is "There will be Hell to pay! Whoever knew Carma was going, will have hell to pay!"

It's really easy to lie when you can't talk.

201

I always hate not being able to use my body but today. . .

Morgan was watching me while Siti and mom delivered food to people from church.

Mo squealed "Special ones!" and woke me from a nap.

She must have been flipping through the channels and stopped on a station when she saw pictures of Downs babies. It looked like hundreds of them in a room looking up at the camera. Round faces, widespread, vacant eyes: really disturbing. Mo got quiet and slowly sat beside me. I know we were both thinking of Ngoc but there was a spark in Ngoc's eyes that was missing from these Special Ones, as Mo called them. She started to weep as we listened to the facts as they were reported.

Romania is euthanizing all the Downs and "undesirable" children. Newfangled gas chambers. Parents are bringing them to be gassed they say but some reports suggest that the military is forcibly rounding them up.

"Iceland has cleansed their gene pool. We will too." The Romanian minister of health said through a translator.

When the story was over, Mo rested her head on my stomach and wept. When her sobs seemed uncontrollable, she grabbed my hand, placed it on her head the way I would have done in days of yore.

We were still weeping bitterly when Siti and Mom came home. Mo for the Special Ones. Me for the impotent memory of comforting the ones I love.

202

It just gets better and better.

They say it's not in retaliation for the DFOB massacre at the Border but it sure sounds like it.

Banner just signed an executive order rescinding citizenship of those without at least two grandparents who were US born citizens! I SHIT YOU NOT!

If it was just the act of a crazy impotent Man, no biggie but he's got the Supreme Court and the legislature under his thumb, so they were standing behind him in a show of force just like when he postponed the elections. Message received: you need not oppose us. That means millions of people are now undocumented and subject to deportation. There's a massive spending bill to authorize building prison camps to hold folks until they can be deported! The order takes effect next month—giving people time to leave on their own or get documentation together to prove they belong. It's of course not clear how they are going to round people up but from his speech that is the plan.

"We have to take our country back!" he said.

To which the crowd gathered and the lawmakers around him gave a loud cheer!

203

Sailor thinks he'll be home by the end of the year. Ever since the N. Korean generals, backed by China, killed their leader, the aggression has simmered down. It's not over but it's much better—and we didn't use a Nuke thank God. I can't wait to see Sailor! It's been almost a year!

The Deportation squads have started in the West. Mainly Asians cuz of the war and of course Hispanics but any yellow/brown/black with an accent really. There's a mass migration Northeast to NY, Mass, VT., etc.—the stronghold of the Resistance. Carma was right. Things are getting worse here.

Thank God for Sailor's check each month. My savings is gone. I get a small disability check that just about pays for diapers. Mark is still working and Manny is back with his company. Beanie and Mo are still working—medical school is postponed for Beans but she's doing a lot of work at the hospital so education nonetheless. Everyone pools money to take care of the family. Sailor's money helps me not feel like all I'm doing is taking from my family.

Sailor mentioned bringing Danilo and his family here when he gets back. Danilo's a nurse so he can help take care of me. All of this was said to Siti whose feelings got hurt and she couldn't remain the objective translator.

"Do you have a problem with the way we've been taking care of her all this time?"

"No! Not at all. I'm so grateful"

"You don't need to be grateful to me for taking care of my sister!"

Siti's still in 'Hell To Pay' mode.

"I know. I just meant . . . I was just saying thank you."

"For taking care of my own sister?"

"For taking care of my wife. I wish I was able to do it or at least help because I know how hard it is and . . . "

"It's not hard for me. That's what family does. But you're welcome."

"I was thinking of bringing Danilo and his family here because things in the Philippines are getting really difficult politically. I thought he could help us both take care of Trina and it would be good for him."

"Umph. Well I don't need help taking care of my sister. If you want to bring him, who am I to stop you but he and his family are Asian so you might think twice about bringing him. Plus, he's foreign. Can he even get in now?"

"He's an American"

"David, they're detaining Asians."

"You honestly think it'll be a problem?"

"All I can tell you is that we are trying to get birth certificates ready in case anybody starts making rumblings about our true citizenship. Its Asians and Hispanics now. Muslims and all black folks can't be far behind."

I closed my eyes and let them talk. I don't want Danilo to come. I don't want to share Sailor with him. I know it's awful; but it's true. Plus, I don't want him cleaning me and caring for me. Siti's right. We're doing fine. I don't know what it will be like to depend on David like that, let alone Danilo. The thought gives me an anxiety attack. I've been having them more and more lately. I get Siti's attention when she's off the call with David. She's pissed still.

"zanac" I spell.

She reaches in her pocket and swallows a pill then goes to the bedside table, preps a syringe and gives me a shot.

Soon the bear that has been chasing me, so my heart was pounding out of my chest, is on the other side of the door. I still hear him growling but I'm not under immediate threat of being mauled. Then sleep comes.

204

Danilo, Maria and Felipe-David arrived. Sailor is ecstatic to have them here.

This is mean. They stink. There's a smell I can't get rid of. It's like when you smell something rotten and days later you can still smell it. It's in your mouth and throat like a vapor. Maybe Felipe is the one who stinks. Hygiene? But it doesn't smell like little boy stink. It's like a deep down woman's funk.

205

Sailor spends a lot of time with them. Especially Maria who is beautiful, voluptuous and feisty; but she stinks. She's the one who takes care of me most of the time. I don't like her. When the men are around the two of us, she is kind but there's a mocking quality to her kindness. She looks at my twisted mouth and loose skin with smiling disgust. She put a mirror up in the room so that I stare at myself all day, physically unable to turn my head and avert my gaze. When she changes me, she leaves me uncovered allowing the horror show that is my body to run on a loop until she deigns to cover me. I can't escape the image of the folds of skin draping the bones that are my thighs; the skin of my breasts and stomach melded into one formless entity; the cracked brown of my nipples the line of demarcation to remind me that I once had real breasts; the never ending stream of saliva that slides out of my mouth and pools in the depression of my left clavicle. Above all I hate not being able to escape the sight of my hands—specifically, my fingers which are perpetually gripping the air. They look as if when the stroke happened, I was desperately trying to hold on to the world, to myself, to life.

With Maria in my home, I wish I'd let go that day.

206

Danilo and Maria make love loudly all the time. It's always in my ears. At first, I thought it was sexy even if embarrassing and I imagined that I even itched down there but way deep inside—wanting. But it stopped being sexy because the itch is uncomfortable and the more they do it, the worse she stinks. The smell permeates my skin and I taste . . . her. So, their screwing makes me sick. I hate it. She's always screaming but I know she's being loud so that I can hear. Taunting me because I can't do that anymore—not even scream. I don't know the last time Sailor touched me. I am beginning to hate him because he brought her into our home.

Sailor did this to me. All of it.

If he weren't such a selfish lover, he would have known I was in extremis and could have gotten me to the hospital and drugs may have saved me. But no, he always gets lost at the end. There could be a tornado ripping the house apart and he'd have to cum before taking shelter. I used to think that was wonderful somehow. Well, wonderful left me trapped in my body unable to even scream. Thanks a lot David! On the rare occasions that he comes in and tries to speak to me it's like he's a phantom, sneaking in and out.

And he thinks I don't see him looking at Maria.

207

They rut like hogs and the stench is unbearable. I wake to it. They get louder throughout the day. It doesn't stop. I hate it. I usually take a nap during the day, but I can't because of their incessant rutting. David was here in the room with me for a change. He doesn't talk to me he just sits and watches. He didn't even acknowledge the screaming coming from the next room! Like it's normal. I don't know who he is anymore.

208

Maria adjusted the mirror last night. Now I see the doorway and the hall. She's up to something. She just smiled at me as she did it. Didn't say anything just did it and walked out of the room.

209

Oh Lord God! I didn't want to believe it, but I saw it with my own eyes!

Maria stood naked in the hallway outside of my room, in full view of the mirror. I tried not to look but she stood there and smiled at me. Her body was so firm. More firm than my body has ever been, and I hated her and myself so much that I started to cry. Then she turned her back to me and flung her arms around Danilo's neck and her legs around his torso. As they went at it with no shame, she began her shouts and then so did he. This time his voice was deeper and huskier than I'd ever heard. Her screams were more unbridled than they'd ever been. Their rutting was violent and animalistic—vindictive. I'd never seen them do it before, but I knew that this was somehow different than what had happened before. I couldn't take my eyes off them and then he placed her on the floor and spun her around to take her from behind. She looked me in the eyes in the mirror and winked. I was so embarrassed that I looked away and that's when I saw Sailor enjoying her body calling her name.

I screamed and sobbed. In my mind I destroyed the room that I now think of as my prison.

210

Today they didn't do it in the hallway. They came into the room and did it on the bed next to me. I could taste the salt of sweat on David's back—a flavor I used to relish but now makes me sick. Her stench felt like a wet rag in my mouth gagging me. Then I heard my family coming down the stairs. David and Maria heard them too and they rolled—still joined—to the floor between my bed and the wall: hiding. Quietly, but not silently, enjoying each other.

Before Mom and Siti got to the room Maria said "we . . . will . . . kill . . . them . . . too," in rhythm with David's thrusts. I knew she was telling the truth. I think they've killed Danilo and Felipe. I never see them anymore. I broke into a cold sweat. I couldn't feel it on my skin, but the chills were so deep I felt them in the deepest part of my spine.

Siti and Mom came in. I thought they smelled Maria's stench. Mommy's face said she knew something was wrong and she asked me, "Honey! Are you ok?"

I looked behind where they sat on the bed facing me and there was Maria inching closer to them. Threatening

Two blinks—yes.

"Why are you crying?"

David stood behind Maria, kissed her neck."

"I ok"

"Does anything hurt? You are pale as a ghost!"

Maria pulled out a knife and stood behind them looking me in the eyes without blinking. When she raised the knife above her head, I knew I had to speak. As quickly as I could I yelled for them to get out— let her kill me.

"Iss Mara. Gon kil me. Salr afare her. kil Danlo n proly Fepe. Gon kil u. has a nif! Run!"

Mommy put her hand on my head and her eyes got big.

Siti kept asking me what I was talking about.

"Kil u! kil U. run!" I spelled as quickly as I could. Then Maria struck and everything was red. There was blood everywhere. She and David were covered in it! I screamed and screamed as they both slaughtered my family. After it was done David stood over me, grabbed a pillow and placed it over my mouth. His demented smile was the last thing I saw before everything went black.

211

I'm really weak and sad but I'm alive.

I had a raging urinary tract infection and was well on the way to becoming sceptic. Mom and Siti caught it. I'm in the hospital but they say I can go home tomorrow.

Sailor didn't try to kill me. He's still in the Pacific on a ship. Danilo and Maria aren't real—at least not the people I conjured them up to be. The doctor said urinary tract infections turned septic can lead to psychotic episodes. So not only am I trapped in a meat prison I'm also psychotic. Lovely.

I know it wasn't real but I'm still afraid of what it will be like when Sailor's home and Danilo and his family are here. Part of me thinks I should let David off the hook of being married to me. He can still be happy. He deserves to be held and loved. I'll never be like Maria. The thought of Sailor and what I can never be for him or to him, ever again, makes me so sad.

Kind of wish they'd let me die. Sounds like I was close to it. They could have just done nothing.

God please take me.

212

The doctor prescribed anti-depressants and anti-psychotics for me along with the anti-anxitey.

Not sure it is helping. I didn't tell him that Maria is still a part of my daily thinking. I know she's not real but I'm not sure I can convince him I'm not psychotic.

My world feels like it is crashing the way the world around me is crashing.

While I was in the hospital, Israel struck Iran so . . . full on war between two nuclear capable powers. We're pulling out of N. Korea fight supposedly. We bombed the mess out of them so their long-range capabilities are destroyed—so they say. Ground war against pockets of resistance but the military has laid down their arms and the people are too weak from malnutrition to pick them up. Sailor's coming home but probably only for a short time because most likely, all hands-on deck in the Persian Gulf. So far, the US has not been drawn completely in to the war but it's just a matter of time.

The Resistance is fracturing. A lot of the backers were Jewish. They saw Hitler in the President like everyone else but with Israel under attack . . . that's a bigger Hitler. If the President fights for Israel, they'll join him and take their money with them. The COD –"Christians of Damnfoolistan"—are firmly with him and see it as a Biblical fight;

which I suppose it really is. Satan is working this thing—just the way God said he would.

I'm praying for the Rapture or death. I'm tired.

213

It's just a Man in a uniform. Just a Man in a uniform! But . . .

GYAT DAY-YUM!

He's beautiful! Service dress blues. Jesus God how did I EVER pull this Man? How can I ever HOLD this Man? Thank you, Lord, for giving him to me.

We took a picture together—his idea—and we looked like a beautiful before and horribly after joke.

He is so shiny and clean and pressed and crisp and upright and strong.

I am frail and crumpled and wrinkled and flaccid.

But there is one picture when he is caressing my bad cheek, and we are looking at each other. Although we are so different there is one thing that joins us. We both look in love. How is that possible?

Only God.

274

Danilo isn't coming. The grandparent citizenship rule has been extended for certain groups. Banner's good friends with the dictator in the Philippines and it doesn't look good to accept the droves of people trying to flee repression in that country so for Filipinos, both maternal and paternal grandparents have to have been born in the US (not naturalized—born). That cancels out Danilo. I know I'm not to blame for Danilo being barred but I feel bad about my hallucinations. I love Sailor for wanting to bring his child here but in my brutally honest moments I have to admit that I'm glad it worked out this way. Maria still haunts me.

Sailor has decreed our home a Good News zone. We don't watch the news.

"It's obvious that things are going to hell we don't need a play by play of the descent," my beautiful Sailor says.

For the most part our family has agreed to it but every now and then there's a slip and someone blurts out an atrocity. We'll get back to reality but He's on R&R for a month and then we'll see what his orders are.

"Until then these are the rules" Sailor said and tacked them up in our bedroom.

The Three No's of the Cook Household.

No talk of the Danilo farce!

No BANNER!

No news!

Aye Aye Captain!

Each morning, he does the physical version of the yoga class we designed the night before. He's much less flexible than I am but he tries and he's getting better. By the time he leaves he should be almost as good as me.

After my feeding, changing and dressing he loads me into the wheelchair, and we go for a run with the girls. He runs a lap as fast as he can, pushing me around the track then he passes me off to Beanie who runs with me and then Milga and then Mogo to bring it home. I'm up to 12 laps! Sometimes the whole family comes, and I can get as many as 20 laps in. I love those days.

Siti and mom have always taken good care of me. I'm always oiled and clean (as clean as they can get me with all the folds of skin). Somebody exercises me twice daily, so I have never had bed sores. My teeth are healthy, and they try to keep my breath fresh—again hard when you can't close your mouth all the way. Somebody is always ready with a tissue to mop up the spit.

In the beginning when I first got locked in, I had acupuncture weekly. Kelly would come to the house, and we all hoped that somehow Chinese Traditional Medicine would fix me. It didn't unlock the door, but it did bring me peace and calm and improved muscle tone and color. As the world situation went tits up it was hard and then impossible for Kelly to come help me on a regular basis. While he's here, Sailor insists on bringing Kelly to the house. I see him 3 times a week for now. Kelly's glad for the work. In a crisis acupuncture and other luxuries are the first to go.

On Sundays, Sailor and I watch the livestream church at MacAllen. The rest of the time, we watch movies, talk, laugh and he makes love to me—emotional and spiritual. Not physical. We agreed, getting freaky with basically a corpse is just creepy.

Last week, Pastor Daniel railed openly against Banner and the COD who he calls apostates. He's been doing that for a while now, so I'm used to it. I'm also used to the fact that when he does it you can see and hear people in the congregation mumble or get up and walk out. It was the first time David heard him speak so openly against what's going on in the country and the church. His reaction was the same as mine had been—he started shouting. Hooting and hollering "My God! My GOD!" waiving his hands and marching around the room getting up close on the screen and talking to Daniel as he spoke the good Word. When I was a kid, I felt uncomfortable when men "shouted" in church. It always seemed so undignified and a bit feminine, but I love it when Sailor gets the Holy Spirit. I forgot how nice it is to be in church with him.

I always knew I was blessed but right now I FEEL blessed.

215

We had to break the rules.

News is on 24/7. There was a major terrorist attack in Maryland—a Resistance stronghold state and where Carma was when she last texted us two weeks ago.

All we can do is pray for my baby because Maryland is a war zone.

It's a mass casualty event at various locations close to DC in the heavily Jewish enclave of Montgomery county. Dead and injured still being counted but so far upwards of 800. They targeted the seven largest synagogues on Yom Kippur.

Beanie sedated Siti. She was losing her mind which meant she was going to kill someone. That someone was most likely going to be Mark because he refused to go searching for Carma. Beanie took one of my syringes full of Xanax and muscle relaxant and dosed her mother. There will be hell to pay when she wakes up but for now everyone, except Carma, is safe.

216

Two days later and we still don't know who is responsible for the bombings.

The obvious suspect is ISIS or some other radical Islamic group—there are so many of them now.

"These crazy Radical Islam sons of bitches hate the Jews—especially My Jews. These good Jews loved me, and I will not let their deaths go unpunished and we will not leave Israel to ISIS and Iran!" said Banner, the President of Damnfoolistan.

The only problem is, ISIS hasn't definitively claimed it and their cagey language has the whole country on edge.

"The Yom Kippur bombing is to our benefit whether we did it or not. Jewish dogs are dead and their houses of worship are destroyed, Allah be praised. But, people of the Great Satan, consider the benefit to your government to destroy the Resistance stronghold of Maryland. Yes. We know of their locations and how they too were destroyed in the bombing. If it was not your government, consider the benefit to the little Satan, Israel, to sacrifice their little ones to draw the Great Satan into the fray against Islam. Allah will grant us a great victory through this act that you call terror, and we call vengeance."

Good points. Valid points. Prophetic points.

217

The latest breaking news.

News commentator: "Just a few minutes ago, President Banner extended the executive order which legalized the detention of Asians 'in protection of the country' to include Iranians and other "suspect" Muslims."

Flash to video in the Oval Office of Banner again flanked by the "government" minions.

"We're going to crush Iran and the Islamist fuckers who hit us folks. I'm making America safe again and Israel, I'm coming to save you to!"

Banner's Jews and the CODs rejoiced by burning down the few mosques that were left, forming search parties to round up and hold, or kill, Muslims until the federal government forces could come and get them.

218

We are officially at war—again. Sailor's R&R is cut short by a week. He left yesterday. He's going to the Persian Gulf. Before he left, he burned a copy of our sex tape onto a CD and put it in one of the boxes with my diaries that he hid under my bed the last time he was home.

"So you know it's there and can watch us any time you want" he said with a wink and a smile the night before he left.

I tried to calm myself down by watching MacAllen but the feed went dark right after the campus pastor who was preaching said the bombings were self-inflicted wounds!

I asked Beanie to give me a double shot of Xanax. I need to sleep through this.

279

Thank God! We heard from Carma. She and Arthur are ok. She sounded so strong in her text.

"Dear Fam. We are fine. Pray for all of us. War is hell but SAA!"

"It's not safe to say Screw America in writing or anything else— you never know who's watching or listening," Siti said.

The new saying is SAA (Screw America Anyway). It may still flag the text as coming from a resister, but everything is a risk now.

Siti reads the text every day and then thrusts her fist in the air and loudly says "Screw you anyway America!" She's bucking for a fight and if one of the neighbors hears and says something, a fight she will have. None of the family is brave enough to tell her to quiet down though. We just pray that God blocks our neighbor's ears.

If Siti could fight she would. But, she has me and Mommy and the rest of her family to take care of, not to mention chronic pain of her own but if she could leave us, she'd be on the front lines, killing indiscriminately and righteously with one hand while stirring vats of delicious food for the troops with the other. Instead, when she's not changing and feeding me, she cooks all day, delivers it to the poor as part of a ministry she and mom started in their church. Then she comes home and watches violent tv all night and does the same thing all over again the next day. As far as I can tell, she doesn't sleep. We're all worried about her. She can't last long like this but I'm not gonna say anything to her about it. The rage emanating from her is palpable.

Right now, I just watch serial killer shows with her until I fall asleep.

MacAllen has been back online for three weeks after being dark for two weeks. But today, Pastor Daniel talked about "just war" and when we are called as Christians to stand against the government. The site went dark again 27 minutes into his sermon, right after he invoked the example of Nazi Germany and Bonhoeffer.

220

New York and Maryland went back to Damnfoolistan because of the Yom Kippur bombings. They are firmly Banner's Jews now and all of that funding left the Resistance. We don't know where Carma is. Hopefully not Maryland anymore.

Even with the loss of New York and Maryland, the Resistance is holding on. They are in control of the far NE from Maine through Vermont. There are other states who are fighting alongside them but not a contiguous block.

221

I think I'm dying.

I saw the doctor three weeks ago and since then, my family has been looking at me like they want to tell me something but they're afraid. Two days ago, I woke up and heard Mommy and Siti whispering and when they realized I was awake, they quickly got busy cleaning and didn't respond to me when I rolled my eyes, our signal for "What is happening?"

222

I'm not dying but the Church is committing suicide.

Siti hasn't let me tune into MacAllen on-line this whole week. She said there was something wrong with the internet, but she was just protecting me from the news that the church Elders had a no confidence vote against Daniel. They've been fighting it out in the media. Apparently, she's been limiting my access to the news too. Today I insisted and she let me live-stream the MacAllen service. That's when I saw Pastor Daniel get arrested in the pulpit.

The COD faction at MacAllen staged a coup and told him he could not preach there anymore. He laughed and actually said, "Get behind me Satan!" as he pushed past a bloated COD and started preaching. A smattering of people applauded him but only a smattering. You could see one of the Cod on his cell phone gesticulating wildly. Then, it seemed immediate, there were cops on the stage. Daniel resisted and they tazed him. When he went down, they cuffed him and dragged him away.

When they left, Pastor Mack took his place and started preaching the same sermon Daniel had been preaching. The Cod called the cops and the same thing happened only this time they drew their guns. Pastor Dale, who used to be a cop, jumped in front of Mack and tried to calm the situation. All of the associate pastors, Nate, Zulu, Carli, Marlon,

433

Adei—all of them—lined up behind Mack waiting to be cuffed then they walked them off the stage. Pastor Dale stayed, trying to calm the congregation. There were a couple of fights but for the most part it looked like a sea of COD. They were shouting then suddenly they hushed and the camera panned back to the pulpit and there on the stage was the devil himself smiling. Then the crowd erupted in a chant— BAN-NER! BAN-NER! BAN-NER!

223

I no longer have a church.

MacAllen has officially become a COD congregation. Seems like Banner had held a grudge against Daniel since the drive by prayer all those years ago. He's been back a couple of times and the pictures of him in the pulpit have been plastered on the news, touting him as a Christian President.

Daniel was released after a couple of weeks as were most of the others, but they were all charged with various crimes. Daniel and Mack got the most serious charges including sedition. The government stopped short of treason which carries a possible death penalty but if they speak in public they could be slapped with treason charges. Mommy and Siti still go to their church, and I can stream their service but their pastor sucks. He has never really said anything powerful and even less so now that there's a level of scrutiny. He just makes me angry so, no thanks. They go for the fellowship, and affiliation rather than the message.

Thank God for the audio Bible and CDs/DVDs of old sermons from pre DFS times. It's not safe to access past sermons online as that can get you marked as a subversive. Old technology is the safest way to do anything in the age of Banner.

224

The Resistance must be making headway because the government is making lawmakers take oaths of loyalty to "America governed by Banner" today. That's how they have to say it. They lined all of the lawmakers up and one by one they had to say it. Mommy and I watched for 2 hours as one by one they pledged allegiance to Banner. Most didn't just say the required words. They tried to outdo each other with the praise and worship. Halfway through the show, the required statement of "I vow my loyalty to America governed by President Banner" had morphed into versions of "I pledge my undying allegiance to President Banner." Many pledged to lay down their lives in support of Banner- not America. The cameras panned the faces of the lawmakers, and most were crying and raising their hands high as if praising the Lord. When the cameras caught glimpses of the few who stood stock still, looking around them in shocked amazement and terror, the camera quickly panned away.

I couldn't take my eyes off the spectacle. I couldn't believe I was seeing this. I fully expected to hear someone call him Lord or God. The sentiment was there, they just lacked the words. I had forgotten that Mommy was sitting next to me until I heard her say, "Even so Come quickly Lord Jesus!" I blinked amen and continued watching—a witness to the end of days, at least for the United States of America.

The last two to take the oath were Hadassah Goldman the Senator from NY and Rafael Castro from Florida. Banner, who had been seated during the adulation raised his hand and immediately the crowd quieted. He walked toward Goldman. I prayed that this woman whose story was well known to the world, would stand firm. Her father, forced to serve as a capo at Auschwitz, had killed himself and Goldman's mother at the Holocaust Museum after testifying that among the thousands he had gassed and thrown into the furnace alive were his father and grandfather. Hadassah said his story motivated her every day to fight against tyranny and injustice. If she bowed to Banner, there was no hope. The only sound coming from the screen was the clack clack of Banner's shoes as he walked toward her. When he reached her, he grasped her hands in his, pursed his lips and stared at her like a fish gasping for air.

Goldman looked like she was about to vomit then began haltingly, "Sir, I . . . I canno . . . " she licked her lips and swallowed again. Tears rolled down her cheeks as she let go of his hand and looked at the ground. "I can . . . not but . . . pledge my loyalty and love and praise you for the love you are showing by saving my people, your Jewish people. You are our Messiah!" she said and fell to her knees.

The crowd erupted in ecstasy. Banner pulled Goldman, a very attractive woman and mother of 4, to her feet, pulled her flush to him and kissed her long and hard on the mouth then walked back to his seat, leaving the Senator breathless and dazed. The camera found and focused on her cheering husband and children who were in the crowd.

Mom let out a shriek of pain and I once again knew in the deepest part of my being why people throw dust on their heads and rip their clothing in mourning. That was it. The only one left was Castro, a minion who was handpicked by Banner. He regularly declared his love for the President. Once seated, Banner grinned broadly at Castro and said, "Last but certainly not least, well, maybe they are the least but that's ok, my Latinos still love me am I right?!" he said to shouts of

Viva Banner from the crowd. "Come on Castro, bring this thing to a close! I'm tired. I never thought I'd get tired of winning but folks, when you win like we do, it's hard to keep it exciting," he said. The crowd erupted in giggles like a demented laugh track.

The camera went to Castro. He looked up and it seemed that he was struggling to keep his composure.

"I confess that I have loved you since you gave me your favor and placed me in the seat of power that I now hold," Castro cried. "I have prayed for you and I will continue to pray for you" The cameras focused on Banner who yawned. "But I refuse to bow down to you and pledge allegiance. This is a blasphemy that we are committing today and it's like the scales have been peeled from my eyes today. We must all Repent. Especially you Mr. President."

The crowd went wild, cursing and screaming even as those who stood closest to the Senator from Florida grabbed him roughly and ushered him toward Banner.

"I tell you folks we have a problem. If not for me, this country we love is going to hell. This guy was a loser and Banner saves him. I saved him. I gave his life meaning and does he thank Banner like the rest of you? No! He turns on me. Get him out of here! I tell you folks if somebody was mean to someone I loved, someone who saved my country, my people . . . I'd beat the living shit out of him. This guy . . . he's dead to me. He deserves whatever he gets."

Given the word, the crowd fell on Castro and began to pummel him with their hands and feet. The cameras went dark as one of them caught Hadassah rearing back, left foot poised, ready to deliver a kick to her colleague's midsection.

Liz was right. The Rapture will be a non-issue for America.

225

Senator Castro died of his injuries. The videos of his beating have strangely disappeared. There is no way to prove who beat him to death so nobody talks about it. CNN's Cooper tried to follow up on the story but he and a handful of other journalists who wanted to pretend we still live in a democracy have been fired and threatened with jail for defamation of character.

226

Rapture Nearness Assessment:

How close are we to the Rapture of the church? Where are we on the prophetic timeline?

"The granddaddy of all the signs—Jews back in Israel."

Check!

"Earthquakes, famines, disease and signs in the sky."

Check.

"Perilous times."

Check.

"Wars and rumors of wars."

Check

"Violence and sexual immorality"

Check.

"False Christs."

Goldman. Feels like at least Check-ish

"The whole world will turn against Israel."

No!

Phew!

227

Yesterday I woke up to the breaking news sounds going off all over the house.

Commentator: "In a stunning blow to the US war effort in the Persian Gulf, three Generals have diverted a yet untold number of troops and weapons headed to the battle-lines against Iran to Resistance strongholds throughout the nation. These warriors join the ranks of National Guardsmen, retired and former military, police, and regular folks who have been waging war against the National government for the past 2 years. This latest defection delivers a serious blow to the Nation's ability to effectively fight our enemies in the Middle East. The diverted troops were to support and relieve fighters who have been in the fray for the past year. Many of the service people who were supposed to be replaced had fought against N. Korea only to be immediately sent to the Persian Gulf where the US is taking on high casualties.

The Generals, led by General Mattias, released a statement affirming that they are fighting for the Resistance."

"We did not take this decision lightly. Out of love of country we can no longer stand by and watch this President demolish our democracy and turn this country into an evil dictatorship that jails its citizens and kills its lawmakers because they disagree with the leader.

The military is called to support the Commander in Chief but we could not let our soldiers continue to die in these trumped up wars based on fallacious and fictitious intelligence," Mattias stated in a video released from an unknown location.

In response to the defection the President unleashed a tweet storm this morning.

@ USAPres: "These Generals- traitors—putting your sons and daughters in harm's way, illegally diverting troops and resources from the frontlines. The soldiers' blood is on their heads."

@USAPres: "Don't believe Maligning Mattias folks. The threat is real. These savages want our blood. Believe me"

@USAPres: "Their actions are turning God from America. He who turns from Israel is in big trouble folks that's what God said. They are cursing you and exposing you to God's wrath."

@USAPres: "I am willing to save the world, I can do it easy, no sweat. But these traitors who have turned from the battlefield to support the Resistance are ushering in the end of days."

228

God, is it wrong that I rejoiced today when I heard that Pastor Daniel was arrested, quickly tried for treason and shot? I mean of course I am devastated but I'm not at all surprised that the Damnfoolistan government would do something so illegal. It is not the first time. I'm rejoicing because after the arrest of the MacAllen pastors they've all been quiet. I assumed they were afraid of the threat of treason and thus had kept their mouths shut in deference to the evil king, thus betraying God. But last week, out of nowhere, Pastor Daniel found his voice or a microphone and a platform. Suddenly, for some reason Banner's media posted him speaking at a Resistance Church service. And boy did he speak! The bottom line of his speech: kill Banner.

"The generals have struck a blow against the evil king but they did not stop him. Today, I call on the Church to Pray to the Lord as the Israelites prayed for relief from the tyranny of Eglon, the Fat King. Pray Church, that God will raise up one like Ehud to slay today's Fat King and the country will turn to the Lord!" Pastor Daniel said.

After that aired, the top three Google searches were "Ehud", "Eglon the Fat King in the Bible" and "what does the Bible say about fighting tyranny."

To be fair, I think the charge of treason was clearly correct, but I also think treason is the correct thing in today's political climate.

I'm happy because my pastor, Daniel Paige, did not keep silent out of fear of man. He spoke up because of fear of the Lord!

Amen!

Halleluiah!

Thank you, Jesus!

229

What do you believe when everything is unbelievable?

Our casualties in the wars—both with N. Korea and Iran have increased significantly. The N. Korea conflict was supposed to be just about handled and we only had support troops helping the Chinese, the S. Koreans and a couple of ships still in the Pacific just in case something popped off. Then a missile hit. How did an enemy "sleeper cell" suddenly appear and take out 15 soldiers on routine patrol at the DMZ? It doesn't even make sense.

Then in the Gulf, suddenly troops are surrounded and massacred? ISIS captures and beheads 10 Navy Seals? No way. But that's what happened and now the wars are super hot again. The fighting is so heavy that they're just sending dog tags home. That's how you find out your loved one has been killed.

Siti says these are sacrificial lambs for Banner's cause and I believe her. It's awful to think that our military would kill its own just to enrage Damnfoolistan against the Resistance but that is what is happening—everyone knows it.

It's not safe to leave the house because you are likely to run into a "militia" who makes you pledge allegiance.

Mogo was going to work the other day and she had to pledge allegiance to Banner three times before she got there.

445

Mark says they are going to start making you sign a pledge at the Bank when you want to take money out.

"Wat haps if refuz?" I asked.

He didn't answer me.

230

@USAPres: USS Silvania destroyed. 450 dead. This is what happens when Generals defect.

231

Each night I pray that God will take me.

Each day I wake and curse God because I'm still alive.

I have nothing to live for anymore.

God, please come tonight and destroy the world! Please Lord! Tonight!

232

Carma is home. If I could, I would kill her.

Her Resistance killed my beautiful Sailor.

There must have been a better way than leaving our troops unprotected. Even if they were unprotected from their own government. Sailor was doing what he was supposed to do.

"No sense fighting for a country if that country is destroyed by foreign enemies," He always said and he was right. Maybe he wasn't but he was alive and now he's dead!

I don't even know what happened to him. They just sent his dog tags. Dog tags I insist Carma wears.

233

Give a niggah a rope he thinks he's a cowboy.

Who the Hell gave Carma's Arthur a rope? I hate everybody. Especially him. Carma cries every time she sees me. Good! But this niggah here!

"I'm sorry about your husband Miss Poohpie. I truly am. There have been a lot of senseless losses in this war. And Mr. Sailor was one of them. But he didn't die because of the Resistance. Those attacks, at least some of them, are a strategy by the government to enrage the people against the Resistance and its working," he said. Then I saw him squeeze my hand like that was a comfort.

"You know it's true Pooblies." It's Siti, happy because her beloved are safe. Well mine is dead so 'Shut fkup' I say.

Siti isn't the only one with palpable anger.

Just like we do with Siti, they ignore my rage and big head Arthur keeps talking.

"You all have to leave here. The loyalist police and militia have been tasked with rounding up Resisters and putting them in detention."

"We'll just lie. I do it every day when I have to go to work," Mogo said.

"We all do," Beanie said.

"It's not just about answering a question or saying an oath." Big head Arthur said.

"They won't make us take a mark will they?" Mom said.

"NO Love. This isn't that! Please listen everyone. They are going to round up anyone with suspected ties to the Resistance. Arthur and I are on a list of known Resisters. They've already taken his family." Carma said.

"They're coming for you soon. We have to get you out of here tomorrow or there's no telling what will happen to you." Big Head said.

"Do you know where they've taken your family Arthur?" Milga scowled at me.

She's pissed that I'm so pissed and trying to shame me for making things hard on Arthur and by extension, her twin. It's working a little. I feel bad for Arthur and I know they are right about who killed Sailor. If Banner was here, I would find a way out of this flesh prison and torture him until he bled out in my hands. But Banner is not here. They are! My anger has to fall somewhere so I roll my eyes away from Milga's gaze.

"My sister told my nephew to run when she heard them coming. He saw militia put my mom, dad, sister and brother-in-law in a van and drive away. We found him hiding behind a garbage dumpster."

Until now my rage was too pervasive to notice the little boy at Big Head's side. I see him now. Scared, wide-spaced, hazel, cat eyes stare up at me from his dark brown pie-shaped face. A slight tremor runs on a loop throughout his little body. Morgan reaches down and picks the child up. She gives him a piece of candy and coos in his ear. He stops shuddering, too engrossed in unwrapping the candy. I think of Ngoc and my anger flickers.

"Maybe they'll just question them and let them go." Manny

Carma and Big Head shake their heads no. We wait for more confirmation than that. Carma looks at Morgan who puts a hand over the little boy's right ear and presses his left ear against her chest, comforting him and blocking out sound. Assured that the child couldn't hear what was being said, Morgan nods to Carma giving her permission to provide the hard truths we need to hear.

"They sent word to the Resistance that they are going to execute our families for our crimes against the state. They sent pictures to our commanders of live and dead family members. Arthur's were listed as captured and/or dead. You all are on the list too. That's why we have to go—now!" Carma says softly, further insulating the little boy from the news.

There was a lot of commotion and crying at that. I checked out. I'm not leaving. There's no sense in taking me with them. I would just slow them down and from the little I could take in of the plan, survival for the able bodied will be a crap shoot. Carma and Big Head said they will try to get everyone to Costa Rica.

I'm trying to get their attention but nobody is looking at me. Finally Big Head sees me blinking and asks if I'm ok.

I signal that I want to say something, and Mo gets the letter board.

"lev me. I no mak e"

In the end, they knew I was right and they convinced themselves that if they left me, I would be put in a hospital or nursing home and they'd come get me when things got better.

234

Carma is the last to say goodbye to me. After all of the tears I'm exhausted so I beg God to let her hear and agree without arguing with me.

She walks into the room and smiles that little girl smile that I love. I think of how I used to hold her in the palm of my hand when she was first born- 32 weeks and 1 day of gestation. How she used to crawl over to me and collapse waiting for her nebulizer treatment. How she and Milga, her twin, would lay in my arms watching cartoons and ask me what was going to happen next. Where did the last 24 years go? How did we end up here?

"I'm sorry Poohpie!"

"I no. no u falt"

"You forgive me?"

Two blinks. Yes.

Three blinks. I love you.

"I love you more"

"favor" I say.

"You want a favor?"

Two blinks. Yes

"From me?"

Two blinks. Yes

"Anything Poohpie!"

"Kil me"

"I'm sorry what?"

"Kil me pees."

"No Poohpie this'll be over soon. We'll come get you."

One Blink—No. "I slep. Pees"

"Poohpie I can't!" she says and dissolves into tears with her head in my lap. "Please don't make me do this."

"U o me"

I know this hurts her. I have never demanded anything of her or any of the babies. I was the one who owed them for the years of love and belonging. This is awful of me I know but I want to die. I want to be with God. I want to be out of this flesh prison. I want to be with Sailor.

"pees bby. Kil me pees"

"OK Poohpie"

What?! Really? Ok then. Tomorrow I die.

"No tel u ma"

"Ok Poohpie."

"Tank u"

Three blinks. I love you.

Joke: How does someone with Locked In Syndrome sob?

Answer: Silently and alone.

235

I'm surrounded by my family. One by one they kiss me goodbye. Mommy says a prayer over me. She's sedated but her tears flood my face and mouth.

They're ready. They'll drive as far south as they can and try to charter a boat to Costa Rica. Manny has been investing along with his clients and they have a hefty sum in cash and gold coin. Everyone has cashed out their accounts as much as possible without drawing suspicion.

I'm ready. I look at Carma. She looks away. I look at her harder and she walks behind Beanie who produces the syringe. Thank God.

"What are you doing?!" Siti asks. She is on high alert, and she startles Beanie who doesn't know what to say.

"It's to keep her calm," Manny says and looks at me intensely.

God how I love my babies. They're all in on this I see now. Mogo is preventing her mom from taking the syringe. Milga is holding Carma, comforting her.

"No! She needs to have her wits about her when they come!" Siti says nonsensically. Even if I have my wits what can I do when they come? The kids try to calm her down, but she won't hear it. Finally, Arthur notices that I'm trying to say something.

"What is it Miss Poohpie?"

I look at Siti pleading.

"Pees. I slep I no can wach u go."

Their sobs are obliterated by darkness.

236

The sound of the military coming to get you—official or militia—is unmistakable. There's a heaviness to their march.

I heard them upstairs after they broke down the door, scurrying around the house looking for Resisters. When they verified that the upstairs was empty, they came flooding down the steps to the basement. Briefly I flashed back to the rat stampede and imagined that they were three and four deep tumbling and running over each other in their hunger to capture and devour their prey. If I could have screamed the power of it would have demolished the house around me.

My family left me alive only to be overrun by rats scratching and biting me. I could feel the coolness of their snouts and the unintended scratch of their claws as they crawled up, over and across the exposed skin of my body; under and over the blankets that covered me.

A man's drawl shook me from the flashback, and I felt gratitude in the midst of fear.

"What do we have here?" the young white man said taking in the accoutrements of locked in syndrome. IV, stockpiles of diapers and Ensure-like bottles. After taking it all in, his eyes landed on me in my pitiful state.

"Good Lord! Can you talk?" another voice asked. This guy was older and Asian.

Two blinks. Yes.

In walked more people—women and men all races but mainly white and middle aged.

The first guy said to no one in particular. "Looks like she got left.

"Bastards. See boys, these Resisters are animals. They just leave their own to die.

"Guess they couldn't take her with them. Would have slowed them down."

"She's still healthy so she must not have been here alone too long. They're probably nearby. Send a group out to look for them. You three go search for any ideas about where they're heading"

"What should we do with her?"

"Well, if her own people don't want her neither do we. Find a way to deal with her but don't make a mess.

A young woman held up a pillow in silent questioning. The head guy shrugged yes.

For the second time in who knows how long, I prepared to die. I welcomed the darkness that was the pillow over my face but, Lord willing would soon be the dark of death before I was with Sailor and Jesus.

"What are you doing? We are soldiers of God captain. We don't take the lives of innocents."

The pressure stopped, and I could breathe again.

"Resisters aren't innocent ma'am.'

"Paraplegics are sir. Her blood won't be on my hands!"

The pillow was removed, and light rushed at me again. Tears of rage, frustration and sadness blurred my vision as they raced from my eyes into my mouth and ears.

The woman who had saved me leaned over me. I could taste her minty breath in my mouth. Tenderly she wiped the tears away from my eyes and for the first time I saw her. She smiled at me. She cautiously looked around to see that no one was watching before whispering in my ear, "Don't worry Trina. I won't let anyone hurt you. God has sent me to save you."

Then Betty, my former friend and fellow IBF leader, kissed me on the cheek before ordering the militia to take me away.

Part III

Please!

PLEASE!

Come Quickly!

237

They moved me to a nursing home after checking me out for a couple of days at the hospital. There's nothing they can treat me for so they can't keep me at the hospital. Nursing home is a bit euphemistic. It's basically a prison camp for the infirm and crazy—a nursing prison if you will. I don't know anyone's story or even how many of us are here but there are a lot of us and I think many of us have family in the Resistance. One of the nursing guards calls us "the Left" (left behind by the Leftists). Pretty clever for a Damnfoolistanian to have a double entendre.

I'm in a dormitory style room. It's like a hangar in an airport or at least what that looks like on TV. I realize I have a lot of knowledge that is based on TV shows. I've never actually been in a barracks or a hangar and yet I know that that is where I am now.

It doesn't smell fresh. Lots of half-washed bodies, including mine. The nurse comes around about twice or three times a week to change my feeding tube. It's enough, I guess. I never feel hungry. They wash me more or less every two weeks. They don't keep my breath fresh like my family did so by the time they clean me, my mouth is rancid. I can go about 3 weeks before the taste of my breath starts to literally drive me crazy. Thank God, they haven't let me go longer than that. I think

I'm developing bed sores. I don't feel anything, but I haven't been moved or massaged since I got here—however long that's been.

Time is hard to tell because there is no natural light, plus they keep me heavily sedated so I don't know how long I am asleep. Could be a day, 8 hours, 20 min I can't tell. I'm not complaining, if I have to be alive and alone, I'd rather be high all the time. Anyway, without anyone to communicate with, I'm dead already. The best way to kill a writer is to never hear her stories.

238

The nursing prison's patient Management philosophy is "Keep 'em high and entertained" so they leave the tv on all the time. It cuts down on the loneliness and allows me to get out of my head which is actually a blessing. The shows are on a loop so it gets to the point that I can recite them—even in my sleep—and then they change the shows.

Right now, my favorite show is I AM Your Voice! It's a game show and discussion all rolled up into one. The contestants are given a tweet and they have to guess what the President is tweeting in reference to. Then they have to explain the meaning and implication of the tweet. The contestant who wins gets a front row seat at one of the President's rallies at Laguna Mar. Yes, I know it's ridiculous, but it reels you in and you actually root for folks to win.

This month there's this little guy named Clark. He is so earnest, and he really is good at interpreting his President. This episode is one of my favorites.

Host: The tweet is "Every time I speak of the haters and losers I do so with great love and affection. They cannot help the fact that they were born fucked up."

Clark, you are really quick on that buzzer buddy. Ok. When did our beloved President tweet this and what is the context and meaning?

Clark: It's a toughie Jim because there's a lots of losers and haters out there. Well, there WAS. Now that our boys is rounding them up there's a lot lesser of them out there (Laugh track). But My President was wondering if people would vote for him if he ran for President cuz lots of people was stupid.

Host: Woooo Clark you are on FIRE! Absolutely correct. For the extra point let's see who can best explain the importance of the tweet. Bonnie, you can answer first unless you want to pass?

Bonnie: No Jim I'll go. I love this tweet because it shows the humility of our leader. He knew how great he was, but he still presented a choice for us. We could either accept his gift to lead and save the nation or not. I think he knew what would happen, but true humility is not assuming or gloating. That's My president Jim.

Host: Wow Bonnie you are so right! Jessica, can you top that?

Jessica: (Wipes tears from her eyes) No Jim. Bonnie has so captured the essence of My President. Good job Bonnie.

Host: Uh-oh! Clark you're smiling do you have an answer that can beat Bonnie?

Clark: I believe so Jim although the humility theme is so strong in this tweet that it's hard to top. Buuuuuttt . . . In this tweet, the traits of love (He says he loves them strait out. In fact, he says GREAT love and affection) but there's also impar. . . uh, imparshe . . . .??? I never remember that big word that means treat everybody the same?

Jessica: Impartiality! OM Gosh! You're soo right!

Clark: Yeah, you see, he loves them and has affection for them losers and haters the same as he does for winners, kind of, even though they's fucked up BECAUSE they was born that way and they can't help it. He'd be wrong if he held it against 'em if they was born like that. He knows he was born blessed remember he said "I consider myself too perfect to have faults" so he knows who he is and he still has Great love and Affection for the haters and losers Because they was born fucked up. That's Love and impar-uh . . . that's My President!.

Host: Amen Buddy Amen! That's a good word and Good enough to get you the extra point and to move you on to the finals! (Applause track plays)

Well folks that's about all we need to say for right now. We're gonna let you chew on the president as humble, loving and *impartial*. Until next time folks remember that Our President has a very good brain and he's said a lot of things! Study up and maybe you too will be a winner on I AM Your VOICE!

(Music blares and dancers come out. They are little black kids doing a cute hip-hop high energy dance to the theme music. I hate to see them, and I hate that they are smiling and really talented. The contestants do a little wiggle along with the music and Jessica gets pulled into the dance with the little pikininnies. She dated black men at some point I'm sure)

Breath-taking right? I just love that Jessica helped Clark out with that big word.

239

There's no way that Beanie thought she was giving me enough drugs to kill me! She'd been overdosing me for months since Sailor died. She knew how much I could take. They never intended to kill me. I get that it was a hard ask but I asked for it. I would have done it for them. They had no idea what they were consigning me to. This is hell. I didn't want to live without Sailor, and I certainly didn't want to live alone. That's why I asked to be killed. Love means doing the hard things for those you love. Not killing me was the easy thing for them. Maybe I just overestimated their love for me. Maybe they never really ever loved me. Why would they? I was alone and always there—the extra. As long as I was around and convenient they "loved" me, but would they go out of their way to be with me? To love me?

It's such an awful thing to realize that your entire life has been a lie. My family never loved me. If they had they would have taken me with them or killed me. They did neither.

I wonder if Sailor really loved me. I think he liked feeling needed. Nobody needs you more than a woman who is locked in her own body. I can't even feel when I shit. It just happens and I sit in it. Of course he didn't love me.

God you're the only one who loves me and that's questionable. I mean is this really love? I'm sorry. I know you love me Lord but I ache.

470

There's so much I need Lord. I don't even know how to begin to feel better. God help me! I'm going crazy. Speak to me Lord. Help me!

"Grab 'em by the pussy!"

Oh for God's sake. I can't deal with I AM Your Voice right now Lord. Can't you see I need you? See me Lord! Let me know you love me! Please help me.

Host: Great answer Jacob. Diane, it's up to you. Do you have an explanation for this tweet?

Diane: I do Jim. This is one of my favorite tweets. I just love it because it brings me such comfort. I am considered a beautiful woman and very accomplished in my field. People look at me and think I have everything. But I don't. And you know there are a lot of us out here like that. For a long time, I prayed that God would send someone who would really see me. When My President said he just grabbed beautiful women by the pussy, I thanked God for answered prayer. He knows that even beautiful women need validation. I thought how special those women must have felt to have someone as perfect and giving and accomplished just reach out to them- to touch them. It's unconventional but that's why we love him. At least that's why I love him. God sent me Banner. He gets me. He's the ONE who SEES ME."

Oh Lord! Put me out of this misery!

Host: Wow. Amen. Each week I'm amazed by the insights of our contestants, am I right folks? (Applause track) Amen. Amen. Until next time folks remember that Our President has a very good brain, and he's said a lot of things! Study up and maybe you too will be a winner on I AM Your VOICE!

Save me from this hell Lord, please!

Enter the dancing pickininnies.

"It's time!"

Jesus! You're here!

It's the gang-banger turned nurse-guard! That can only mean one of two things: Food or drugs. Lord, please let it be drugs. Let me escape!

He makes his way down the corridor of the Left rolling a tray.

Please please please let it be drugs! Please Lord let it be drugs. Take me out of this misery at least for a few minutes. Please!

He stops beside my bed and holds up a syringe! I imagine myself a junk fiend. Dancing and itching for it. Tying the rope tight around my emaciated arm, hitting the crease of my elbow, readying the vein. "Come on daddy. Umph! Give it to me. Ooo don't wait."

It hits like a wave, tossing me about as I worry that it won't be enough then smoothly the under tow pulls me slowly away from the hellish shores of consciousness out into a placid sea where not even waves disturb me.

Thank you, Lord. Only You are El Roi, the God who sees me.

240

I don't know if I'm asleep or awake as I recite the words along with Jim.

"Until next time folks remember that Our President has a very good brain and he's said a lot of things! So, study up and maybe you too will be a winner on I AM Your VOICE!" Then I hum the upbeat version of "Lord speak to me that I may speak" as the Pikininnies dance.

"Do you like that show Trina?"

My name! How long has it been since anyone called my name?

I look to the right. Betty smiles at me. She's in fatigues with a gun casually slug across her back. I see the muzzle behind her right shoulder.

"I'm so glad you woke up before I had to leave" she said in the drawn out nasally whine of a Louisiana drawl.

My eyes grow big. Is she here to give bad news about my family— the family she used to speak so highly about? Or was she going to kill me? Please God let her kill me!

She noticed the fear in my eyes. She must be used to that look. Few things are scarier in Banner's America than a petite, Bible carrying white woman with an automatic weapon.

"Oh. The gun? Don't worry. I'm going on patrol when I leave here."

So, the news is right. They are really patrolling and looking for Resisters behind every rock. I wonder what she does with them when she finds them. What would she do to Carma or Siti or Mommy? I hate this bitch and I tell her so with my eyes which are squinted almost shut with rage.

"Your family? We still don't know where they are. We're looking for them though. Me especially. I want to bring them back and get them healed."

I imagine ripping her head off and pissing in it!

"Jesus is coming back soon Trina and the Resisters are going to hell. I know your family and I know they've just taken a wrong turn. I believed they knew Christ. It would be a shame for them to miss out on heaven because of a misunderstanding."

She rubs my forehead and bends to kiss it. When she recoils at the stench of my unwashed locs and unbrushed teeth (going on 2 weeks from the taste of my breath), I thank God for Jesus and the other nurse/guard's lack of work ethic.

"Don't worry Trina. I'll keep looking for them."

DIE BITCH!! The phrase is like a loud bell ringing over and over, bouncing around my brain, banging against my skull.

"I'll be back as soon as I can."

247

A new I AM Your Voice started today. That means on top of being a murderous, blasphemous bitch; Betty is a liar too cuz I haven't heard a word from her since that day she went patrolling for my family.

I don't want to see her.

I don't want her company.

I want information, particularly about my family. And I want her to see the unadulterated hate in my eyes.

242

Still no sign of Betty.

I've been paying more attention to the news which is terrifying. Either my family is dead, or Betty is. The fighting between Great America and the Resisters looks gruesome. The news vacillates between pictures of dead Resisters or videos of frenzied Resisters burning Bibles, lining up for free abortions or frolicking naked in sexually confusing orgies (women with penises screwing men with vaginas) around campfires. Actually, the newscasters have taken to calling Resistance strongholds Sodom and Gomorrah.

I have no idea what is going on in the Arab-Israeli war. All they do is show the president walking with troops saying "we're winning guys!" A clip like that comes on between every show and at least twice during the news. It looks like he's never in the US because he's always on a different ship or at a different camp. He was even out in a battlefield once.

So we're winning the war abroad and we're killing the brutal, godless Resisters and insurgents here.

243

I woke to Betty reading the Bible to me today. As much as I hate her it was good to have someone pay attention to me. It was even better to hear God's word read to me. She was reading from Genesis 2:

> The LORD God said, "It is not good for the man to be alone. I will make a helper suitable for him."
>
> Now the LORD God had formed out of the ground all the wild animals and all the birds in the sky. He brought them to the man to see what he would name them; and whatever the Man called each living creature, that was its name. So the man gave names to all the livestock, the birds in the sky and all the wild animals.
>
> But for Adam no suitable helper was found. So the LORD God caused the man to fall into a deep sleep; and while he was sleeping, he took one of the Man's ribs and then closed up the place with flesh. Then the LORD God made a woman from the rib he had taken out of the man, and he brought her to the man.
>
> The man said,
>
> "This is now bone of my bones

and flesh of my flesh;
she shall be called 'woman,'
for she was taken out of man."

That is why a Man leaves his father and mother and
is united to his wife, and they become one flesh. Adam
and his wife were both naked, and they felt no shame.

Such a sweet passage and such sweet memories and thoughts. God created the desire in Adam before he created Eve. Jehovah Jireh. Kind provider. How lonely Adam must have gotten when he'd finished naming the animals and they all went off with their mates. I've known that pain. I know it now. It sucks. Did Adam even have words to express desire? He had never wanted for anything. Did he feel sad in paradise? When Siti and Beans and I were studying Genesis together, Beans' lesson was that God makes what we need out of nothing. So true. He brought My Sailor to me out of thin air. I was so focused on LOKIE and Fallu that I barely noticed Sailor. When I was with Sailor, I could be naked and feel no shame—even twisted and locked in—I was not ashamed.

God is amazing because he has provided connection and comfort for me using this woman who I hate. I hope she'll come back and read His word to me again soon.

244

She came back! Betty is really trying to ingratiate herself and it's kind of working—damnit!

Today we talked about signs of the times. I used to love to think about this. Hearing Betty talk about it was exciting and reminded me of the wonder of God and the hope of Jesus' Second coming.

Rapture Nearness Assessment: (I haven't done one in a while. Here goes.)

How close are we to the Rapture of the church? Where are we on the prophetic timeline?

"The granddaddy of all the signs—Jews back in Israel."

Check!

"Earthquakes, famines, disease and signs in the sky."

Check

"Perilous times."

I think of diminutive Betty, who had sat with an Ak47 in her lap reading the Bible to me before going out and killing resisters. I want to laugh and cry. Check and double check!

"Wars and rumors of wars."

Checkarino!

"Violence and sexual immorality"

Way done been checked!

"False Christs."

People act like Banner is their Christ, but no one has actually called him that. It feels like he is—a false Christ—but I don't want to admit it. So . . . not checked.

"The whole world will turn against Israel."

Not checked. My Sailor died making sure of that.

PLEASE come quickly Lord!

245

Betty came back today! It was right in the middle of a special report on the news, so we just watched it together.

> Reporter: So, Mr. J.C. Windham, you claim that you escaped from Vermont, the Capitol of the Resistance stronghold, correct? Yet you also claim that you went there willingly. So, why did you need to *escape*?
>
> Windham: I was being persecuted for my faith. My *Christian* faith.
>
> Reporter: That's just terrible but we've been reporting that the Resistance was hostile to Christians since this whole thing started. If you were a Christian, why did you go to the Resistance?"
>
> Windham: I was foolish. I didn't believe the reports. I thought it was just propaganda and I thought the President was vulgar and mean for kicking out Hispanics and locking up Asians and Muslims. As a black Man I thought my family was not safe here. But

once I got there and saw what was happening, that everything you reported and worse—so much worse things were—happening. I knew I was wrong to leave America, to doubt the president . . . and I tried to leave.

Reporter: What happened when you tried to leave?

Windham: They wouldn't let me. My children were brainwashed. It was horrible. They watched me all the time.

Reporter: Can you tell us what it's like there? What's an average day like?

Windham: It's kind of like you see in the movies. Everyone has to get up and do exercise like they do in the factories in China. Then you have an assigned job. I'm a gynecologist so I saw patients, but my primary job was to perform abortions. I . . . I told them I didn't want to. When they asked why, I was afraid to tell them that I thought abortion was murder.

Reporter: Why were you afraid?

Windham: I knew the official stance on abortion and there were rumors . . .

Reporter: What rumors?

Windham: I . . . I . . . uh . . . rumors of re-education camps.

Reporter: Yes, we've heard that the re-education camps are actually torture camps where you are beaten and starved, and your family threatened until you renounce your faith in Christ. Is that what you'd heard?

Windham (almost inaudible): Yes

Reporter: Did you ever see these camps?

Windham: Yes

Reporter: Were you in one of these camps?

Windham: Yes

Reporter: Were you tortured?

Windham nods his head, yes.

Reporter: What did they do to you?

Windham hesitates then unbuttons his shirt and turns his back to the camera, exposing an angry, raised, red and oozing "C" crudely carved into his back. Then he removed his cap showing a similar, smaller mark on his forehead. Lastly, he showed the same markings on the palms of his hands.

Windham: They called it the Mark of the beast. They said I could escape the mark if I renounced Christ, but I couldn't do it. After they marked me, they had my children beat me as a sign of loyalty to the Resistance—

otherwise they'd also be marked. They held me for a month in a cell but when I still refused to renounce my faith, they made me walk behind a car, hands tied to the bumper for miles until we were in sight of America. Somehow, it must have been God, the rope broke, and I was able to run for the border and make it to safety.

Reporter: Ghastly! And your family is still there?

Windham: Yes

Reporter: What is going to happen to you now?

Windham: I'm to stand trial for treason. I will likely be killed but I'll be killed in America. I deserve death for what I've done.

Reporter: What? Um . . . ok. Sure. Ladies and Gentlemen, we have a special call from Our President! (Reporter and Windham stand)

President: I heard the story—terrible terrible. These monsters are, for his Christian faith folks on the shores of AMERICA. Can you believe it this is why we gotta get them. WE gotta kill them because they're gonna kill us. That's what they want. But this guy I tell ya he's suffered. You've suffered. So now you know that I'm you know you're sorry right? I was right. Right?

Windham falls to his knees: Yes sir. I am so sorry. I was wrong. You are good. You are great. Long live Banner and your whole family.

President: See folks. This is real gratitude and this guy should die but I'm gonna save him. He knows how to be thankful and repent. So . . . I'm gonna save him. Yeah! You're saved!

A movement in my peripheral vision caught my attention. I looked and saw Betty on her knees, hands upraised in a posture of worship, tears running down her face as she silently mouthed prayers to God. I watched for a second, scowling internally and wondered what she could possibly be thanking God for, when Jesus, who was bringing my shot, guffawed loudly. His disdain cut into the praise to my right and Betty looked up with an anti-beatific visage.

"What are you scoffing at (her eyes swept over his tattooed arms, brown face and name tag) HAY-ZUES?"

"Nothing. Nothing ma'am"

"It seemed to me you were mocking my prayers."

"No. Nope. Nope"

"Then what were you laughing at?"

"My friend had told a joke, and I was laughing"

"Is this an imaginary friend, HAY-ZUES? Cuz I just see YOU! HAY-ZUES."

"No, my friend is back in the nurse's station. I was thinking about it all the way here and I. . . I just got it and laughed. I'm sorry I interrupted your prayers. I'd be happy to pray too. Always happy to pray," he said and got down on his knees.

This seemed to satisfy Betty who smiled sweetly at me then turned to leave. When she got about three feet away from my bed, she turned abruptly and eyed Jesus who was still on his knees.

"HayZUES! What was the joke?"

He rose slowly and caught my eye. I wish I could whisper a joke to him. He swallowed deeply, obviously thinking then he smiled broadly.

"Why is Harvey Goldman gonna burn in hell? Because he Resists the light."

After a beat, Betty chuckled.

"Tell your friend that's a stupid joke. But it's good theology. HayZues Ma-jill-a" she said as she smiled sweetly and went out to patrol the streets of Woodbridge, Virginia.

246

I haven't seen Jesus in a while.

I see Betty almost weekly now.

I'm glad I can't ask Betty about him. God help me I look forward to her visits. She remembered that I love the passages where Jesus calls himself God and where God shuts down his enemies. Last time we read 1 Samuel 5 when the Ark of the Covenant was taken into the temple of Dagon and the next day and the day after that, Dagon was on his face before the Ark, dismembered.

Today we read John 8 when Jesus says before Abraham was, I AM! She giggled remembering how I would thrust my fist in the air when I read that. My conquering king Jesus! I imagine riding on a horse alongside Him proclaiming that He is God. It doesn't matter that I didn't ride in my functional body. In my locked in self, I'm a horsewoman. Powerful core, straight back, tight buttocks and strong thighs astride a beautiful stallion as I follow Jesus into battle.

Warm peppermint scented breath in my ear interrupted my reverie.

"Everything is gonna be alright. Jesus is coming back soon Trina!"

Yes, he is Betty. Yes, he is.

247

Thank God. Jesus came back!

He has a sort of "I don't give a damn" attitude now. Not sure what happened. He still has no work ethic. My teeth haven't been brushed in I don't know how long but I'm used to it now. He brings the drugs on the regular so I'm not gonna complain about it.

I think he feels connected to me because I saw the fear in his eyes, and he saw the fear in mine, when Betty questioned him. Today he sat with me and watched "I AM your voice" before he gave me the shot.

Host: Alright this is our last question of the last episode for this season. The winner gets to go to a rally at Laguna Mar and sit on the stage behind Our President! Clark, Jesse, Brienne. You've all done phenomenally, and I know Our President is proud of you. He watches the show faithfully, so he knows all of you by name and your adoration is a sweet smell to him. But. We can only have one winner. Who will it be? For the win, what prompted Our President to tweet the following?

"The only lies that count are the lies I tell the public not the lies I tell myself."

Jesse, you got to the buzzer first. What is the context of this tweet?

Jesse: It was in response to the lie about the size of the inaugural audience Jim!

Host: Sssss . . . .noooo. Wow. I'm sorry Jesse that is incorrect. Clark or Brienne?

Brienne: uhhh. Was it in response to revealing that Otieno had NOT wiretapped the White House?

Host: Ohhh, good guess but no. Clark? It's up to you buddy.

Suspenseful rendition of the theme song plays as Clark wracks his brain until the buzzer goes off.

Host: Clark? What you got bud?

Clark takes a deep breath: I thought it was the wiretapping oh Man! Ummm was . . . it . . . when he . . . Oh God . . .

Host: Give it a try.

Clark: Ok. Was it when he backtracked and said that the Access Hollywood tapes were a fraud?

Host: You know he had admitted to the statements on that tape a year earlier, right?

Clark: Yeah

Host: And there were many lies he could have been referencing?

Clark: Yeah. I know.

Host: But you're going with the Access Hollywood, "grab 'em by the Pussy" thing? You're sure?

Clark: No but it's the best I got right now so . . . Yeah, I'm going with it.

Host: It's a good thing because . . . you are right! You're going to Laguna Mar!

Golden balloons fall from the ceiling and the audience shouts their approval as Clark falls to his knees and thanks his god.

Host: Listen folks that's it for now but remember that Our President has a very good brain and he's said a lot of things! Study up and maybe you too will be a winner on I AM Your VOICE!

Cue music and dancing pikininnies.

"I hate that I like this show!"

489

It's Jesus! He's talking to me!

"I hate that I like it too Jesus!"

"The other stations have shit for shows. It's awful! Only Touched by a freaking Angel or the one with the white karate dude. Can't think of the name of it. It was ok in the 80s but it sucks now. The Banner channel is the best in TV programming. Sad!" he said and giggled at his mocking of the president. I giggled too. Good one Jesus.

"But TV had gotten so good before everything changed. This is Us, the Walking Dead, Queen Sugar, Homeland, Outlander?" I said, continuing the conversation.

"The Walking Dead is still on, so I guess it's not all crap but it's either this or serial killer and disaster shows. You wouldn't know this but it's all propaganda. Everything is orchestrated to make us scared. The only light shows on tv are this and *Banner World*."

I hate *Banner World*.

I caught myself laughing at the episode where Pocahontas was massacred along with her tribe of Snowflakes which included a little guy who was crotch level to everyone else, a Man with a rocket for hair, a Man who obviously had Parkinson's and a woman who was always being chased by a crowd yelling "lock her up". I usually pray or exercise when that's on.

"Anyway, you're lucky to be trapped in there rather than out here. It's a shit show but hopefully soon things will change."

What does that mean? What will change? What's going on Jesus? Tell me something! I yelled at him, but our moment had passed. He was shooting the contents of the syringe into the IV port.

248

Betty is back!

I hate to admit I've missed her. But I have.

It's been a while. At least 2 rounds of the new I AM Your Voice have come and gone. She looks weary. Jesus said the battle is changing so maybe that means the patrolling is getting harder. Anyway, I hope she's ok. I can't believe I'm saying that but it's true. She's sweet like she used to be before the world changed.

"I was thinking about you the other day and laughing," she said. "You remember the rap you made up? I swear it was driving me crazy one night on patrol trying to remember it then, thank God, it just came to me:

> 'I AM God,
> there
> is none higher
> all the
> little "g" gods they call
> me sire!'

"I started marching to that little beat and Bob, you never met Bob, my husband. Your sister did. He wasn't in the best mood back then.

Nor now, truth be told. Anyway, he sees me bopping along and he gets mad and starts yelling. 'You think you're at some club? What the hell are you doing?!' Like to scared me to death cuz I was so into your little rap, I didn't notice him. I'm no dummy no matter what he says, so I got it together quick, but later on, I taught it to some of the others and they really liked it. We bop down the road looking for Resisters singing it now—of course only when Bob's not around."

I forgot that Siti said she thought Bob was abusive. There's confirmation Siti. Hopefully he isn't physically violent, just scary and volatile like Fallu was. I hate to think of poor little Betty being beat up, but I wouldn't be surprised.

I do remember that rap. I loved it. Poor Betty, she remembered the words but not the cadence. This gives me a chuckle cuz I imagine a line of good old COD's bouncing up and down off beat, tripping over their feet, everybody clapping at different spots to the "beat" Betty made up. But it goes like this.

> I AM GOD
> There is none
> Higha!
> All the little 'g'
> gods
> They call me
> sire!

You gotta recognize God's swagger.

249

Jesus was sitting with me when Betty came today. We were watching Banner's World. It's such an awful show. It's basically a Banner-themed South Park. It appeals to the basest humor. Today "Little Mario" the one who is crotch height—was again trying to find a way to possess power (his story line is always that he's chasing after power like Wylie Coyote is always chasing after the Road Runner). In this episode, Little Mario goes around "orally pleasuring" senators and judges and whoever else would allow him to. Just when they are about to complete the action, he gets them to bestow their power on him. If they refuse, he bites off their pleasure bits (male or female). When he gets to the top of the power chain, there's this giant with a big golden phallus. Mario is dying to do him. The giant allows him to and when Mario demands the giant's power the giant laughs and drowns Mario in golden semen.

Jesus and I were sitting there in stunned silence watching Mario cry out in ecstasy and terror when Betty walked up and broke the spell.

There is such animosity between her and Jesus! But the tables have turned a bit. Jesus is not afraid of her and there's a no more white Girl Superiority popping off Betty when she looks at him. She's actually a bit kowtowed. I wish I knew what happened!

Jesus looked her up and down, slowly stood up and said to me, "I'll let you visit a while with your friend then I'll be back with your shot."

I blinked twice in agreement and thanks, but nobody pays attention to my communication. For all he knew I was begging him to knock me out. He still would have left me with her.

When he was gone Betty whispered in my ear, "I don't trust him."

No Duh, Captain Obvious! Tell me WHY!

"But let's not talk about Hayzues."

No! Let's!

"God is really good Trina. He gives us a word when we need it. And I'm so grateful that he sent my unit to get your family cuz if he hadn't, you'd probably be dead and so would my faith. God has used you mightily Trina."

Oh shit. Is she gonna tell me she's a Resister? Has she finally seen the light about Great America (the new name they're using—yes, it is disgusting. Banner says he has already made America Great). Lord, please let her see the light. I'm sorry I haven't prayed for her before. Please multiply this prayer. In Jesus' name amen.

"You know your little rap? It really caught on and a couple of people asked me what it meant. I had to think and think to remember why you said it. Then I remembered another part of the rap. "it's my prerogative to elevate Cyrus" and that's how I remembered it! We were studying Isaiah!

Isaiah 45:22. I am God. There is no other!

You were always so clever. I was so sad that we lost touch after IBF. But. . . that's a conversation for another day. Anyway, I told my group of ladies in the patrol where the rap came from, and we decided to do a little study of our own. We started with Isaiah 45. Do you remember what it says?

She pulled out her worn Bible and began to read. In that moment, I loved her scary, gun-toting, Banner-crazy, country ass!

"Cyrus is my anointed king.
 I take hold of his right hand.
I give him the power
 to bring nations under his control.
I help him strip kings of their power
 to go to war against him."

Oh Betty! Yes! I do remember this! I love the story of Cyrus. I love the fact that Isaiah prophesied about this, hundreds of years before Cyrus was even born!

"Cyrus, I am sending for you by name.
 I am doing it for the good of the family of Jacob.
 They are my servant.
I am doing it for Israel.
 They are my chosen people.
 You do not know anything about me.
 But I am giving you a title of honor."

I wish I'd written the book I wanted to write about this. How awesome it must have been for the Israelites to know scripture and then to hear rumblings of Cyrus. And then put two and two together when you're in exile and know God was going to deliver you! Dog! Talk about the drama of the Bible!

"How terrible it will be for anyone who argues with their Maker!
 They are like a broken piece of pottery lying on the ground.
Does clay say to a potter,
 "What are you making?"
Does a pot say,

"The potter doesn't have any skill"?
How terrible it will be for anyone who says to a father,
"Why did you give me life?"
How terrible for anyone who says to a mother,
"Why have you brought me into the world?"

"I see why this type of passage gave you such pleasure Trina. It's nice to remember that God is in absolute control of everything. Even the mess we're in now."

Dag Betty. Why did you have to follow Banner? Remember how we used to talk about God like this before times changed? I loved you. More than that, I respected you as a woman of God. As my teacher. But no matter. You're back and we are again able to dissect scripture together. Thank you God.

"I will stir up Cyrus and help him win his battles.
I will make all his roads straight.
He will rebuild Jerusalem.
My people have been taken away from their country.
But he will set them free.
I will not pay him to do it.
He will not receive a reward for it,
says the LORD who rules over all."

"I don't know what you think but I feel like God is speaking directly to America in this."

I guess but . . . not really Betty . . . I mean, Israel is Israel and . . .

"Haedon S. Banner is our CYRUS, Trina!"

What!?!

"I know it with all of my heart and just when my faith was faltering, God, using your little rap, encouraged me and strengthened my faith in his promised savior."

496

NO NO NO NO NO NO NO NO NO!

"The battle looks bleak right now Trina. We've taken a lot of losses both here and abroad. We are getting to desperate times, but God has said he will save us, and I believe that he's going to use Our President—our CYRUS—to do it!"

I can't believe what I'm hearing. How can she so horribly twist scripture and use me to do it? I haven't been this terrified in a long time. I want to run and scream and hide from the terror that is coming. It feels like my heart is going to come out of my chest! She notices and places her hand on my chest to calm me, but she's riled up and her voice is rising as she continues to extol the virtues of her leader.

"It's Ok Trina! I know you're worried about your family. They're probably dead and that's ok. It's what had to happen. I know the pain of loss. My sons are gone too! Two because of the Resistance and one killed by the Muslims. But don't you see? God is going to repay it all. Your family and my boys dared to argue with the Maker and his Chosen One. They had to die. The Muslims will be killed—they're already gone from our Great America, thank Our President! And soon we'll blow them to kingdom come, them and the rest of the Resistance who took our loved ones Trina! God has promised and OUR PRESIDENT—OUR CYRUS—WILL DELIVER!"

She is screaming now.

I can barely understand all that she's saying because tears are flooding my ears. Then I feel the warmth invading my veins and from far away I hear Jesus saying " . . . has to rest now . . . can come back another time if you want."

250

I had a nightmare.

I was screaming at Betty to tell me what she knew about my family. She just kept saying, "They're probably dead like my sons . . . but it's alright. God's gonna use his Chosen One to save us!"

For the second time in my recent conscious memory someone put their hand on my chest to calm my breathing.

"Don't worry, she's gone," Jesus said.

"Your friend sure lost her shit. I wouldn't be surprised if I didn't see her in one of the beds down here soon." He laughed and put his feet up on my bed, reclining in the chair to my left.

"Her husband had to come get her. He's a mean son of a bitch and he was embarrassed cuz she was still nucking futs when he got here: trying to strip off her clothes and yelling 'He's our Cyrus!' You know what mean sons of bitches do when their women embarrass them? Beat the shit out of them. That's the second time I've done that to her. I almost feel sorry for her."

So do I and not just because Bob most likely beat her. Lord will you count her blasphemy against her if she's crazy? Is faith in Banner pathological or just evil? Is she saved or is this like accepting the Mark of the Beast?

498

"Have you noticed she's a little scared of me? Yeah, I had to knock her down a peg or two."

Sorry Lord, let me come back to you in a second. What's Jesus saying?

"She thought she was all high and mighty. After that day in here when she demanded to know why I was laughing, she showed up at my house. Yeah . . . she didn't tell you any of this did she?"

One blink—no!

"Yup and she came in heavy with a whole group of militia. Arrested me in front of my wife and son"

Jesus, you look like you're 15. You have a son?

" . . . they had masks on—cowards—but I recognized her voice, 'way-yer ee-uzz HayZUES Me-Jill-a!' I opened the door so they didn't break it down—it's what they do you know? They come in loud and heavy, that way your neighbors are afraid to help you, and your family is left in the cold if they arrest you. I knew I was in trouble when I left here that day, so my family was ready. I went with them—no struggle. They beat me up a bit. Charged me with mocking the president and 'casting aspersions' on the claims of Great America (that's an actual charge). I had to prove that my grandparents on both sides were US Born and still they beat me. They held me for a couple of days until my cousin walked in and vouched for me."

Who the heck is your cousin?

"I bet you want to know who my cousin is huh?! My cousin is none other than J.C. Windham."

Get the heck outta here! THE J.C. WINDHAM? The guy who gets trotted out at every opportunity to testify against the Resistance? The J.C. Windham who was tortured and refused to renounce his faith? One of the President's "saved ones"?

"Your eyes are as big as theirs were. He's like a god to them—all he's gone through and the way the President loves him? They couldn't get enough of him. Taking selfies with him. Listening to the story of his torture. They even got to touch the "C" on his hands. It was Biblical. When he told them I was his cousin, practically raised in his house, they had to let me go. Your friend's husband even made her apologize to me. He had the same look in his eye then as he had when he picked her up from here. She'll be lucky if he doesn't kill her. Poor thing."

What?! J.C. Windham is real? All of that really happened to him in the Resistance?

"It's funny. You don't really know people. I grew up with JC—of course I knew him as Sam. I had no idea he was that good an actor. Even I believed he'd been tortured. But it's all propaganda. He got caught trying to go to the Resistance but they 'made him an offer he couldn't refuse.' So now he's J.C. Windham, puppet of the president and my trump card."

Wow!

251

I know she was crazy, but I can't help thinking about what Betty said.

Does she know my family is dead? She said, "They're probably dead" so maybe she was just hypothesizing or projecting.

I wonder how her sons died. What if Bob killed them? What if he made HER kill them? That would have driven her crazy. That would have also made her question her faith in Banner. Then to have her other son killed 'by the Muslims'. I guess that means he was fighting in the war.

What did she mean that all the Muslims were gone in Great America? I know they were detaining all of them. Did they kill them? What about the Asians? There's been nothing on the news about it, but the News is what they want us to see. Maybe Jesus knows. How do I get him to tell me?

252

Shit! I have no idea how to get information from Jesus!

253

I've been watching the news closely for any information.

Nothing on the fate of the Muslims or Asians in detention. But Banner said something that reminded me of Betty.

"It's time to win this war! We're gonna blow them to Kingdom Come folks! Kingdom fucking Come! It's time to win!"

254

Where did this dream come from? I haven't thought of the nightclub Havana Village in YEARS and yet now I'm dreaming of it. Not the wonderful live salsa that they played. Not the sweet and tart taste of a cold Caipirinha. Not the ease and beauty of my hips swaying to the beat of the drums. Not the freedom of rum-fueled gyrations. No, I'm dreaming of the stench of beer and vomit breath wafting up to me from the small Guatemalan men who try to lead me in a drunken salsa which in their minds is guided by the sound of a marimba—not a Conga. I hate this dream, so I force myself awake only to find that it's not a dream. Jesus is whispering in my ear, but his breath is so rancid that it takes a moment to focus on the words.

"Zhey did it! The Ghenrles! Iss ova. Zheycomin" then he noisily weaved through the barracks proclaiming, "the ghenrles did it!"

When he left there was something I hadn't heard in a while—silence. The TV was off. Well, not off but there was nothing but a blue light emanating from it. No sound. Just light.

255

The TV came back on with a bang. Literally.

Banner in front of a firing squad runs on a loop. Over and over. One minute it was just the blue light of the tv and then a close up of Banner's face, bloody and scared. No defiance now, just terror. His mouth worked like a fish gasping for breath. If he was saying something they didn't broadcast it. He's guided around corpses on the ground and pushed up against a white wall spattered with red and black. Then,

BANG!

He falls.

The camera pans to a large jubilant crowd.

Then the loop starts. Different angles of the same scene.

256

According to the TV, the Generals from the Resistance made a deal with the Generals of Great America, and they are both in control of the soon to be unified country.

"Blow them to Kingdom Come" was the trigger.

Banner was planning to nuke Iran, Turkey and Lebanon. The Resistance strongholds would have been next. His Joint Chiefs of Staff and a group of ten Resistance Generals made a pact that they wouldn't allow him to go nuclear—when he tried to, they killed him and his closest allies. The other flunkies were arrested. The troops were always loyal to the Generals above Banner. There's still fighting going on, but DC has been captured and all of the military bases are under the control of the Generals.

Video of Bannon's execution is joined by scenes of other executions now. Firing squads. Hangings. All of them public. At first, I was horrified but when the reality of what was happening hit, I was embarrassingly elated. Now I look forward to the execution videos.

God forgive me.

257

Jesus never returned and neither have the nurse/guards. Neither has Betty.

The death of Banner is great news for those outside of this barrack. For us, the bedridden, it means that we lay in our filth literally dying of thirst and withdrawal. Our bodies are dependent on the sedatives they've been pumping in us. Now the groans of the vocal ones vie with the news of liberation coming from the TV. It is truly an awful way to die; particularly now that it seems life may be preferable again.

258

I must have lost consciousness before the Saviors came. That's what I'm calling them. Soldiers and nurses—separate people, not one and the same. Today a nurse brushed my teeth! I don't know the last time that happened.

The last thing I remember before awaking to find order being restored by the Saviors were the stories Lin and I heard all those years ago during our first trip to Guatemala; especially the ones about the 10 children who died as their mothers fled the army in the Cuchumatanes Mountains of Guatemala. Maria Consuelo, a midwife, told us how they evacuated the maternity hospital. Then, night after night ladies came and told me and Lin the names and stories of their children.

Inocente or Inocenta—preborn—miscarried as Pamela ran up the mountain.

Consuelo or Consuela—preborn—miscarried as Celeste ran up the mountain.

Trinidad—preborn—miscarried by Aquavida when the group stopped to drink water by the stream.

Augustin—6 years old—shot in the back as he ran up the hill, carrying his baby brother.

Auxilio—3 days old—shot by the same bullet that killed his brother Augustin who was carrying him because his mother, Maria Inez, was too weak.

Ignacio (Nacho)—3 years old—lost in the chaos as the women gathered up his mother, Panchita, who had been shot in the back while running up the mountain.

Pax—30 minutes old—shot in utero. When the women got to a clearing, they delivered the baby from Panchita's corpse. He survived 30 minutes.

Sueno—preborn—miscarried when Ana reached the top of the mountain.

Jesus—2 days—thrown in a well by soldiers when they raided the hospital. Paula, a midwife, was carrying him when she tried to stop the soldiers. She, along with Jesus, his mother Juana, and several other women were thrown into the well. Their deaths allowed about 15 women and children to escape.

Maria Paz—2 years—trampled to death by the soldiers chasing the women who fled. Little Maria got separated from her mother, Conciencia, in the chaos.

"Tell their stories. If people hear their stories, it's proof that they existed, that they were real. That they mattered." Maria Consuelo implored me and Lin as we left that last village in the Ixcan all those years ago. We promised we would, but we didn't. I never forgot them though.

Maybe I was saved to finally tell their stories. Maybe sanity will be restored in the country. Maybe life will be worth living again.

So be it now Lord please, see to it.

Let's Connect!

I hope that along with making you laugh, cry and think, *Y'all Chose This* left you wanting and *needing* to talk about what you read. If it did, let's start a conversation at <u>Dorcasrenee.com</u>. Join my mailing list and receive a deleted scene from *Y'all Chose This*.

Enjoy this book?
You can make a big difference!

I'm so grateful for my committed and loyal readers! Your reviews are one of the best thank-yous I can receive. Reviews are the most powerful tool I have as an author when it comes to bringing my books to the attention of other readers.

If you enjoyed this book, I would be grateful if you could spend three minutes leaving a review (it can be as short as you like) on the book's Amazon page.

An excerpt from

Wait! What?

The Decimation of Lady Liberty

by Dorcas Renee

Now Available on Amazon

PROLOGUE: FALLU

It had been a long difficult flight from Ireland to DC. The last two hours so turbulent that Fallu thought he might be sick or go crazy with fear that they were going to be thrown to the ground. Finally, the jumping and bumping stopped. Now it just felt like he was sitting in a restaurant. A very tight restaurant. A very tight restaurant full of white people. Fallu hadn't noticed how small the plane felt until now. He'd been too preoccupied with the turbulence. Now all he could think about was how close he was to everyone and how close they were to him. Even after being in Ireland for three months, being surrounded by so many white faces still freaked him out. Especially here, where everything was so tight. The seats, in front and beside him seemed to squeeze him. The ceiling felt like it was squishing down on him. Even the air felt thin. No matter how hard he sucked it in, his lungs didn't seem to fill.

He started to sweat. His mind raced, searching for exits…a way out. Somewhere he could get air, but there was none. He closed his eyes trying to shut out how close the walls, ceiling and floor had suddenly become. His legs bounced from the effort of willing himself to not run down the aisle screaming. What would the white people think if he did that? The thought of the panic he'd cause made him giggle but when he saw how the man seated beside him looked at him, Fallu feared he was truly losing his mind. Only crazy people laugh when they are suffocating to death.

Terrified, he began rocking back and forth. Surprisingly the motion helped. He closed his eyes and focused on the movement then he noticed there was a slight whistle when he breathed in. So, he focused on that. Soon an image appeared behind his closed eyes. The Statue of Liberty. Yes. The symbol of freedom and peace. Lady Liberty, Oisin had called her.

"You'll be safe with Lady Liberty. Better than being in this shite hole I'll tell yeh" the Irish aid worker had said as he completed Fallu's paperwork at the refugee camp in Guinea. "You'll stay in good old Erin until we can get yeh a flight to America. Start life all over. Have a pack of kids. Bring your mum right over, yeah? Get her fixed up good. Don't worry Fallu. The Lady…She'll keep you safe under her skirts boy-o, yeah?"

Fallu fought to keep images of his mother, ravaged by war, at bay. "Why would she do that for me?" he asked the kind man who looked a little like Father Christmas.

"Because it's her fecking motto" Oisin had said before reciting the poem.

'Give me your tired, your poor, your huddled masses yearning to breathe free, The wretched refuse of your teeming shore. Send these, the homeless, tempest-tost to me,'

If that doesn't describe you, I don't know what does. She has to accept ya. Yeah?"

Fallu had never considered himself to be wretched refuse, basically garbage, the way Lady Liberty apparently did; but war had taken everything from him so he would gladly accept the succor she promised.

"Yeah" Fallu answered the memory of Oisin's question aloud just as the plane landed with a bump and skidded to a stop at the gate. "Is this America?" he asked no one in particular.

"Yep, sure is. Where are you visiting from?" His seatmate asked.

"Sierra Leone Sah. Come to take the 'Mother of Exiles' up on her offer of world-wide welcome!"

About the Author

I love Jesus and cuss a little . . . ok a lot.

There's a lot to say about me but where is the mystery in that? The most salient fact is that I am a writer.

I write to be seen.

I write to be heard.

I write to make a difference.

I write to change the world.

I write to make sense of the world and my place in it.

I write to BE.

Thank you for reading *Y'all Chose This*. I hope that along with making you laugh, cry and think, *Y'all Chose This* left you wanting/needing to talk about what you read. If it did, let's start a conversation at Dorcasrenee.com. If you join my mailing list I'll send you a short story (deleted scene from *Y'all Chose This*).

Footnotes

1. https://www.theguardian.com/global/2008/jul/24/barack
obama.uselections2008

2. https://www.christianpost.com/news/david-platt-prays-
for-president-trump-after-he-unexpectedly-shows-up-at-church-
service.html

www.ingramcontent.com/pod-product-compliance
Lightning Source LLC
Chambersburg PA
CBHW021836010726
47493CB00005B/1422

www.ingramcontent.com/pod-product-compliance
Lightning Source LLC
Chambersburg PA
CBHW021444240626
47153CB00001B/283